INSIDE OUT

Based on a true crime

by

"DOC" HOLLOWAY

CALICHE RESIDENTS, ENJOY THE ROAD SGT. DOC Holloway ARIZONA HIGHWAY PATROL ~ RETIRED,

Brighton Publishing LLC
501 W. Ray Road
Suite 4
Chandler, AZ 85225
www.BrightonPublishing.com

Inside Out

Based on a true crime

by

"Doc" Holloway

Brighton Publishing LLC
501 W. Ray Road,
Suite 4
Chandler, AZ 85225

Copyright © 2012

ISBN13: 978-1-936587-67-4

ISBN10: 1-936-58767-X

First Edition

Printed in the United States of America

Cover Design by Tom Rodriquez

∽REVIEWS∾

"Fast paced, superbly written book. Filled with telling details and a masterful control of pacing and story structure. I found this book difficult to put down. Highly recommend for those who love crime novels and suspense books, as this one will keep you on the edge till the last page."
Amazon.com reader review

"I was more than enthralled, I was spellbound. I didn't expect the surprise ending."
Gregg Girard, Sergeant/Retired, Arizona Department of Public Safety, Highway Patrol.

"A great read. The author's personal colorful history gives him a wealth of material and his easy style is very comfortable."
Ron Hollar, Lieutenant/Retired, Arizona Department of Public Safety, Highway Patrol.

I am a retired law enforcement executive with thirty-eight years' experience. Through the years I've read hundreds of books written by current/former law enforcement personnel.

I read Holloway's book Inside Out. It was riveting, thunderous, compelling, yet heartwarming.

He skillfully mixed fiction and non-fiction, weaving a story that was easy to enter into its description. Holloway's depiction of conversation between characters allows the LE reader to recall conversation from their experiences that were similar, thereby quickly getting into the framework of the storyline.

Inside Out is an excellent read and a gravity-defying book; it's hard to put down.
Ron Zuniga

ᥫ INTRODUCTION ᥫ

My name is Cod Overture. I have been a law enforcement officer for over forty years. And just like any other police officer with my tenure, I've done just about everything there is to do in police work. I worked the beats, dispatched police cars, worked the jail, rode solo motorcycles, was assigned to helicopters, was a criminal investigator, and worked Internal Affairs. I now work homicide.

I am not your typical TV police hunk. I have gray/brown hair and blue eyes, and my mustache is almost white. I am five-foot-eleven and weigh about two hundred pounds. I am sixty-three years old. I wear glasses, and I am not as spry or as stout as I used to be. I have a tattoo of a human skull thumbing its nose on my upper left arm, a reminder of my younger Navy days. I don't smoke or drink beer; I'm a rum and Coke kind of guy. And I drink too damn much coffee. I am not a Charley Chan or Sam Spade. I am just an ordinary, everyday, hardworking cop—but I get the job done.

The only thing I would not do was work narcotics. I knew working the streets as a police officer was dangerous, but I always felt working narcotics could be more dangerous because of the money involved.

I was a beat cop working the streets when the Supreme Court created the Miranda warning. I've investigated everything from child abuse to homicide, arson to prison escapes, from bribery to crooked cops, and rape to petty thefts.

I am also no-nonsense. You break the law, I put you in jail. But I am also honest. During my career I kept several suspects out of prison because I proved they were innocent, when others were more interested in arrests and convictions in spite of the evidence. You see, I always thought the system has forgotten what it existed for, and that's to find the truth no matter where the chips fall. The system is called 'criminal justice' for two reasons. One is to prosecute the offenders, and the other is to clear the innocent.

I am also very particular about who my friends are. I was once told by the mayor of the city, Lance Wilson, in front of a crowd of people, "Cod doesn't have any friends because he is too particular."

To which I replied, "Mayor Wilson, if you politicians took my lead instead of sucking up to every two-bit lobbyist in the world, the citizens of this community would be a lot better off."

At the time, Wilson was an icon in local, state, and federal politics. He'd been mayor for twenty-five years and no one messed with him. He built a political machine so strong, US congressmen sought him out for help. Mayor Wilson was so embarrassed by my comment; he called the chief of police and demanded that I be fired. The chief told the mayor he couldn't fire me because of my tenure on the department. But to satisfy the mayor, the chief ordered me suspended for five days.

At least, that's what the brass thought. But what the brass didn't know was that I knew the payroll clerk, Esther Cruz. I had kept her son out of jail on a bad possession charge when I was a young street cop. She never forgot. When she got my suspension order, she ignored it and paid me anyway. I got five days off with pay and no deduction from my vacation or sick time. I couldn't figure it out. Why did I get paid when I was on suspension? Then I ran across Esther at a meeting.

She told me, "I know they were fucking with you, Cod, but I paid you anyway. Let's just keep it our secret. Besides, I consider it payback for protecting my son."

And that's the way it was left.

Cod is my given name. It was my mother's brainstorm. Mom was born in Twillingate, Newfoundland. Her father—my grandfather—was a cod fisherman who sailed out of Twillingate on *The Dart and the Dove*. My grandparents had nine kids, but my mother, Verna, was the only one of the nine who would go cod fishing with her father. Hence, my name.

Cod fishing had been my grandfather's life, however, there was never enough money, and he always had to work for someone else because he couldn't afford his own boat. Eventually, my grandfather got tired of fishing and immigrated to the United States looking for a more stable life style for his family.

My grandfather emigrated from Newfoundland through

Pennsylvania and picked Detroit, Michigan, to settle in, because of the auto industry. He went to work for the Dodge Corporation building Dodge trucks. My mother and the rest of her family followed soon after.

When my mother met my future father, their courtship lasted about five months, before they married. When I was born, my mother insisted that I be named Cod. My father, who came from the poor south, wanted to name me Gravy, because as he once told me, "Gravy was all we had to eat, and it kept me alive so many times." Fortunately, my mother won the argument, and I became Cod. Can you imagine being called Gravy Overture? I would have been known as Soppins Overture. Are you kidding?

And you guessed it: As soon as I went to work for the police department, everyone started calling me Fish, like Fish on Barney Miller. But I stopped that nickname cold in its tracks. No way was I going to be nicknamed after that grouch. However at times, I must confess, I could be a real Adam Henry, which is cop-speak for 'Ass Hole.'

A few years into my career, I acquired a reputation as being abrasive. I got that from a major, who thought I was too gruff when I answered his questions. I wasn't being gruff, I was giving him honest, constructive criticism, and he didn't like it. The major called my boss and raised hell. And, as most street cops know, some people do not like honest answers, especially police department brass. They don't want to hear about problems. They want all peaches and cream, no ripples. Some of them have become so isolated in their own little worlds that they forgot what it was like to work the streets.

⎰⎰ CHAPTER ONE ⎰⎰

On July 17, I transferred from Robbery-Homicide to White Collar Crime. I was in Robbery-Homicide for twelve years. Of course, it is no longer called Robbery-Homicide. Because there had been such an increase in armed robberies, the powers-that-be thought it would be better to have two separate sections, one called Robbery and one called Homicide. That never made much sense to me, because every time there was a robbery and the victim was murdered, we in homicide caught the case. So in reality, if homicide caught the suspect, we solved two crimes. So why not leave it Robbery-Homicide? You know: if it's not broke, don't fix it. But who knows how and why bureaucrats come up with their ideas?

The only thing I would miss about leaving Homicide was my partner, Nate Randal. We had been together the whole twelve years. Big Nate, as he is called, is a good guy to have around, because he is six foot six inches tall, weighs 260 pounds, and is all muscle. He is African-American, as black as coal and as bald as an eagle. He looks intimidating, but in reality, he is one of the easiest going guys around. It was really humorous to see some bad-asses think they were tough as nails . . . until they saw Big Nate. Then their mouths would drop to the floor as they stared in disbelief at this big hunk of man. When Big Nate showed up, no one gave us any shit.

In our early years, Nate and I made our reputations as being straight-arrows over a case involving two uniform cops and a young street punk named Percy Guido. Guido got into it with his brother and mother over his reluctance to hold a steady job. Guido beat the hell out his brother, breaking his nose and giving him a concussion. A neighbor heard the disturbance and called the police. When the two uniform cops entered the second floor apartment, Guido took a punch at one of the cops. He missed and got his ass arrested.

Then the two cops decided to teach Guido a lesson. They cuffed his hands behind his back and picked Guido up like they were carrying a log, one carrying Guido by his head and shoulders and the other by his feet and legs. When they got to the stairs, they threw Guido headfirst down the flight of stairs. The fall broke Guido's neck, and he died instantly. When the officers went down the stairs to pick Guido up and take him to booking, they realized he was dead.

Then they concocted a story that Guido fought with them, tripped, and fell down the stairs. Unfortunately for the officers, there were two nuns and a priest standing at the opposite end of the hallway watching the whole episode.

The press had a field day with it. The headlines read, *Cops Kill Handcuffed Teenager*. What they didn't say was that Guido was nineteen, a convicted felon, and had spent time in the joint. When Big Nate and I confronted the two officers with the witness testimony, they both confessed and ultimately pled guilty to involuntary manslaughter. Guido's mother sued and collected a hefty sum from the city.

For a long time after that, Big Nate and I were kind of outcasts with the rest of our brothers in blue. We actually had targets on our backs for a while. And, of course, we got the silent treatment. There was a feeling among the cops that we didn't protect our own. However, nothing was farther from the truth. Those two idiots who tossed Guido down the stairs were giving all the cops a bad name. After a while, everyone realized what we did was the right thing for everyone. Eventually Big Nate and I were invited to a uniform party in our honor, kind of a 'sorry we treated you like shit' party.

Nate was married to a gal named Leona. She was a shade over five feet tall and weighed in at ninety pounds. What a couple they made! Talk about a pair of head-turners. When they walked down the street, everybody looked.

It's common for police officers who work together to also hang together. It was no different for Big Nate and me. We barbecued and partied together. Our kids went to the same school, and we even traveled together. Nate and Leona went with my wife, Louise, and me to Twillingate, Newfoundland, to track down my Newfoundland ancestry.

What a great trip! We saw icebergs and whales, and we met some of the friendliest people in the world. To pay Nate and Leona back for going with us, we promised to accompany them to Africa whenever they wanted to go.

I always knew Big Nate had my back, and I sure as hell had his.

Leona was after Nate to retire. He put in twenty-seven years, and she wanted him out. She did not want him to end up like so many others, dead after they reached retirement age. The politicians gave police officers and firemen a twenty-year retirement plan because they realized it was tough to work the streets after a certain age. Come on, how many fifty-year-old cops could take on a twenty-year-old bad guy? Not many, and as a consequence, a lot of my friends in blue who were retirement-eligible were killed on the job. Leona knew that, and wanted her man alive. Her idea was to get him to retire, and start planning their trip to Africa.

Big Nate finally gave in to Leona's wishes. Nate turned in his papers and went on terminal leave. With Nate gone, I didn't want to work homicide with anyone else. I decided that since he was gone, I'd transfer to White Collar, where it would be safer. I had my time in too, but I just couldn't bring myself to give it up. I really loved what I was doing. I guess you could say it was an ego thing, and you would probably be right.

I reported to White Collar Crime on July 17 at 0800. My new boss was Cory James. While I was waiting to talk to him about my new assignment, I noticed that he had a pretty good setup. All the furniture was new, and the office had paneled walls with carpeted floors. Sure was a lot different than Robbery-Homicide. The secretaries here were attractive too, and he had four of them. I thought, *Why does anyone need four secretaries?* The one doing all the phone answering was blond and, I would say in her early forties. She also had a voice like a damn peacock, loud and shrill. But she was friendly. When I checked in, she offered me a seat and a cup of coffee. Very hospitable. I took the seat but declined the coffee. The second gal was Hispanic. I heard her making appointments for James. A brunette was running the NCIC computers doing background checks, I assumed, on suspects. And the fourth was another brunette who must have been his personal secretary, because she came out of his office with a steno pad.

The blond with the shrill voice told me, "Captain James will be with you in a few minutes. He's on the phone with the chief."

I told the blond, "On second thought, I will have that coffee you offered me, with cream please." I took the coffee and sat down to wait.

James had been promoted to Commander about three years ago. He was assigned to the West Side Patrol Precinct when he first joined the department. He was another guy who had skeletons in his closet but for some reason, namely the mayor, he was able to get promoted. You see, his wife got tired of him always working nights, so she started chasing around on him. When James found out, he beat the hell out of her. Almost killed her. But James' sister was married to one of the mayor's first cousins, so it was hushed up. James got sent to the mayor's security detail to get him out of the West Side Patrol Precinct.

I had to hand it to him, though. He'd taken the ball and run with it. Now he was the commander of White Collar Crime. Some guys get all the breaks. I knew who James was, but we had never worked together.

Well, I shouldn't say never. He did follow up a family fight call an old partner and I had several years ago.

It was the Fourth of July. I was working nights and was partnered with a guy named Richard Dukes. Dukes and I responded to a family fight call on Baldwin Street. When we arrived, the house was dark with no sign of life anywhere. We went to the front door and rang the bell. No answer. We beat on the door with our flashlights and announced who we were. Still no answer.

Dukes said, "I'll try the back door."

"Okay." I said.

As soon as Dukes got around the corner of the house, the front porch light came on, and the front door opened. A skinny teenage boy was standing there, covered with blood.

Before I had a chance to say anything, the kid said, "My stepfather was beating my mother, so I hit him in the face with a Coke bottle and split his face open."

"Where is he?" I asked.

"He's in the back bedroom,"

Stupid me, I was a rookie then, and I didn't have enough street smarts to ask if the stepfather was armed. I walked into the bedroom, and the stepfather stuck a .257 Caliber Weatherby custom-made rifle in my

8

face. I thought I was a dead man.

The stepfather's face was split wide open. The laceration started on his forehead and ran down to the left side of his nose. There was blood everywhere. Coke bottles are thick. It must have taken one hell of a wallop to break a bottle on this guy's face. He was really pissed off and wanted to kill his stepson.

Dukes finally made it into the bedroom and kicked the rifle out of the guy's hands. We had to wrestle the prick to the floor before we could get him handcuffed. I had blood all over me; it ruined my damn uniform.

When the sergeant finally showed up, it happened to be Cory James. The department's policy was to have a sergeant follow up all serious calls, to make sure the cops were doing things right. It was as if the department didn't trust us. I can't imagine why, after all, they trained us.

Anyway, Dukes took the stepson into the kitchen to interview him, I took the wife into a second bedroom, and Sergeant James stayed with the stepfather in the back bedroom.

While Dukes and I were interviewing the mother and son, we heard a gunshot. I thought the stepfather got loose and shot James. Dukes thought I got shot. We both charged into the room where James and the suspect were. Thank God they were both okay.

Sergeant James had a brain fart and decided to unload the rifle. While he was unloading it, the fucking thing went off. The bullet went through a wall into a third bedroom, where it traveled under a crib with a baby boy sleeping in it. Fortunately, the kid was not hit, and he didn't even wake up! What a damn mess! We must have looked like the Keystone Kops.

And what did Sergeant James say about this? He didn't say he was sorry. He said, "I hope this doesn't fuck up my career. I will do whatever it takes to get promoted."

I remember wondering about that. *What the hell does that mean? He would sell his wife and kids, sell us out, get down on his knees, or what?*

And after all this, the stepson and wife wouldn't testify, so the asshole stepfather walked.

Soon after this incident, Richard Dukes told me, "I've had enough of the Corey James types in the department. I didn't tell you, but four months ago I applied with the San Diego Police Department. They called yesterday and offered me a job, and I've decided to take it. I report the first of next month."

I told Dukes, "Every department has a Corey James."

"But San Diego pays you enough to put up with their assholes. I'll triple my current salary."

"Point well-taken. I'll buy you a drink after work to celebrate."

ᐸᑭ CHAPTER TWO ᑫᐳ

The semi-truck came to a slow stop in front of the bar. The sign read *Windy's Bar, Ice Cold Beer, Food, Air Conditioning.* The driver had stopped at the bar twice before, looking to sell stolen equipment. It was scorching hot at 115 degrees, and the sun was blistering with not a cloud in the sky. And to top it off, his truck's air conditioner had quit working. *I have to get that fixed,* he thought to himself.

Today would be a good day for a cold beer, he decided. He hadn't had one in several weeks because they were taboo where he lived.

He left the semi running, exited the truck and removed the magnetic signs from the doors, and placed them inside the cab. He had three different sets of magnetic signs that he used for cover: one for the state, one for the city, and one for the US Postal Service. Today he was using the city government sign and wearing a city uniform. He knew the police didn't bother or check government vehicles, especially postal vehicles. The signs gave him the uncontested run of the state. The semi was white, just like a thousand other semis. Nothing to make it stand out. It was a Plain Jane, which was just what he wanted.

He walked to the back of the semi to make sure the trailer was not blocking the driveway. He didn't want any police nosing around, looking for parking violations. He knew the military jeeps and equipment inside the sixty-five-foot-long trailer would be safe, but he decided to check the load anyway. He opened the trailer doors. The jeeps appeared to be secure.

A homeless man who was digging through a dumpster behind Windy's saw the military jeeps inside the trailer. He wondered where they were going. Then he went back to his digging.

11

After locking the trailer door, the driver entered the bar through the back door. It was dark inside, just like the last two times he'd been here. He couldn't see very well in the darkness, but found his way to the bar and sat down. He pulled out a pack of KILZS cigarettes and lit one.

He ordered the cigarettes over the internet, with a computer he used at the local library. The cigarettes were sent to his post office box. *What a place,* he thought. *Make up a phony name and you can do whatever you want. People are so stupid, they'll believe anything.*

When the bartender saw the driver he said, "Oh, it's you again."

He responded, "Sure is dark in here. It'll take a minute or so for my eyes to adjust. It's really bright outside."

"What are you selling today?"

"I'll have a Coors Light. And to answer your question, I don't have anything to sell. I just want a cold beer and to relax a little bit before I go home, but next week I will have two commercial freezers, do you think Windy would be interested in them?"

The bartender left to get the beer. By the time he returned with the Coors, the driver's eyes were beginning to adjust to the darkness.

The driver scanned the familiar barroom and the long mahogany bar running the length of the room. Matching stools lined the bar rail. The cash register was brass, with white marble keys, and it looked like something from out of the past. He saw the same old dartboards and the long shuffleboard game against the opposite wall. Tables and chairs were pushed against the far walls. A mop and bucket were sitting in the middle of the floor. A wooden dance floor covered the back of the room, with a small bandstand for musicians. No other customers were in the bar. *Same as the last time I was in here—good,* he thought.

"Do you miss your transmission shop?" the driver asked.

"Sometimes I miss the work, but the headache of being a business owner is a real pain in the ass. Keeping employees happy, scheduling, and handling customer complaints was too much, so I sold out."

"Have you ever met the people who bought your shop?"

"No, I haven't."

12

"The new owner is a woman. A dwarf. She's about three-foot-six, a little tiny shit. But she buys some stuff from me. Mostly trannies and small engines. The stuff I wanted you to buy when you owned it."

"I didn't know that. But how does the city come by so much property to sell?"

"We get the stuff from the military. It costs the military too much to keep, so they give their entire surplus to the city. My job is to sell the stuff direct to business owners. It saves owners money and puts money in the city coffers. The military gives us all kinds of stuff to sell. It's amazing how much waste exists in government agencies, in particular, the military. No wonder my taxes are so damn high."

What a joke, he said to himself. *I don't even pay taxes.*

The bartender shrugged. "Well, Windy isn't here. He's off for the day. He should be here tomorrow. Why don't you leave your business card with your number, and I'll have him call you."

"I don't have any business cards."

"Just write your name and number down on a napkin. And speaking of your name, what is it? We've been talking on and off for about two years, and I don't even know your name."

"My name is Gregory Pauper, but just call me Greg."

"Nice to meet you Greg. I'm Carsey Jackson. Just leave your number."

"Nah, I'm not in the office much. I'll come by some other time."

"Okay."

The driver saw a Mexican enter from a back room and go over to the mop and bucket and start mopping. *Must be the handyman,* he thought.

Then the front door opened, a flood of light entered the bar, and two uniformed police officers stepped into the door way.

"Holy shit!" the driver yelled, right before he pulled a gun and started firing at the officers. The officers fell. The driver, now a murderer, heard a commotion behind him. He turned and saw the handyman trip over the bucket of water, overturning it. The handyman scrambled to his feet and started running toward the back door. Quickly, the killer fired at the fleeing handyman, missing him. The bullet hit the door frame, shattering it. The handyman made it out the back door and ran for his life.

The killer turned to the bartender, who stood frozen in terror, his mouth wide open, not able to speak. The killer said to Jackson, "You're coming with me."

Before leaving, the killer picked up the Coors bottle, taking it with him. But he forgot his partially smoked KILZS cigarette.

The killer and Jackson exited the bar through the same door as the fleeing handyman. Once outside, the killer forced Jackson into the back of the semi-truck's trailer and locked him inside. It was like an inferno inside the trailer, but the killer was not concerned about Jackson. He was concerned with getting away.

The homeless man heard the gunshots and took cover behind the dumpster. As the killer was closing the semi-trailer door he saw the man emerge from behind the dumpster, they locked eyes. The homeless man had a chrome grocery cart with American and Confederate Flags attached to it. He grabbed his grocery cart and fled down a back alley.

The homeless man was wearing a beat up Diamondbacks baseball hat with a "Buddy Poppy" attached to it. He had on baggy brown pants held up with a rope instead of a belt. He was 5'10" and maybe 130 lbs. soaking wet. He had long gray hair and a stubby beard. He looked as if he hadn't had a haircut or shave in months. His cart was full of his "beautiful junk," as he called it. Junk that he planned to sell later

The killer thought to himself, *I'll have to deal with him later, but he should be easy enough to find.*

He drove away, heading north to the Johnson Truck Stop.

Justin Cunard, AKA Gregory Pauper, now a cop killer, was in his late fifties. He was a little over five-foot-eight and weighed just over a hundred and fifty pounds. He had silver-gray hair and large green eyes. He was slightly built and walked with a hitch in his step. He looked more like a grandfather than a killer.

He'd been using the Johnson Truck Stop as his fueling station for three years. He'd originally selected it because it was the biggest truck haven in the state. He reasoned that he would be just another truck driver there, unnoticed and insignificant. He could also use the truck stop as a place to swap out his enclosed Fruehauf trailer for his flatbed trailer, if the need ever arose.

During the three years he'd been using the truck stop, Cunard had gone out of his way to make friends with the truck stop manager, Lavelle Paynter. From time to time, he would buy Paynter lunch and had even sold Paynter one of his stolen M151 military jeeps.

It was all part of his plan to use the truck stop to hide some of the money he received from selling the stolen military property. Cash was Cunard's problem: he had nowhere to hide it. He had a small checking account, under his assumed name, but he could only put small amounts into the account for fear of alerting the feds. He was afraid to leave it at the "Place" because it was so far away and isolated.

Cunard knew that it was common practice among truck drivers to leave property in truck stops to be picked up by other drivers. Cunard figured Paynter would let him use the truck stop safe as a hiding place for some of his money stash—a plan that would eventually prove fatal for Paynter.

Justin Cunard made his phone call from the Johnson Truck Stop shower room.

"Jason, it's me."

"What do you want now?"

"It's me. I shot Mike and some other cop. I think they're both dead."

"Mike Townsend?"

"Yes, what other Mike do we know?"

"What? Why did you do that?"

"What was I supposed to do? What if he recognized me? He knew I wasn't supposed to be here. What the fuck was he doing checking bars? I thought he was a detective."

"Fine, I guess you had no choice. You have to protect the operation. What were you doing in a bar? You know that isn't allowed."

"I was hot and thirsty. I wanted a fucking beer. What I was doing in there is beside the point. I was there. So what? I had no choice. If he would've recognized me, it would've been all over. Is that what you want?"

"No, that isn't what I want, but what are we going to do now?"

"I don't know. You're the brains behind all this. And there's another problem. There were three witnesses: a Mexican handyman, a homeless guy, and the bartender. I have the bartender with me. He's locked in the trailer. The Mexican got away. I can find the homeless guy later."

"All right. But you will have to kill the bartender and then try to find the homeless guy."

"Okay, but I will need help. Can you meet me at the 'Place'?"

"You know I can't meet you."

"You never want to help me. You've always been the careful one, never take a chance."

"You did it, you take care of it."

"Well, you told me to do it."

"I did not."

"You did, too, you asshole. You never did like to help me."

"Go fuck yourself, Justin."

Before leaving the truck stop, Cunard stopped by Paynter's office to ask him to hold onto his duffle bag for him. The duffle bag contained $27,000 in cash. Paynter did not know what was in the bag, but agreed to put it in the safe. Justin Cunard told Paynter he would pick it up the next time he was in.

Three hours later, Cunard arrived at the "Place." The Place, as he called it, was twenty acres of land in Callaway County. He had acquired the property two years ago as a place to store stolen property and to conduct his illicit business. He found it through one of his foster brothers.

The twenty acres was surrounded by a ten-foot solid fence topped with barbed wire. It contained a small portable communications building that Jason used as an office. He had acquired the communications building from a military base. The small building was self-contained, with portable electric generators, fresh water tanks, and a rest room.

Justin Cunard and his brother, Jason, were raised by foster parents, along with several other young boys, who because of their situation, considered themselves to be foster brothers. The Cunard brothers were raised at the Fontaine House Foster Home since they were five and six years old. Justin was younger than Jason, but he was the most reckless, always pushing the system, just barely avoiding the law. Jason was the opposite; he was unusually cautious and wouldn't dare taking a chance on anything. He certainly would not think of breaking the law. But he was a notorious bully.

After entering the fenced lot, Cunard exited the semi and opened the trailer doors. He found Jackson lying on the floor. He was unconscious and near dead from heat exhaustion. Cunard carried Jackson to the front of the trailer and placed him inside a large military ammo storage container. He shot Jackson twice in the back of the head, killing him instantly. Skull fragments, blood, and brain matter covered the floor of the container.

"I did you a favor, buddy. I put you out of your misery." Cunard mumbled.

He rolled Jackson's body in thick black plastic and sealed it with duct tape. He carried the body into the trailer and placed it in the back of one of the jeeps. He backed the jeep out of the trailer and drove to a seldom-used hiking trailhead on Callaway County land. Cunard carried the body into the forest, dumped it, and covered it with leaves.

What Cunard didn't know, was that he had been seen from the top of Slate Creek Hill by Mayor Lance Wilson's ranch foreman, Ellis Walker. Walker heard what he thought were gunshots and wondered what was happening. *Probably local hunters,* he thought. He stopped the Bronco and reached for his Bushnell binoculars. He stood up and peered down at the fenced lot, but did not see anything but stored military vehicles.

Then movement caught his eye: a vehicle backing out of a trailer that was attached to a white semi-truck. *What's a jeep doing inside a semi-trailer?* He asked himself. He watched as the Jeep drove out of the gate. There, the jeep stopped, and the driver exited the jeep so he could lock the double gates. Then he returned to the jeep and drove down the dirt road disappearing from view.

Walker had stumbled across the fenced property several days ago and had been watching it ever since. He wondered about the whole thing. *Who is this guy and what the hell is he doing? Why all the military vehicles and equipment? Does the Mayor know about this? I'll have to talk to him, next time he's up here.*

ᑕ᠊᠌ CHAPTER THREE ᑫ᠍᠌

Two lovers were just finishing their sexual encounter when one of them asked, "What's that noise? No one knows about this place. Christ, I hope it's not your father. He'll kill us if he catches us."

They had heard the sound of a vehicle coming to a stop near their love nest. They ducked behind a fallen log so as not to be seen.

Then they saw a man who was carrying a large bundle draped over his shoulder. The man dumped the bundle on the ground and started covering it with leaves.

"Hurry up, Jason," the man said. "We have to cover him and get out of here."

A moment later, they heard an identical voice say, "Shut up, Justin. I am hurrying."

"No, you're not. You always take your time. You've done that ever since we were kids."

"Well, too bad. I have to watch where I'm walking."

"Who is he talking to?" one of the lovers whispered to the other.

"I don't know. I can't see anyone else."

"He must have someone helping him."

"It's getting dark, the other guy must be in the shadows."

"They sure sound alike."

"Maybe they're brothers. Be quiet! They may hear us."

As the solitary man returned to the jeep, the lovers heard him say, "Get in the fucking jeep, Jason. We don't have time to waste."

The two lovers heard the vehicle leave. They waited for several minutes before they decided it was safe to go. But the male, being nosy, wanted to see what the man dumped. He told his lover that he probably

19

dumped a dead animal.

"Let's go look," he said.

The girl, being more nervous, said, "No way. Let's get out of here before they come back."

"No, I'm going to check and see what it is. You wait here."

The boy left his girlfriend by the fallen log, but it was getting dark, and she was getting leery about being alone, so she followed her lover to the site where Jason Cunard had dumped Carsey Jackson's body.

The boy brushed away the leaves and found the black plastic package. He ripped the package open and exposed a man's head that was half gone, he gasped and his girlfriend let out a bloodcurdling scream that roused roosting birds from their nests. Then they both ran like hell.

After dumping Jackson's body, Cunard drove back to the Place. He cleaned the ammo storage container that he had killed Jackson in and headed back to his place of residence. But first he had to stop at Mason's Storage Facility. He had leased two storage rooms as well as parking space under his assumed name, Gregory Pauper. He had paid a year's rent in advance.

He entered the storage room and changed out of his civilian clothes into his everyday working uniform. He returned to the truck, gathered up his magnetic signs, and stored them in the building, along with his .38 caliber revolver. He drove to the back of the storage lot where all the travel trailers were parked. He parked his covered trailer, hitched his state-issued flatbed trailer to the semi-truck and headed to his house.

He returned to his place of residence, knowing he would be safe from the police. *Those dumb fucks will never find me,* he thought to himself. *I have the best of both worlds. I have free rein. I'm never stopped or checked. How could they be so dumb and so pathetic? Give them money and food and they'll do anything I ask. The "Man" is so blind, he doesn't realize I have his protection.*

As I waited to see James, his staff members started running around like scared chickens. I was wondering what the hell was going on. Phones were ringing off the damn hooks. Cell phones were beeping like crazy.

James peeked out of his office and shouted, "Overture, get in here!"

I was not used to people barking orders at me, so some of that abrasiveness I was famous for was about to come out. I was upset anyway, because I'd had to wait so damn long.

Before I could say anything James said, "Two uniform officers have just been shot. They're both dead, and the bartender is missing."

"Who are they?" I asked.

"Townsend and Jessop."

"Townsend?" I exclaimed. "I just had coffee with him last week. I don't know Jessop."

"They were shot in a bar called Windy's while following up on an armed robbery at a drugstore. You're ordered back to Homicide to handle the case."

"Windy's Bar on Sheridan?" I asked.

"Yeah."

"Hell, I know Windy. I used to have that beat. But back to Homicide, why? What are you talking about? I just got here."

"Your transfer has been cancelled. You're going back to Homicide." James added, "These orders are from the mayor's office, via the chief. That was him on the phone. They'll be waiting for you in Homicide."

Yep, the same mayor who said I did not have any friends, who wanted me fired for embarrassing him. I didn't know what to say. Hell what could I say? I was dumbfounded. *Two dead cops, that's not good. The whole city would be on lockdown until the asshole or assholes who did this got caught.*

And it was going to be up to me and whoever my new partner was to get it done. *But maybe,* I thought to myself, *just maybe, I can talk*

21

Big Nate into delaying his retirement. Nah, he'll never go for it. And I know Leona would never allow it.

Well, I did as I was told. I beat feet back to Homicide, and sure enough, the Chief, Larry Flint, and Mayor Wilson, were waiting for me in the Homicide Commander's Office.

The Homicide Commander was Captain Baylor 'Bones' George. He was an old-school cop like me. He had been around the block once or twice, and he'd made it on his own. He did not have a mentor, and he did not kiss anyone's ass. He was direct and to the point—my kind of guy. No bullshit, no spin, say it like it is.

He was about five feet eight inches tall, and was as skinny as a rail. Years ago when Bones was hired, he was so skinny, he had to conceal three hand guns in his pants, to make the police departments weight requirement. Some people called him Bones George behind his back. I didn't; I called him Bones to his face. And he seemed to like it. At least, he never gave me any grief over it. He motto was, "Do what the fuck you are paid to do, and do it by the book, and I will go to hell and back for you." And he did, more than once.

Bones once got into a fight with a small time street thief. Bones ended up on his back, with the punk on top of him. Bones' elbow was jabbing the punk in the side. His elbow was so skinny, the punk thought it was Bones' gun, and started yelling, "Don't shoot! Don't shoot! I give up!"

I've known Bones for a long time. We were street cops together in two different precincts. We worked together at the Scott Hotel fire that was started by an arsonist. Bones and I carried twenty-eight dead people out of that building. All of them died in that inferno, some by fire and some by smoke and some had even jumped to their deaths to avoid being burned alive.

I loved working for Bones. In a way, I was glad I'm back in homicide. However, I missed Big Nate. Bones saw me coming down the hallway and waved me into his office.

He said, "Cod, you know the Chief, and I heard that you already know the Mayor—no pun intended." Of course, they all let out a little chuckle with that comment.

The Mayor started off with, "Detective, I want you to forget about our little altercation. As a matter of fact, I have ordered the Chief to restore your pay and to have your suspension erased and your record cleared."

I thought, *Holy shit, what am I going to do about that? I've already been paid. What about Esther Cruz? Will she get into hot water?*

"Mayor Wilson, don't worry about it. I needed the time off to think about retiring." That was all I could think of to say.

"Oh, no," the Mayor said. "I can't let you retire. I need you to solve these killings. And you were right. I need to be more selective in who I associate with. Besides, I like your bluntness. If some of my assistants would stand up to me like you did, instead of agreeing with me all the time, I would probably make better decisions."

It took me a moment to realize it was an election year. Anyway I let it go.

The Mayor continued, "We have two dead police officers: Mike Townsend, a twenty-five-year veteran, and Henry Jessop, a rookie. This kind of lawlessness cannot and will not be tolerated by my office. Detective Overture, I have instructed the Chief and the commander to give you all the resources you need to solve this case. Be assured, I do *not* like being interviewed by the press over these kinds of issues. Do whatever it takes, and don't worry about money—spare no expense—but nail whoever did this.

I said, "Mr. Mayor, I will do everything I can, within legal limits, to find whoever did this."

When the Mayor and Chief left, Bones and I sat down to discuss the case and my plan of action. Bones wanted to know how I was going to handle all the notoriety this case was going to bring.

I thought to myself, *That's an easy question to answer. Don't talk to the press.* Of course I didn't tell Bones that.

Bones said, "You're to concentrate on the cop killings, not the robbery at the drugstore. I know you'll have to go to the drugstore because that's where it all started, but don't get involved with the robbery itself, except to interview the victim about the perp."

"What does the drugstore robbery have to do with this?" I asked.

"Townsend radioed that he had information that the drugstore robbery suspect ran into Windy's Bar. From that, we assume that the robbery suspect killed Townsend and Jessop."

I told Bones, "I'll sit down and write out a plan of action, which will include getting Big Nate back." I knew that writing a plan was a lie. I have never written a plan of action on a case in my entire career. I think Bones knew it too. But I did want big Nate back.

"What are you talking about? Nate retired," Bones said.

"The Mayor said 'all the resources I needed', and Big Nate is a resource. Can you get him reinstated?"

"It's an unusual case and request, but the Mayor did say any resource. Why didn't you bring this up when the mayor and Chief were here?"

"I guess I didn't think of it."

"I don't think the Mayor will care. He can't afford any bad publicity. The election's coming up."

"Okay, then. If you'll take care of that, I'll get a car and head to the scene."

Bones yelled after me, "Keep me informed, God dammit!"

I went to the motor pool to check out a car and head for the crime scene. But first, I had to call Esther Cruz. I asked the cop at the motor pool desk if I could use his phone for a private call. He grumbled a little bit but left to have a cup coffee. He also told me that he got a call from the Chief's office saying that I was to have a car assigned to me permanently.

I said, "Thanks." Then I called Esther. When she answered I said, "Esther, its Cod. We have a problem."

She said, "What's that?"

"Have you heard about Townsend and Jessop"?

"Cod, everyone has."

"The mayor called me back to Homicide. I was transferred to

White Collar Crime today. But the mayor stopped the transfer. He wants me to investigate the Townsend and Jessop killings."

"Well, good for you, Cod."

"But Esther, he also wants my suspension cancelled and my pay reinstated."

"Don't worry about it. I'll just make it retroactive on the books, and no one will know the difference."

"Esther, are you sure? I don't want you having any problems because of me."

"I'll be just fine, Cod. I know where some skeletons are, too. Remember, I've been here about as long as you have."

Well, I let that one go and said, "Thanks Esther." Then I picked up my assigned undercover car and headed to the crime scene.

⌒CHAPTER FOUR ⌒

There had been a reported armed robbery at 441 E. Sheridan, between Beals and Goethe Streets, on the east side of town, normally a crime-free area. The original call advised a drugstore had been robbed of money and prescription drugs, and the owner of the store, Arthur Phillips, was pistol whipped by the perpetrator. The crime occurred at 1230, in broad daylight. The day had been very hot and extremely bright.

When a robbery or serious crime occurs, police procedure is to pinpoint the exact location and create four quadrants around the crime scene. The quadrants are identified as northeast, southeast, northwest, and southwest. After the quadrant locations are identified, uniformed patrol cars are sent to each quadrant to canvas the area, looking for suspects, witnesses, weapons, or anything that would be helpful in solving the crime.

Patrolman Mike Townsend, a twenty-five year veteran, and patrolman Henry Jessop, a six-month rookie were assigned to the southwest quadrant. Townsend was Jessop's training officer. Their job was to scour the quadrant for anything that would help in solving this crime. It could be anything: a car leaving a parking spot, a fast-walking pedestrian, or someone with packages or bags. They were to contact any citizens who were on the streets in an attempt to gather information about the crime and suspect.

When Townsend and Jessop first arrived in the sector, the veteran officer spotted an old woman bent over, picking up some items. He told Jessop to stop the car so he could talk to her.

Jessop asked, "Why?"

"She might have been knocked down by the perp."

Townsend got out of the car and approached the lady. "What happened?" he asked.

"Some kid was running and bumped into me and knocked my bags out of my hands."

"What did he look like, where did he go, did he say anything?"

"The asshole didn't even say he was sorry or offer to help. I saw his face, but I didn't recognize him. I believe he had on a blue jacket with some kind of decal or writing on it. I don't know what it said. But I think he ran toward that bar across the street. He's just a kid, real short. He's white."

Townsend told Jessop, "Park the car and follow me. We're going over to Windy's."

As Jessop followed Townsend's instructions, Townsend called in the info to communications and headed to Windy's, with Jessop close behind. They both entered Windy's, looking for the suspected robber of the drugstore. What they ran into was a hail of bullets. They were both shot to death shortly after entering. Townsend left a widow, three kids, and two grandkids. Jessop was not married and still lived with his parents.

Windy's Tavern was a local gin joint frequented by the neighborhood residents. Windy's had been around a long time. It was a typical local bar. It sponsored softball teams and bowling teams and conducted dart tournaments. It even had horseshoe pits.

As far as anyone knew, the owner, William "Windy" Benifield, appeared to be a law-abiding citizen who did not tolerate any illegal activity in his establishment. Benefield's nickname, Windy, did not come from his first name William, as most people thought, or because he talked a lot. It came from the fact that he farted when he got excited, hence the name "Windy." Windy couldn't help it. He had some damn problem that the medical system could not solve. You could push Windy's buttons, and all of a sudden, he would start farting. He just could not control it.

When I got to the drugstore I contacted the robbery dicks who were on the scene. I was told that as far as they knew no one else was in the store at the time of the robbery and that the owner was in the hospital in serious condition. They had a patrol car on the way to the hospital to check on the victim and to take his statement, that is, if he could talk. Crime scene technicians were already processing the scene for evidence. There was nothing else I could do at the drugstore so I headed for Windy's.

Windy's was three blocks west of the drugstore, but on the south side of the street. When I got there every damn cop in the country seemed to be there. Cops, fireman, paramedics, they were everywhere. I talked to the uniform Sergeant in charge and asked him to try and clear some of these people out of here. I know they wanted to help, but now they were becoming a problem.

I went into Windy's. Leo Lapaka from homicide was talking to Windy Benefield, the owner of Windy's. I went over to talk to Lapaka and Benefield.

"Hi Wendy." I said as I approached.

"Hi Cod, how the hell are you? Long time since I've seen you."

"Yeah, it's been quite a while."

I first met Windy when I was a young street cop assigned to a beat that included his tavern. In those days we had to make bar checks to make sure no young kids were being served. I hated those bar checks and I am sure the bar owners didn't like us nosing around either.

That's when I first found out about Windy's farting problem. He would get so upset when I came in to check his bar he would start farting and screaming about harassment.

Finally, I said to him, you want me or would you prefer Liquor Control doing this? Well he must have preferred me because he quit his bitching and farting.

Lapaka saw me and said, "What the hell are you doing here Cod? I thought you went to White Collar."

"I did, for about twenty minutes. The Mayor and Chief cancelled my transfer and assigned me as lead on this case."

Lapaka said, "Huh?"

"Hey, I didn't ask for this, I was ordered here. I'm not here to step on any ones toes."

"No problem" Lapaka responded.

Just then Lapaka's cell phone went off. Lapaka answered, said a couple of "yeahs and okays" and handed me the phone. "It's Bones he wants to talk to you."

Bones said, "First, Lapaka will be your new partner. Second, the Mayor and Chief have approved for Nate to come back, however there are a couple of catches."

"What are they?"

"Nate can only come back on contract. He cannot legally carry firearms and he will not have arrest powers. And you are the one who will have to convince Nate and more importantly his wife to accept those conditions."

I thought, *That's never going to happen.*

I looked at Lapaka and said, "It looks like you and I are partners, at least on this case."

I knew there was no way Leona would allow Big Nate back on the job. Not without a gun anyway. But who knows, anything is a worth try.

When the call came into headquarters that two cops had been shot at Windy's the caller would not give his name or address he just said, "Dos polica have been shot at Windy's Bar," then the caller hung up. The caller spoke with an accent. Dispatch called the number back but got no answer, it wasn't Windy's phone number, it was a cell phone.

A police car and fire paramedics were dispatched to Windy's to follow up the anonymous call. When the Officers got to Windy's they found the bodies of Townsend and Jessop. They immediately secured the scene and called for a supervisor and detectives.

Townsend had fallen backwards, his arm pinning the door ajar. Jessop fell forward into the bar. Blood covered the floor. The fire paramedics, who saw death many times before, knew it was hopeless to check the bodies for a pulse. They were right, there was no sign of life in either Townsend or Jessop.

Leo Lapaka was the first homicide detective on the scene. He found Townsend and Jessop's as they had fallen. Their blood everywhere. He called for crime scene technicians and had dispatch call the owner of Windy's. He asked dispatch to pull the tapes on the 911 call and to notify the Medical Examiner's Office.

Lapaka found an upside down mop bucket with water all over the floor with the mop lying next to the bucket. There was a bullet hole near the back door. The cash register drawer was open and full of money. There was a cell phone next to the cash register. There was no weapon or shell casings. And there were no drinking glasses or bottles on the bar. There was an ash tray with a cigarette butt in it.

When I finished talking to Bones, Lapaka and I continued our interview of Windy Benefield. I thought, *If he gets excited and starts farting I'm outta here, Lapaka will have to put up with him. After all, the Mayor put me in charge. And who am I to challenge the Mayor? I did that once, remember?* But for some reason Windy was calm and collected, and never farted.

Benefield was not very happy about his bartender being gone. We know the bartender was here, but we do not know for sure if a customer other that the perp was here. Windy told us the bartender was Carsey Jackson, a white male in his fifty's, five foot ten inches, gray-brown hair and blue eyes. He worked for him for about a year. He said when he hired him; he did a cursory background check to make sure he was not a thief. He told us that he never had any problems with him; he was always on time, honest and very hard working.

He also said that Jackson wanted all the work he could get. Sometimes he would work double shifts for the tips. Windy identified the cell phone that was lying next to the cash register as Jackson's. Windy also told us that the till money was all there. Jackson lived at 3479 Beals Street, about six blocks from Windy's. Windy told us that Jackson was married to a woman named Yvonne. He thought Yvonne was pretty sick with lung problems.

But what happened to Jackson? Did the killer kidnap him? Did Jackson run because he was wanted somewhere and didn't want to talk to the police? If he ran why didn't he take his cell phone? But if he was kidnapped or ran, who called 911? If the shooter was the same guy who robbed the drugstore, why didn't he take the money from Windy's? If the killer took Jackson, Jackson was probably already dead.

I said, "Windy, does the bartender have an accent?"

"No, why?"

"We know someone else was here. Who was it? What about the spilled mop bucket, do you have a maintenance man?" Windy started to wiggle and began to fart so I knew he was hiding something.

"Windy, we are going to listen to the 911 tapes, we already know the caller has an accent. If you had an illegal working here we don't care, but we need to know who he is, we are not interested in anyone's immigration status."

"Yes, I have a cleanup man, he is an illegal from Mexico, poor guy has five kids, and his wife is pregnant. He's just trying to make a living. About six months ago I found him going through my garbage cans looking for food for his family. I felt sorry for him and gave him a job." Windy added, "His name is Juan Lopez, he lives in Mexican Village near Mack and Van Dyke, I don't know the address, I have his cell phone number."

Lopez had a pre-paid cell phone, there was no way to get his address from the phone.

"Windy" I said, "You are going to call him and do whatever it takes to get him to talk to us. I will have a Spanish speaking officer here to help you and listen in, promise him anything. We have two dead cops, the department will do whatever it takes to help him and his family. The Mayor needs this case solved. I will talk to the Mayor and push for legal status for him and his family. The Mayor told me no holds barred, I will have his family put up in a hotel if wants it, but get him to talk to us. Convince him to trust us, have you got it?"

"Yes, I will do what I can. But what happens to me about having an illegal worker?"

I said, "Damn it Windy, the Border Patrol can't catch illegal aliens now because they are too busy catching drug dealers. Do you think they will care about a guy that will help put the killer of two cops in jail, they will probably give him a medal."

Before Windy made the call to Lopez I called dispatch and told them to locate a Spanish speaking officer and send him or her to Windy's as soon as possible. I didn't want Windy misinterpreting anything that Lopez might tell him. I wanted the Spanish speaker on the line. Then I had a uniform car sent to Jackson's address with instructions to sit on the place to see if anyone fitting Jackson's description showed up.

Windy told us that when he met Yvonne Jackson she appeared to be in very bad health. He said she was ash white and coughed all the time, like she had lung trouble. He figured that's why Jackson wanted to work all the time, to help pay medical bills.

I called Bones to give him an update. "Bones," I said, "We have a lead on a witness. He is an illegal alien, named Juan Lopez, he is from Mexico. He was working for Windy Benefield as a janitor and cleanup man. We think he made the 911 call because the caller had an accent. However he is gone. He is probably afraid he will get sent back to Mexico without his family. Christ, the guy has five kids and a wife he is trying to support. Windy doesn't have his address but he does have his cell phone number. I have asked for a Spanish speaking officer to be sent to Windy's."

I continued, "Windy found him going through his garbage cans about six months ago looking for food, he felt sorry for him and gave him a job. Lopez probably trusts Windy so we are going to have Windy call him, but I want the interpreter on the line with them. Would you run Lopez' name for us? And you need to talk to the Mayor about Lopez staying in the country legally. He may be our only witness. There is a possibility that the bartender, Carsey Jackson, has been taken by the shooter. Lapaka and I are getting ready to go to Jackson's house to interview his wife."

There was no one else for Lapaka and me to Interview. No witnesses to either crime. At least no witnesses we could talk to. The two cops were dead; the pharmacist was out cold and could not talk. Jackson was gone, probably kidnapped and dead by now and the illegal had fled, hopefully not back to Mexico. Lapaka and I decided to get a cup of coffee and figure out what the hell we were going to do. Then we'd go talk to Mrs. Jackson. Before we left I gave the crime scene guys some instructions on what I wanted.

I wanted photos from every angle, all the paper and trash processed, every cigarette butt collected, and everything dusted for prints. And of course the bullet dug out of the door frame, if it was still there.

I had uniform cops canvas the entire neighborhood looking for possible witnesses. They came up with nothing.

❧ CHAPTER FIVE ❧

Lapaka and I went to Ma's Restaurant, a local police feed bag over on Jefferson Street. We took the police booth in the back room and sat down to figure out what we had, which was not much.

I asked Lapaka, "Do you have any kind of plan?"

"No, and if the Pharmacist dies and we cannot locate the illegal, we are fucked. Besides, you are in charge; you are supposed to be the man with the plan. All we are going to have is the ballistics report and the testimony of the old lady. Who, by the way we need to interview."

"Put her on the list to do tomorrow," I said.

The waitress who took our order had been working at Ma's ever since I could remember. Her name was Joann; she was a short red head, with a million freckles. Poor gal looked like she had been rode hard and put away wet. She was just like a lot of others who work hard and can't seem to get anywhere. She was back in seconds with our coffee. And she saw to it that our coffee cups were always full. She was a great waitress.

Lapaka was a black haired, brown eyed Hawaiian. He was just over 5' 8" and weighed about 230. I had never worked with Lapaka but I heard he was pretty sharp and his name always intrigued me, so I said, "I know you are from Hawaii, but what part?"

"I'm from Honolulu?"

"How did you get to the mainland, and more importantly why?"

"I was over here on a football scholarship, I was a middle linebacker for Tennessee Tech in Cooksville, Tennessee, ever hear of it?"

"No, afraid not."

"I blew my right knee out and my football career ended, so I entered the Criminal Justice program at Tech. I got my degree and here I am."

"But why leave Hawaii?"

34

"I'm like a lot of guys, I wanted to change and see other parts of the country. I could have played at Hawaii, but I wanted to see the mainland."

"How did you get into homicide?"

"I was lucky, I caught a couple of guys wanted by the FBI, and got a medal. You would have thought I caught John Dillinger, Clyde Barrow and Bonnie Parker at the same time. I'm not stupid; I know why I got the award, because I am the only Hawaiian on the department. It was a minority thing, the Chief asked me what I wanted to do and I said homicide. Here I am. You know political correctness."

We paid our tab, which included a decent tip for the red head, and were on the way to Jackson's house when dispatch called and told us that a Spanish speaking officer was on the way to Windy's. Her name was Victoria Redondo, and she was fresh out of the academy. We changed directions and headed to Windy's.

Redondo was waiting for us when we arrived. She was about 5'2" and was probably 115 Lbs. She looked like she was twelve years old. I thought, *Where do they find anyone this young?* I introduced myself and Lapaka, as well as Windy, to Redondo. I explained to Redondo what we were up against and she understood completely.

She told us she used to interpret for the courts before being hired by the police department, and her grandfather had been here illegally but applied for and been granted amnesty under President Reagan. She was the perfect person for this job.

I called a friend at the Sheriff's office to ask if we could use their interrogation room and communication taping systems. His name is Oscar Smith. We met at a Homicide Seminar two years ago in Las Vegas, and had kept in touch with each other. We also belonged to the Homicide Investigators Coalition.

When we got to the Sheriff's Office, Smith was waiting for us and had an interrogation room and taping system set up for us.

When a police officer is killed, the whole police community closes ranks. We then become one big department, instead of a bunch of small ones. I knew Smith would help us. I didn't want to go to our office because I didn't want any interference from Bones or anyone else. I like Bones, but sometimes he wants to take over the cases. He is a supervisor now, not a lead investigator. Besides, someone from the Mayor's Office would probably be nosing around.

The first try to get Lopez was made at 1830. No answer. We tried ten minutes later, still no answer. On the third try I told Windy he was a jinx. At 1900 he got through. A woman answered speaking in Spanish, and I put Redondo on the line. Redondo went into her Spanish mode and told the woman on the other end of the line who she was and that she was looking for Juan Lopez, the maintenance man for Windy's Tavern.

There was no response. Redondo heard the woman talk to someone else, a man's voice was heard in the background along with crying babies. The woman said he was not there. Redondo told the woman she heard a man in the background and wanted to know if it was Juan.

Redondo started talking really fast in Spanish, relating to the woman that Mr. Lopez was in danger of being targeted by the man who had killed the two police officers.

Then she told the woman, "Your kids will be murdered by this man when he finds you, we will protect you, you have to trust us."

That did it, the woman's motherly instinct took over, she was not going to let her kids get hurt. The woman, Lopez' wife, put him on the phone while screaming at him in Spanish about "Hijos." Redondo was good, she got Lopez to agree to talk to us and he gave her his address.

Redondo told Lopez to stay put, we would be there shortly. I arranged to have Windy picked up at the Sheriff's Office and taken home. We left for Lopez' house, 2610 Mack Avenue, Apartment 12 C. On the way to Lopez' house, I called Bones and filled him in.

Mack Avenue was once a nice area of town, but over the years it had become seedy, and run down. The apartment was just off the corner of Mack and Van Dyke behind a burned out Greek Restaurant. Across the street was a boarded up former movie theater called "The Maxine". The theater still had an old movie title on the marquee.

Lopez and his family lived in the basement of the apartment building. Redondo knocked and Lopez answered the door. When he saw Redondo, he smiled, I guess because she was Mexican. She seemed to put him at ease. He reminded me of Leo Carrillo, the Mexican actor who played Pancho, to the Cisco Kid, in old Western movies. Short and stocky with a big smile. Lopez and his family lived in a one bed room, one bath apartment. All those people in such a small place. But he must have felt they were better off here than in Mexico, because they left Mexico looking for a better life.

Windy was right, he had five kids, but number six was on the way, his wife looked like she was ready to deliver. We found out her name was Rosa. They had more kid stuff lying around here than a day care center, I mean it was everywhere. It was apparent that Mrs. Lopez was not the best house keeper in the world, but who would be, with five kids and one on the way?

Lopez explained to Redondo, half in English, half in Spanish, that he and his family came here from Acapulco, Mexico to find work. They had been here about a year. For the first six months the only work he could get was day jobs. Standing on a corner hoping someone needed a worker. About six months ago Windy caught him going through his garbage cans. Windy took him in, fed him and gave him a job as a cleanup man and dish washer. He said he has been there ever since and no longer had to stand on the corners hoping for work.

He told us that he was at work today. He had been talking to Jackson but before the suspect came in he went to the back room to get his clean up gear. He didn't see the suspect come in the bar or how long he had been there.

Lopez said, "Then I went to work mopping. While I was mopping two Polica came in. They couldn't see because it was so dark in the bar."

"What does he mean when he says they couldn't see?"

Redondo asked Lopez the question.

"When it is bright outside and you go into a dark room you cannot see until your eyes adjust. It happens to me every day when I go in the bar, it is so dark in there it takes a while to get used to it."

"The guy at the bar, his eyes were used to the dark. When the man saw the polcia, he said, "Holy Shit," pulled out a pistol and started shooting." The polica fell, I got scared, the man with the gun turned at me. I started running and fell over the mop bucket, he shot at me but missed, I ran out the back door. I called 911 about the Polica. I don't know what happened to Mr. Jackson. I did not see the gun."

Redondo asked Lopez to describe the gunman.

"Gringo, about 6 feet tall, maybe 160 pounds. White shirt and blue jeans with a dark baseball hat.

I wanted to know if he had on a light blue jacket with writing on it. Lopez said he did not think so, all he remembered was a white shirt. He thought his hair looked white against the dark hat. He did not know the color of the shooters eyes. He thought he was about sixty years old.

I had Redondo tell Lopez that we would arrange for him to meet with a police artist so we could get some kind of picture of this guy.

Now that we knew Lopez was a witness, what was he going to do? He had five kids and a pregnant wife, he just couldn't pack them up and head back to Mexico. He knew he was in a pickle. He knew he had to trust us. He knew he had to help us for the sake of his family. He also knew if any of his kids got hurt, Rosa would probably become his widow, after she killed him. He didn't want any part of that.

I told Redondo to advise Lopez and his family that we would have 24 hour surveillance on his home until we could get him and his family moved to a safe house and that they should pack enough clothes for a least a week. I called dispatch and had them send a surveillance detail. We did not leave until the surveillance unit arrived.

I told the two uniform cops that Lopez was a witness to the Townsend and Jessop killings, and they said, "We will watch over him like a couple of mother hens."

It was too late to call Bones, I would call him tomorrow.

Immigration, another damn problem our politicians cannot seem to solve. So I would have to figure a way to get Lopez and his family legal status, even if it is temporary. And I was going to start by moving him and his family out of this fucking dump.

There is a state organization called "Friends of Criminal Justice." They were funded by a group of wealthy families to help members of the Criminal Justice System, in the event of a line of duty death of a police officer or fire fighter. Bones was a member of their board of directors. I'm sure he could convince them to put up money so this family would have a decent place to live.

Later, I thought to myself, Lopez is right about the bright sunshine and darkness; it does take a while for your eyes to adjust. That's what we did on The Segundo, the submarine I was on. In the Navy it's called, "Rig for Red". During the dark hours, all the compartments are lit with red lights. Watch standers who are going on deck for a night time watch must wear red glasses thirty minutes before watch time, that way their eyes are already adjusted when they enter a dark space.

So the theory is, that when Townsend and Jessop entered Windy's, they came out of bright sunshine into a darkened bar and could not see anything. Their eyes did not adjust in time. But the shooter's eyes were accustomed to the dark. When he saw Townsend and Jessop he opened fire and brought them both down. Townsend, who was first in, was hit by three shots, two in the chest and one in his right arm, Jessop who was behind and to the right of Townsend was hit with one shot, but it hit his Carotid Artery, he bled out instantly. Townsend was dead when he hit the floor. Their weapons were still in their holsters, never drawn. Unfortunately, Townsend did not believe in protective vests, so he didn't have one on. Jessop did, but it did not help him.

✑ CHAPTER SIX ✐

It was well after midnight when we decided to call it a day. We had found a witness and interviewed him, and it was at least a start. I decided that Lapaka and I should go home and regroup. Tomorrow we could start with a fresh outlook. I wanted to go home, see Louise, take a shower and have a rum and coke. Lapaka dropped me off and took the car home.

Time away from the job is good, it gives you time to reflect. An old grizzled Lieutenant once told me, "Son, you have to go home and have a beer, hug your wife and kids and forget about this job for a while or it will eat you alive." You know, he was right. But even when you are home, you still think about the cases, you just can't help it. Some of my most perplexing cases were figured out at home while I was in bed.

One such case, the victim, was shot in the end of his little finger, the bullet traveled up the little finger and exited at the second joint of the finger, tumbled and struck the victim between the eyes, killing him. I racked my brain and I racked my brain trying to figure out how the hell this guy got shot in the end of the little finger.

Then I found out that the shooter was playing Russian roulette, and was waving the gun around, then it hit me like a ton of bricks. The victim must have put his hand and arm out in a defensive position toward the suspect, saying don't point that gun at me, then of course the gun went off, the bullet hitting him in the end of the little finger, eventually killing him. That suspect got ten years, but was out in two.

When I got home Louise was waiting up for me. I'm lucky, I have a wife who is so supportive of me in everything I do. When I was working full time and going to school full time, she took care of the kids, it was no easy task, we had three kids under three. She worked really hard. I'm surprised she did not throw in the towel and call it quits.

Louise and I had met after I returned from the Navy. I was standing on my parent's front porch when I saw a young lady come out of a field that separated our street from the next one. She started up the road past my parent's house. I asked my dad, who was living at the time,

"Who is that girl?" He said that's Louise, she used to play with Terry. I said, "Little Louise that played with our Terry?" "Yes," he said, "look at her, she walks just like a model."

I thought, *Wow, she has really grown up. She is the most beautiful thing I have ever seen.* So I cooked up a scheme for my Dad to take me over to her house on the pretext of my Dad playing checkers with Louise's dad. It worked. We dated the next week and the rest is history.

The next morning, July 18th, my phone rang at 0700.

It was Bones. "You didn't call me last night." He screamed.

I said, "Bones, we didn't get done until after midnight, I didn't want to bother you that late, all we got was a generic description anyway. But I do have a theory to run by you, and I need Redondo transferred to us. The Lopez family really likes and trusts her, she will really help them get through this case."

"Consider it done."

"Oh there is one more thing, I want the Lopez family moved to a safe house. Can you arrange that with The Friends of Criminal Justice?"

"You don't want much do you?" he said.

"Hey, remember what the Mayor said, anything I need."

"Okay, Okay, I will see what I can do. What are you doing today?"

"Well first, we are going to the morgue and then to see Mrs. Jackson, after that I don't know."

"Okay, but keep me posted damn it."

Lapaka picked me up at 0900. He was drinking a cup of coffee that had a rather pleasant aroma. I asked him what is was and he said Kona. It comes from Kona, Hawaii. It is really good stuff, you should try it.

"I don't know." I said. "I'm kind of traditional, I don't like to change. But bring me some and I'll try it."

"I'll do it."

I said, "Before we go see Mrs. Jackson, we need to go to the morgue and find out what they came up with."

"Okay." Lapaka said.

We got to the morgue at 0930. I've always called the morgue the "Morgue". But the new term is, "The Office of the Medical Examiner." However, I still call it the "Morgue" not the Office of the Medical Examiner. Old habits are hard to break.

We contacted the on-duty Medical Examiner, Stanley Baines. Baines had been around a long time and really knew his stuff. But, sometimes he talked over a layman's head, and had to be slowed down a bit so the uninformed could understand what the hell he was talking about.

Baines said, "Jessop was shot once, but it hit his Carotid Artery, so he bled out, he didn't have a chance. He probably would not have survived if he would have been on an operating table when it happened. Townsend was hit three times, two in the chest, and one in the right arm. I noticed he did not have a protective vest on, that might have saved him. I have the bullets and the fragments for you. The report will be done sometime tomorrow."

"Call us when you have it ready and we'll come by and pick it up." I said.

Baines said. "Before you leave, I want to show you something on the bottom of Townsends left foot. He has an unusual tattoo on his heel."

Baines uncovered Townsend's legs and lifted up his left foot. On the heel of Townsend's left foot was a tattoo of a "Five Pointed Star." The center of the star had the initials "FF." Each point of the star had an initial at the point. Five initials W.I.T.C.H. The word Witch. What the hell does that mean? Was he into Witch Craft? I thought to myself.

"What do you make of this Lapaka?" I said.

"Beats the hell out of me. Could he have been into Witch Craft? But wouldn't the background investigation on him when he was hired uncover something like that?" Lapaka asked.

"I don't know." I said.

Baines said. "I have been doing this for over thirty years and I have never seen a tattoo like that, let alone on some one's heel. Beats the hell out of me too. But if you ever figure it out, please let me know."

"We will." I said. Baines gave us a photograph of the tattoo and the bullets and we left.

We arrived at Mrs. Jackson's house about 0945. We knew she had already been advised about the killings of Townsend and Jessop and that her husband, Carsey, a possible witness, was missing.

3479 Beals was a large gray clapboard home probably built in the 1920's. Mrs. Jackson lived in the rear apartment. We followed a long narrow sidewalk that led to the back of the house. We walked up onto a small porch and I knocked on the door. I noticed the back yard contained a large garage that had a coal bin attached to it. At one time the only source of heat for these old houses was coal stoves that sat in the middle of the front room floor. At least that's the way our house was heated when I was a young boy.

As I stood there thinking about the old coal stoves, the door I had knocked on opened, bringing me back to reality. A slightly built woman in her fifties answered the door. I asked for Mrs. Jackson and she said that she was Mrs. Jackson. It was apparent that she was a very sick woman. On top of her illness, she was now beside herself with grief, worrying about her husband. We introduced ourselves and she asked us in. She had been sitting with a woman she introduced as Mrs. Wallen, her land lady. Her home was small, well kept, and sparsely furnished. She offered us coffee, which we declined.

Mrs. Wallen got up and told Mrs. Jackson to call her when she needed her. She excused herself and left. She lived in the front part of the house.

We exchanged pleasantries and then got down to the task at hand. She knew why we were there. I could tell she had been crying.

I asked Mrs. Jackson, "Would you please give us some information regarding you and your husband's background, where are you from, how did you make your living, how long have you lived here?"

She told us, "Carsey and I have been married for twenty-two

years. We never had any children. We are originally from Vermont, but we have been here for about fifteen years. We owned a transmission shop on the east side of town. We were bought out by a national transmission chain about a year ago. It was a pretty good sum of money."

"Why did you sell?"

"Too much trouble getting honest and capable help, workers always quitting, calling in sick, or just not showing up. Scheduling was a nightmare. Customer complaints and too much stress. Carsey said he was getting pressure to buy used transmissions from some guy who worked for the city. He said the guy had about 300 transmissions he was trying to sell. He wanted $100 apiece. Carsey turned him down. He was afraid he was a mobster and that the transmissions he was selling were stolen."

"The same guy came in a week later and told Carsey that he only had 50 transmissions left. He offered Carsey a deal, if he bought all 50, he could have them for half price. But that was still $2,500.00. We didn't have that kind of cash lying around, besides Carsey still felt that the transmissions were stolen. He seemed like he was in there every other week with something new to sell."

"How do you know he worked for the city?"

"He told Carsey he was from city surplus and was authorized to sell surplus military equipment to small businesses."

"Military equipment?"

"Yes, he told Carsey the military gives the surplus to the city and the city sells the stuff to business people."

"Did Carsey tell you the guy's name or anything else about him?"

"No, but Carsey told me that the same guy had been into Windy's two or three time. He recognized Carsey and they talked about the shop. But he did not have anything to sell. Carsey was working the bar that day, and the guy recognized him. They started taking about the shop. Carsey told him it was too much pressure running your own business so we sold out."

"He told Carsey he was sorry that he had to sell, but it was a blessing for him, because the new owners of the shop were buying his transmissions and engines."

"Are you positive he said military surplus?"

"Yes, Carsey told me the guy said it was military. He told Carsey that he gets the surplus from the military bases and sells it."

"Why would the military give all this stuff to the city?" I said, thinking out loud.

Lapaka responded. "I don't know, maybe it's some kind of public relations program."

"Do you know the new owners names?"

"I have the sale papers in the other room, but the name of the new owner is Vestel, Margaret Vestel, a woman bought the franchise. We never met her."

"What is the address of the shop?"

"4000 Concord Street."

"Thanks, but Mrs. Jackson, if Carsey thought the transmissions were stolen, why didn't he call the police?"

"I tried to get him to. But as I said, he was afraid the guy was from organized crime. He was afraid they would burn down the shop. He felt it was safer to sell."

"Look, Carsey and I may not be the two smartest people in the world, but we certainly aren't the dumbest. We knew that guy didn't work for the city. He had to be a crook. Who else would have 300 transmissions to sell? I don't think he got the stuff from the military, do you?"

"I can't imagine how."

"I can't either." Lapaka said.

"How did Carsey end up at Windy's?"

"After we sold the shop, Carsey went to bartender school. He always wanted to work in a bar. The school set him up with the job at Windy's. He has been there about a year."

"Then I got sick. Lung disease, not cancer, but still pretty bad. Well, we did not have health insurance. You know what that means?"

"The bills were outrageous. Some of my meds are six hundred dollars for a thirty day supply. We lost everything, our house and all of our savings."

"Thank God Carsey got in at Windy's. He worked every shift he could work to help with the medical bills. But it didn't do any good, we were just getting in deeper and deeper. Carsey even had to walk to work, we couldn't afford a car. That's why we live here, it's not great. But it is all we can afford."

Christ, I thought, another fucked up system in America, health care.

I asked Mrs. Jackson, "Do you have any friends, family or a Minister you can call on for help?"

She said, "I have two nieces in Vermont, but I can't ask them to come out here, they both have families and jobs."

"Our landlord, Mrs. Wallen, told me to call if I need anything. I do go to church when I am able. Reverend Bowles called when he heard about the killings. Carsey, being a bartender did not feel right about going to church. Reverend Bowles said the church would give me all the support I need."

I said, "Mrs. Jackson I hate to ask these questions but I have no choice. Do you think Carsey just got tired of the situation that you and he were in and this gave him an opportunity to run away?"

She said, "No. I don't think he would do that, he was too proud, always took care of things, he would not just leave. I know he loves me. Detective, I realize he was probably taken by the killer."

When she said that, my heart went out to her, there was nothing I could say to ease her pain.

Mrs. Jackson started to cry again. I gave her my handkerchief. I always carried a handkerchief just for that reason.

The hardest part of this job is telling a parent that one of their kids has been killed and is never coming home again. A hanky seems to comfort them. It's a strange reaction. It's as if the hanky has become part of the child or loved one, it's something a parent or spouse can clutch and hang onto. Mrs. Jackson was no different.

Lapaka asked, "Do you know of any enemies Carsey might have had?"

"None that I know of."

I said, "Mrs. Jackson, if what you say is true, the only answer to Carsey's disappearance is that he was taken by the killer of Townsend and Jessop. And you already know that. I have to be honest with you, if that's the case, Carsey may be in grave danger. We don't know what Carsey looks like. Do you have a recent photo we could have? Does he have any scars or tattoos?"

"Yes, I'll get you a photo. He also has my name, Yvonne, tattooed on his left upper arm." When she came back with the photograph she was crying again.

I decided it was time to leave Mrs. Jackson, there was nothing else Lapaka and I could do or say to ease her heart ache. I gave her my card and asked her to call me if she thought of anything that would help us. I told her that we would be in touch.

She wanted to give me my handkerchief back. I told her, "Keep it, I have lots of them."

She smiled and said, "Thank you for your kindness."

On our way out we stopped by to see Mrs. Wallen. We gave her our cards and asked if she would continue to look in on Mrs. Jackson from time to time. She assured us she would. I asked her to give us a call if she or Mrs. Jackson needed any assistance.

When we left I said to Lapaka, "We need to go see Bones, I have a couple of theories we need to knock around with him."

"Yes, and we need to visit a transmission shop."

"Oh yeah," I said.

ᑲ CHAPTER SEVEN ᑲ

On the way to Bones' office Lapaka and I discussed a couple of different theories. What if the shooter was not the drugstore robber? What if the shooter knew Townsend or Jessop from an earlier case?

Lapaka said, "What if the shooter was wanted somewhere else, and he thought Townsend and Jessop came in looking for him, but they really weren't? The suspect didn't know that, and he sure didn't want to be taken, so he kills them."

"Not a bad theory." I said.

When we got to Bones' office we had two messages waiting for us. One from the crime lab, they wanted to see us. And one from the hospital, the pharmacist had regained consciousness. Finally, I thought, some leads. And of course, there were 2300 call in tips to the 800 hot line. We had to call in police reserves to handle the back log of calls. The citizens were really up in arms over this crime, and they wanted the killer caught. Of course over half of the calls were from nut jobs, but they still had to be weeded out.

Lucy Wales, Mayor Wilson's Administrative Assistant was in Bones' office when we got there.

I told Lapaka, "This means trouble. Just what we need, a stuck up bitch sticking her nose into this investigation."

"Now, Now, Cod". "Just because everyone in town knows that the Mayor is banging her, does not mean she is a bitch."

"Well, everyone knows but the Mayor's wife," I said.

We stood outside the door until Bones motioned us in. Bones introduced us to Ms. Wales, however we already knew who she was. Lucy Wales was the Mayor's squeeze. She was twenty years his junior.

Before anyone said anything, Wales demanded to know what progress was being made on the investigation.

"The Mayor wants to make a public announcement tomorrow and he needs some assurance that the case is progressing in an orderly fashion and will come to a swift conclusion."

I said, "Miss Wales, we are doing everything in our power that we can, however, some things are not within our control. We only have one witness and he can barely speak English and he cannot identify the shooter. The pharmacist is just now able to talk."

"We are not even sure the drugstore robbery and the killings of Townsend and Jessop are connected. We haven't heard from the lab about DNA or fingerprints. We can't just snap our fingers like a magician and find things out. If we are lucky, we might have a ballistic report, but that will only tell us the caliber of the weapon, not the owner. This is not a TV crime show where the case is solved in sixty minutes. Maybe the Mayor should hold off on his press conference."

"Detective, that is not your call. Maybe you guys should ask the FBI for some help."

"Ms. Wales, are you talking about the FBI that did not solve the Jimmy Hoffa Case? The FBI who had three agents killed in Florida because they didn't know how to make a felony stop? The same FBI that had a female agent killed in Arizona, by one of their own, because of poor planning in a felony arrest? If you are I don't want any part of them thank you."

Then all of a sudden Lapaka jumped in and said, "You know what, it is not your call to be sticking your nose into this case. We have more important things to do than sit here and discuss an ongoing investigation with you. I know you work for the Mayor, however, you are really not in any position to be telling us what to do."

With that, Ms. Wales got up and said, "We will just see about that Detective," and left in a huff.

Christ, I couldn't believe my ears, and people call me abrasive. I thought Bones was going to shit his pants.

I said to Lapaka, "What the hell got into you?"

Lapaka said, "I can't stand that bitch, she thinks her shit don't stink."

And Bones said, "Lapaka, if I hear from the Chief's Office over

49

this, I am going to have a piece of your ass."

Lapaka said, "It'll be worth it boss."

Bones asked, "Where are you on this damn thing? What theories have you come up with? I have to tell the Chief something."

"We have a new piece of information you need to know about. When we were at the Morgue, Baines, the Medical Examiner, showed us the bottom of Townsend's left foot. He has a tattoo of a five pointed star with the initials FF in the center and the letters W.I.T.C.H. one letter over each point of the star. The word WITCH."

"Witch, what the hell does that mean? Why on the bottom of the foot? Was he a fucking Warlock?" Bones asked.

I said, "I don't know about that, but it seems to me if it was on the bottom of his foot, he didn't want anyone to see it. It was hidden, but why? It's another crazy angle to this case that we'll need to figure out."

"We have a couple of other ideas we are working on. What if the drugstore robber and the killer are not the same person? What if there are two different suspects? What if the drugstore perp did not go to Windy's? What if the killer was just sitting in Windy's having a beer? Maybe he was wanted somewhere else, and thought Townsend and Jessop were in there to get him. They weren't of course, but the killer didn't know that. What if the killer knew one of them from a previous case? Maybe the killer was protecting himself from an earlier crime. If it was a previous crime it was probably Townsend that he recognized."

Bones said, "It looks like you two have come up with some pretty good theories. But I would still pursue the drugstore suspect until you get something more concrete. By the way, don't forget to call the lab and hospital. Also, have you had a chance to call Big Nate?"

"Hell no, we've been too busy."

Before we left Bones' office the Chief called. Bones yelled, "Lapaka, stay, Cod get out." Well I know what that meant; Lapaka was in for one hell of an ass chewing.

While I waited for Lapaka I called the crime lab to find out what they had. The news wasn't good. There were no prints. They found two partially smoked cigarettes. The name on the cigarettes was all but gone. The letters ZS were all that remained of the brand name. The lab tech told me that neither the tobacco nor the cigarette paper was from a commercial American company. At least he had never seen any similar samples. The lab tech felt it could be a foreign brand. He had an ongoing computer search trying to locate the manufacturer of the cigarettes. They were still working up the ballistics report.

The crime lab was able to get saliva from the cigarettes for a DNA test. However, there was no match in the National DNA Bank. I really wasn't surprised about the DNA match, not everyone has had a DNA sample taken. But there should have been fingerprints, then I remembered there were no drinking glasses or bottles on the bar. Whoever did the killing was really thinking, the killer must have taken them.

When Lapaka came in, I filled him in on the info from the crime lab.

Then I asked him, "What happened?"

"Bones chewed me up one side and down the other. I have never been chewed on like that."

Then Bones told me, "Lapaka, I don't hold grudges, but would you please hold your tongue the next time you see that bitch. And believe me, there will be a next time, I guarantee it. Now get out of my office and catch a cop killer. Consider yourself reprimanded."

I told Lapaka, "Bones was just doing what he had to."

Lapaka said, "Cod its Six O'clock, let's call it a day. We can see the Pharmacist tomorrow." After that ass chewing I need to go home and have a beer, and what was that business about Big Nate?"

"I'll tell you tomorrow." I called my wife Louise and asked her if she wanted to go out for dinner. She said yes. With that I headed home to get Louise.

I picked up Louise, and we went to Mario's Italian Restaurant, a favorite place of ours. I had my usual, spaghetti and meat balls, Louise had pasta and broccoli. Over dinner I filled her in on the case. Louise was always my sounding board. I can figure out a crime, but I can't figure emotions. Louise can, she is the one who always brings me back to reality.

What is it about women, that makes them so good at emotional reality? Thank God I married a good woman. I also wanted to find out Louise's feelings on my trying to get Big Nate back. Louise was like Nate's wife, Leona, she was not having any part of it. I blew that thought off. When we got home it was after ten, we were both bushed so we showered and hit the bed.

I must have been dreaming. I was back on the Segundo and we were about to dive, the diving alarm was blaring over and over, and wouldn't shut off. Finally I awoke and realized it was the damn phone that was ringing. I wasn't on the Segundo at all, I was home in bed. Jesus, what a dream! I have been out of the Navy for over forty years and I still dream about it.

It was daylight. I reached for my cell phone and knocked the bed side table lamp over breaking the light bulb. Another mess I would have to clean up.

"Hello, I said, this better be good, I was having a hell of a dream you interrupted."

"Bones here, are you awake?"

"I am now damn it! What is it Bones, I mumbled into the phone?"

"I hate to start your day off like this, but a dead male body has been found up in Callaway County, you need to saddle up and head up there. It looks like its Carsey Jackson. Lapaka is on the way to pick you up. He should be there any minute."

"The homicide guy up there is Carl Bowden. He will meet you at the Sheriff's Office."

"Are you sure it's Jackson?" I said

"No, not positive, there was no ID on the body but the physical sounds a lot like Jackson. The Callaway County Sheriff's Office called because of the FAXES we sent out and all the publicity about Townsend and Jessop. Did Jackson have a tattoo of "Yvonne" on one of his arms?"

"Yes he did."

"So does the body they found, so it is probably him."

"Okay, I'll get ready," I said.

Bones said, "Take some extra clothes, you may be there a couple of days," and then hung up.

My lovely wife, Louise, was already up and had the coffee going. I told her about the lamp. She said she would clean it up.

After all she said, "I have been cleaning up after you forever." I couldn't argue with that, so I headed for the shower.

Then I began to think that Big Nate was right, it is time to retire.

As I was finishing my second cup of coffee, Lapaka showed up. I asked him if he wanted some coffee.

He said, "No, I have some in the car, I brought some for you too. I got the Kona Coffee you wanted. Strong as hell, but it wakes you up. We'll need it; it's 125 miles up there."

"Holy shit," I said, we'll be up there all day."

Lapaka said, "What else do we have to do, it's not as if we're busy."

"Yeah right."

It took us three hours to get to Callaway County. On the way Lapaka asked about Big Nate again.

I told Lapaka, "When I was ordered back to homicide to meet with Mayor Wilson, the Chief and Bones, the Mayor said I could have anything I wanted to help with this case. After the meeting I asked Bones if he thought he could get Nate back to help me. Nate and I worked homicide together for a long time and I felt he would be a good asset to have."

"Does that mean you are not comfortable with me as a partner on this case?"

"No, no, not at all. But I have never worked with you before. I really don't know your hang ups, just as you don't know mine. However, over the past two days, I think it has been a pretty good two days, don't you?"

"Yes I do." Lapaka said.

"I don't have a problem with you at all."

"Oh, by the way, I really liked you getting into Lucy Wales' face, I thought that was great. As a matter of fact, I thought I heard myself talking."

Lapaka laughed. And said, "Yeah I think we'll do all right as partners. You know, maybe you should talk to Big Nate, at least he could give us some unofficial assistance."

"Well I guess I could think about it," I said.

ℰℴ CHAPTER EIGHT ℰℴ

We got to the Callaway County Sheriff's Office just before noon. We parked in police parking and headed for door that said "Sheriff." This building had to be from the 1810's. It was built with blocks made from solid granite. All the windows were encased with black steel grating. It was a damn fortress. There was a long winding sidewalk with Elm Trees on each side. Each Elm tree was surrounded by black steel ornamentation that matched the steel casing on the building's windows.

We entered the Sheriff's Office through a large oaken door. Immediately inside the door was a long counter, similar to a bank. Behind the counter sat a young man in a Sheriff's uniform. He was busy reviewing reports and didn't notice us. Real observant, I thought. I banged my car keys on the counter and he jerked to attention.

"Sorry," he said, "I was going over my crime scene notes from the body we found yesterday. We don't find many homicide victims up here. I was just making sure I didn't miss anything."

We identified ourselves to the Deputy as police officers and I asked, "How do you know the body was a homicide victim?"

"Because he has two bullet holes in his head, at least that's what Monroe said."

"Who is Monroe?" I asked.

"He's the medical examiner."

"Oh," I said. "Sounds like a homicide to me too."

"Why are you here?" He asked.

I said, "We are here to see Detective Bowden about a dead body that was found up here, it must be the same one with the two bullet holes."

The Deputy said, "Here in Callaway County our officers are referred to as Deputies, not Detective or Investigator, just plain Deputy."

"Excuse me for not following protocol. We are here to see Deputy Bowden, is he in?"

"Wrong again. Deputy Bowden is a she."

I said, "We were told Carl Bowden, sounds like a man to me."

"Yep," Deputy Dog said. "It's spelled Carole but its pronounced Carl, a lot of people make that mistake."

I was about ready to crawl over the desk and punch this little ass hole right between the eyes. Finally I said, "Look we came a long way, I don't give a fuck what he or she is, just tell he or she we're here."

The Deputy got this stupid look on his face and said, "Well you don't have to get uppity, just cause you're from the big city."

"Would you please tell Deputy Bowden we're here," I said. Finally the Deputy called back to Bowden's office.

About three minutes later, the door opened and a voice that sounded like a gorilla said, "Is someone out here looking for me?"

It was Deputy Bowden. This woman, was about 5' 10," weighed at least 230 pounds and could have been a middle linebacker for the Chicago Bears, I shit you not, this was one big woman. She was Callaway County's answer to Big Nate, only she was white, female and had hair.

I said, "I'm Cod Overture and this is Leo Lapaka we're Detectives from the Police Department, we are here to see you about the dead male body that was found up here. We were told you notified our department this morning. Are you the lead investigator, oops excuse me, the lead deputy on the case?"

Bowden came over and said, "Yes I am." She shook our hands and I thought she was going to break mine. Jesus, what a grip this woman had.

She also said, "I hate being called deputy, I should be called detective or investigator. I have been trying to get the sheriff to change it for two years, but he is a fucking hard head. I should know, he's married to my twin sister."

I thought, *Jesus, there can't be two women this big!*

56

Bowden escorted us back to her office and offered us coffee. I took the coffee but Lapaka was too stunned to talk. The last time he saw a woman this big was back in Hawaii.

Bowden said, "We got your faxes about the missing bartender and of course the publicity on the two officers who were killed. We are going to send a rep to the funeral, its least we can do. We're a small outfit, but we like to be involved with other agencies."

Bowden continued, "The body was found yesterday morning by a couple of eighteen year olds out hiking. As soon as they found it they called. They said they did not see who put it there. They waited at the trail head and escorted the Deputy to the body. You met the Deputy, he's the one on the desk."

"Oh yeah, we met him, all right."

"You'll have to excuse Deputy Cocran, sometimes he is a bit much to deal with," she said.

Then I wondered, *Does he carry one bullet or two?*

Bowden told us that the body had two bullet holes in the back of the head, execution still killing. They did not find any shell casings or any other evidence to speak of. The body was wrapped in black plastic and sealed with duct tape. The body was covered with leaves. The plastic covering his face had been ripped open.

Bowden added. "At first we thought it was critters that tore the plastic, but there were no claw or teeth marks on the face. The person who did this left no foot prints, at least we didn't find any."

Bowden figured the killer walked on the leaves to avoid leaving any tracks. Cocran found a cigarette butt at the scene, but doesn't know if it was connected to the killer. She said the cigarette butt had the initials ZS on it. She wanted to know if that meant anything to us. I told her yes that was the same as the brand found in the bar where the two officers were murdered.

I told Bowden that we were not releasing any information about the cigarette butts to the public, so we would like her to do the same. She agreed it was a good idea.

I asked Bowden, "Do you think he was murdered where he was found?"

"No, I don't think so. There was not much blood at the scene, so I think he was killed somewhere else and dumped up here?"

"Did you find any tire tracks?"

"No."

Bowden went on, "As I said we are small agency, we don't find many dead bodies up here. And we sure don't have a crime scene unit, so we had to process the scene by ourselves. I will take you out there if you want."

I said, "First we need to see the body to make sure it's Jackson's. If it's him, then we would like to see where he was found."

"The mortuary is across the street, we can go over there now."

We walked across the street to the mortuary. The Funeral Home Director was also Callaway County's Medical Examiner. He confirmed that death was due to two bullet holes to the back of the head. He had removed the bullets during his autopsy. The bullets were so damaged that a ballistics check would be impossible. He did mark them as evidence however.

I checked the decedent's left upper arm. The tattoo, "Yvonne" was there. The photograph confirmed it was Carsey Jackson.

I asked Lapaka to call Bones and tell him we found Carsey Jackson. Bones told Lapaka that he would have Mrs. Jackson notified.

I turned to Bowden and said, "It's getting pretty late, can we go to the crime scene in the morning?"

"Sure, meet me at my office at 0700 tomorrow. There is a motel just down the street. It belongs to the sheriff's cousin. Tell them who you are and he will give you a discount."

I said in jest, "His name isn't Floyd is it?'

Bowden got it. She laughed like hell and said, "Floyd was the barber, there wasn't a motel owner in Mayberry." All three of us laughed at that one. She at least could take a joke.

We met at the Sheriff's Office at 0700 sharp. Bowden had deputy dog with her. His real name was Shelby Cocran. As he was the deputy that handled most of the crime scene, Bowden wanted him to come along. I didn't have a problem with her reasoning; after all it was their crime scene. We all piled into Bowden's patrol car and headed to where the body had been found.

After getting in the car Bowden told Cocran that we were not releasing any information concerning evidence found at the crime scene, and he was to keep the information confidential as well.

On the way to the scene Lapaka asked Bowden, "Where is the High Sheriff, how come he is not in on this?

"The sheriff is back at the Traffic Institute at Northwestern University. He won't be back until next week. I call him every day to update him on everything that goes on."

"Traffic Institute, how many wrecks do you have up here?"

"Next to none. It was a Federal Grant from Homeland Security, so he went."

"Why didn't he send a deputy? The sheriff isn't going to investigate accidents."

Bowden said, "Hey its politics, it will be good for his resume."

I interjected, "Yeah, I once had a supervisor who never left the office, but he was the first one to get all the equipment even when the street cops had to wait. He even got body armor and never used it. Go figure."

When we got to the area, I was pleasantly surprised at the scenery. It looked like a rain forest up here. I didn't realize the northern part of the state was so heavily forested. This could have been the backdrop for Robin Hood movies, it was really impressive.

I should bring Louise up here, she would really like this, I thought to myself.

The body was found off of a little two lane road that looked like it could have been a lover's lane. It was dumped about thirty yards off the dirt road, and about one quarter mile away from the main highway. There were trees and thick underbrush everywhere.

The ground was heavy with fallen leaves that looked like they had been there forever. The area had been roped off with the standard yellow crime scene tape. I could see where some of the leaves had been disturbed.

I asked Cocran, "When you got here were the leaves disturbed?"

Cocran told me that when he arrived and checked the area, he could see that some of the leaves had been disturbed. He attributed that to the hikers. Also some of the leaves under the body had been moved, but that was caused by the weight of the body. But most of them were moved by the ambulance workers. He also said that when he got to the body the plastic wrapping had been ripped open exposing the head. He said he did not think it had been done by animals because there was no scattering of body parts.

"Did anyone help you secure the scene?"

"Yeah, Bowdin. I called for the State Police, but they have a five day backup. As you know, we couldn't wait that long."

"Yeah, I guess you're right." I said.

I had misjudged Cocran. He might have acted like deputy dog but he knew what he was doing. For the limited resources he had he did a pretty good job. At least I didn't see how I would have done anything differently.

Cocran said, "I canvassed the whole area, from the spot where the body was dumped, all the way out to the main highway. I didn't find anything, this was a pretty clean scene."

Lapaka and I decided to walk from the scene back to the main road looking for anything that could be helpful. I asked Cocran and Bowdin to accompany us. For a lover's lane area, the place was pretty clean, not much trash lying around.

We walked about 100 yards when Lapaka saw it. Not really obvious, but it was there. A tire print.

"Overture," Lapaka yelled. "Come and check this tire print. Didn't Mrs. Jackson tell us that the guy who was selling the transmissions got them from the military? Look at this, it looks like a Jeep Tire Print."

"Yes she did." I looked at the print and noticed that is was unusual. Not the usual tread, it had an alternating lateral pattern that crossed the tire from side to side, like the old WW II Jeeps. It had been raining on and off the last couple of days, so the print had been partially eroded, but it was still distinguishable. It was on the outside edge of the dirt road, as if the driver was trying to miss the dirt and stay on the grass.

This was four wheel drive country however, so it might not mean anything. There was something about that tire print that told me it was important. I didn't know what it was, but I could feel it. Kind of like a sixth sense. There had been a lot of vehicles over this dirt road, but that print was different than all the rest.

I asked Cochran and Bowdin, "Can you make a casting of this tire track?"

"No." Cocran said. "We don't have casting capability; I can photograph it for you though."

We had to settle for photographs. Maybe our Lab would be able to identify the tire that made that track from the photos.

Bowden asked, "Why are you so interested in that particular tire print?"

I told her. "Because we think the killer has been dealing in stolen military property and this is a military tire track if I ever saw one."

"So, if I should see someone running around in a military vehicle, I should stop whoever it is." She said.

"Sure, any information you can come up with would be helpful."

Before heading back to the Sheriff's Office I asked, "Who are the two hikers who found the body?'

Bowden said, "Two Junior College sweethearts, Jerome Richards and Judy Carlson out on a day hike. I know who they are, I have known them since they were little kids. Do you want to talk to them?"

"You said, you did not think it was animals that tore the plastic, do you think the two kids could have torn the plastic to see what was inside?"

"I wouldn't think so, but anything is possible. But be assured, this is a small community and if they did, it will come out. One of them will tell someone and it will get back to me."

"Okay, if you know them why don't you interview them and press them a little to see if they tore it open. If anything comes of it call us.

"Okay, we'll get on it."

Back in Bowdin's office the four of us discussed jurisdiction. A decision had to be made on who was going to do what. Of course Bowdin would have to discuss that with the sheriff. Jackson's body was found in Callaway County, so they had jurisdiction. If what we thought was true, and he was murdered somewhere else, that agency would have jurisdiction. But where did that leave us? So far we only had jurisdiction over the Townsend and Jessop killings.

How many agencies would this entail? Sounds like a task force brewing to me. Just what we need. However, because, our case involved two dead police officers from our department, we would probably be the lead agency, which would be a good thing.

I was concerned about the cigarette butt and the bullets that had been gathered as evidence. Bowdin assured me that they would be preserved. There was nothing else to do but head back home.

Prior to saying our good byes, Cocran wanted to know if our department was hiring. He said he was interested in going to work for a bigger police agency. I told him to call the Personnel Department and ask for Donna Douglas, she was in charge of hiring. Tell her I said to call. He thanked me, we said our good byes and left. It was now July 20th.

☞ CHAPTER NINE ☜

When we got back to town it was 2200, so Lapaka dropped me off at my place and headed home. I was supposed to call Bones from my house and fill him in. When I entered the house Louise was waiting up. She was reading "Better Homes and Gardens," her favorite magazine.

We kissed hello and she asked, "How did it go?"

"Not bad, it was Carsey Jackson. He was shot in the back of the head, execution style."

"Well, I don't need to know the gory details, did the trip help?"

"Yeah I guess so, we found a tire print I think might be important, but we knew most of the other stuff. The sheriff's office found a cigarette butt similar to the one found at Windy's, so it is probably the same killer."

I asked, "Would you like to go up there sometime? It is like a rain forest, it really is beautiful."

"Sure, it would be a nice get away." Louise got up and went to the kitchen and came back with a rum and coke. What a peach she is. I decided not to call Bones. Instead, I got up fixed Louis a glass of wine and invited her to the shower.

I got up the next morning with a big smile on my face and really feeling invigorated. Who wouldn't after the shower I had last night.

July 21st. It had been five days since the killing of Townsend and Jessop, and we were no closer to the shooter. And now there was another killing to contend with.

However, the pharmacist was awake now and could be interviewed. We had a generic description of the shooter from Lopez, as well as an artist's rendering, which was worthless. The drawing did not show the face, only a pulled down baseball cap. And we now had the ballistics report. But, ballistic reports from ammo do not give you serial numbers to hand guns so there was no way to identify the weapon or the owner. It was probably a stolen gun anyway. The ballistics people thought it was a 38 Caliber hand gun, make and model unknown, probably a revolver.

I thought to myself that Lapaka and I have a lot to do today. We need to interview Arthur Phillips, the pharmacist, Myrtle Hemmings, the lady who was knocked down by the drugstore robber, and go back and visit Mrs. Jackson. We also needed to research all of the cases that Townsend and Jessop were involved with. Redondo could do the research on the case files and phone logs, and that would really take a load off of Lapaka and me. And, we really need to talk to Big Nate. Fuck, we need a scheduling secretary.

The weapon used to kill Townsend and Jessop was a small caliber hand gun. There was a good chance the same weapon had been used on Jackson. There were no shell casings at either crime scene. So the shooter must have used a revolver, or if he used an automatic, he picked up the casings. But, I don't think he would have taken the time to pick up the casings at Windy's, because after killing two police officers, he would have been in one hell of a hurry to get out of there. The weapon must have been a revolver, and at least that is one premise to go on.

While I was waiting for Lapaka to pick me up, I called Bones to fill him in on the Callaway County trip. I told him everything that transpired, even about deputy dog, and the bull shit about being called deputy.

"There are no other titles up there, except for the Sheriff," I said. "Really small town stuff, but they did know how to process a crime scene, I have to hand it to them."

Bones was not too receptive of my description of Callaway County. He seemed to have other problems on his mind. I asked him, "Are you okay Bones?"

"Hell no. The Chief called the Mayor wants Lucy Wales made part of the investigative team."

"You've got to be shitting me."

"Afraid not, the Mayor wants her to be the liaison between us, his office and the press. He wants her in on everything. I want you and Lapaka to come straight to my office, we have to do something about this."

"10-4," I said.

When Lapaka showed up at my door he had some more of that damn Kona Coffee, he really liked that stuff. I gave him the bad news about Lucy Wales, I thought he was going to blow a gasket. He did spill some of his precious coffee. I laughed like hell over that.

When we got to Bones' office, the Chief and the bitch herself were waiting for us. Only this time Wales had a lap dog named Porter Homer with her. Homer was a political hack who had been hanging on the shirt tail of the Mayor for several years. Wales must have thought Homer was going to intimidate us. That fucking prick could not intimidate anyone, he was a little weasel who was 5' 1" and weighed about 110 pounds. He had a nose like Cyrano de Bergerac and eyes like BB's.

Lucy Wales had a look on her face that said, "I'll show you two ass holes who's in charge here." The Chief looked like he had lost his best friend, of course he's political. He had to go along with His Honor and His Honor's squeeze. However, I did not.

Bones started to explain what was going on when he was interrupted by Lucy Wales.

Who said, "Let's cut to the chase here gentlemen, the Mayor has said that I am to be a major part of this investigation. Whatever you do or whoever you talk to must have my approval. I am to review every report. Isn't that right Chief?"

The Chief, nodded and said, "Yes, that is the Mayor's wishes, but not mine."

Not only was this bitch going to be involved with this case, but she thought she was going to run the fucking thing.

Well that really got my temper up. I said, "Look Wales, If you think we are going to get permission from you on everything we do on this case, you are nuts. You may be the Mayor's aide, but you are not going to fuck with us or this case. The Chief may have to take your bull shit but we don't, at least I don't. I don't have to, because I have one of these." With that I pointed to my twenty year ring. Which really meant I could retire.

"You are not the only one who has contacts in the press. I have a lot of friends in the press, and they will not look kindly on interference from the Mayor's office. Neither will the Fraternal Order of Police, The Friends of Criminal Justice or the Homicide Investigators Coalition. And if you think I won't call them you're wackier than I thought. It's your call lady, and I use the term lady lightly."

I looked over at Homer he was busy taking notes. His eyes were now as big as marbles.

Lucy Wales' face got red as a damn beet, she stuttered a couple of words, got up and left. BB eyes was right on her ass.

Bones looked up at the ceiling shaking his head. And Lapaka, just sat there and grinned.

I looked at the Chief and said, "Well Chief, do you have anything to say?"

The Chief just said, "I wish I had your balls Cod. I have wanted to tell that arrogant bitch off for years."

The Chief really could not say too much about what I said to Wales, because he owed me big time, from a long time ago.

Years ago when we were all working the beats, I got a call about a drunk naked man walking down Iriquois Street. When I got to the scene, and found the guy, it was Larry Flint, the future Chief of Police. He was drunk, but he wasn't naked, he still had his underwear on. I saw to it that he got home with no one else knowing about it.

Where he had been and what he was doing, I had no idea, and I didn't ask. A few days after I found him wondering the streets he called me and thanked me for saving his ass and career.

If the truth be known, that is probably why he wouldn't fire me when the Mayor wanted him to. Because he felt he still owed me. He couldn't have anyway, because I had my twenty in.

After that we never heard another word from the Mayor's Office or Lucy Wales. I did hear later that the Chief got reamed out a little bit, but too bad, he's the one who said he wished he had balls.

The next morning when I got to my office, I went to see Bones to find out if he had Redondo transferred yet. He said he had and that she should be roaming around in here somewhere.

I found her in the break room drinking coffee and bull shitting like most cops do.

She saw me and said, "Hi Cod."

"Hi Victoria, I need to talk to you about your assignment."

"Okay."

"Let's go down to my office."

In my office I explained to Redondo the primary reason she was transferred to my detail, which was to interact with the Lopez family. But I also wanted her to do some case file research. I told her I wanted her to look at Townsend's and Jessop's cases to see if she could find anything that might give us a clue to who the killer might be.

Unfortunately, all I could give her to search for was a damn cigarette butt with the initials ZS and the tire track. I told her that the information on the cigarette butt and the tire track was to be kept confidential. That's all we had at this point. She couldn't thank me enough for having her transferred to the detail. I assured her it was only temporary, and that she would have to go back to patrol when this case was finished. She was happy to be here.

I called Bones from my office and told him Lapaka and I needed to interview both Arthur Phillips, and Myrtle Hemmings. We also needed to go see Yvonne Jackson. I told Bones that Victoria Redondo was going to search the case files of Townsend and Jessop, and check the phone logs of the 800 call in line.

He said, "No problem."

Lapaka and I headed to East Side General Hospital, where Phillips was taken after he was assaulted.

When we got there Phillips had visitors, his wife, mother and father were there. Phillips looked like he had been put through a meat grinder. Two black eyes, a broken nose and a fractured skull. IV lines and wires were running everywhere. But he was on the mend. We introduced our selves and explained what we were up against. I asked

Phillips if he felt like talking to us and he said yes that he felt okay.

Lapaka asked him to tell us what happened.

Phillips said, "I was working on some prescriptions when I saw the kid come in and start to browse. He had been in here before with his mother."

I interjected, "Do you know him?"

"No but I know his mother by sight, she shops in my store once in a while."

"Do you know where she lives?"

"No" Phillips continued, "Anyway I saw him stuff something in his pocket, so I went out and asked him about it, he told me to go fuck myself and pulled a steel pipe out of his jacket and started hitting me with it. That's all I remember."

"He didn't have a gun?" Lapaka asked.

Phillips said, "If he had a gun I didn't see it."

"What does he look like I asked?"

"He is a little guy maybe 5 foot 6. About sixteen, white kid, light brown hair, he was wearing a light colored jacket."

"Then this wasn't an armed robbery?" I asked.

"No, he was shop lifting."

"Shop lifting." I echoed.

"Yes." Phillips said.

I wondered to myself, why would a guy caught shop lifting beat the hell out of someone with a pipe? Could it have been a gang initiation?

"We were told you were robbed of money and drugs, where did that come from?" I asked.

Phillips said, "I don't know, my wife said everything appeared to be there. At least there is no money shortage. The drugs were locked up, he couldn't get them. Must have been someone's imagination."

We thanked Phillips for his time and input and left.

I said, "At best, all this is a strong armed robbery."

"Yeah," Lapaka echoed.

Lapaka and I agreed, the drugstore thief is not the killer of Townsend and Jessop. Well at least we can eliminate him as a suspect and let the assault detail take care of it.

We were on the way to Mrs. Jackson's house when Bones called me.

"Your sister called trying to reach you. She wants you to call her."

My sister, I thought to myself, we haven't talked in years, we have been estranged because of my career and her habits. She did live with our mother, maybe something is wrong with ma. Bones gave me the number and I called.

"Grace?" I said into the phone.

"Yes this is Grace."

"Hi, it's Cod, did you call looking for me?"

"Yes," Grace said, "Mom is in the hospital, she is dying, I found her last night in the bathroom, passed out, she has Leukemia. You need to come home."

"How is she?" I asked.

"She is in and out of a coma and asking for you."

"Okay, I'll make arrangements to come." That ended the call.

I told Lapaka he would have to see Mrs. Jackson by himself because I had to go home. My mother is in the hospital with Leukemia.

I could not believe it. Forty years earlier, my sister Terry, died of the exact same disease. I will never forget that cold February night. My sister was walking across the living room floor when she collapsed and couldn't get up. Her legs would not work, they were paralyzed. My father carried her to her bedroom and my mother comforted her.

My father called our family doctor, Dr. McCall. In those days doctors made house calls. Doctor McCall was a tall stately man who always wore a black suit, black tie, and a black Fedora hat. He also carried a large black leather bag with all his medical instruments inside. After my mother explained to him what had happened to Terry, he examined her.

Dr. McCall wanted to know why my sister had so many bruises? He even asked my brother and me if we had been hitting our sister. Of course we hadn't.

His initial assessment was Acute Leukemia. He ordered her to the hospital for testing.

As it turned out Dr. McCall was right. All the tests indicated Terry had Acute Leukemia. She lasted three days, she was nine years old.

My mother and father were with her when she died. My mother later told me that Terry had said, "Just let me die momma, I hear the birds singing and I smell the flowers, they are so pretty." At the time, my sister Terry was undergoing a blood transfusion, as the last drop of blood entered her frail body, she passed into eternity.

My parents were devastated, they had lost their only daughter. They never got over the loss. Our lives were changed forever. Who could get over losing a child? My mother and father lost two before they passed away. After seeing what they went through, one of my goals in life is to never outlive my kids or grandkids.

I caught the red eye that night. When I got to the hospital the next morning Grace was there, she had been there ever since mom was in the hospital. We said our hellos and hugged, after all, blood is thicker than water. And she is still my sister.

Grace shook mom and said, "Mom, Cod is here."

My mother raised her head, smiled at me, and lapsed back into a coma. She never said a word and she never woke up. I was with her that evening when she passed. Just as my sister before her, my mother only lasted three days. She must have been holding on until I got there. I am convinced she is with the angels and my younger sister Terry, my brother Larry and my father.

Later, I talked with the doctor and asked if this disease could carry over to my immediate family? I mean we have already lost two in this family to Leukemia. The Doctor wanted to know if my mother and sister Terry had ever been exposed to anything. I didn't know, I was only eight or nine years old then. Are you serious? In the nineteen forties you could have been exposed to anything. There was no EPA back then.

My sister Grace made the final arrangements and after the service I flew back to my home. I got back on the 26th. I was gone three days and out of touch with the cases.

❦ CHAPTER TEN ❧

L apaka was waiting for me at the airport when I landed. He gave me some bad news about Yvonne Jackson, she had hung herself. She left a note thanking Lapaka and me for chasing her husband's killer and our kindness to her and Mrs. Wallen. The note said that she could not go on without Carsey. She did not work and had no way to pay her medical bills. "This is the only way, she wrote. I do not want to burden anyone else."

Jesus Christ, is anyone else going to suffer over this case, I asked myself?

Lapaka said there had been no head way on anything, the call log, the research on Townsend's and Jessop's cases, unless you wanted to call going over tons of paper work, head way. At least that much got done. He said some homeless veteran wanted to talk to me about information he had.

I asked Lapaka, "Why didn't you talk to him?"

"He wouldn't talk to me, he wanted the lead investigator."

"Well did he give you any clue at all?"

"Yeah, he said he saw a guy with military equipment on a truck near Windy's"

"Who is he?"

"He said his name was Doc Hendrix, a retired Navy Medic."

"Where does he live?"

"Did you hear what I just said? He is homeless. He told me we should look for him down on 2nd Avenue near Woodward, he said to just ask anyone around for Doc."

"Okay." Put it on the to do list."

Then I wondered, how the hell can a retired Navy veteran be homeless? What is wrong with our society, why can't we take care of the people who protect us?

Lapaka also told me that the funerals for Townsend and Jessop were going to be held together, and that they were scheduled for tomorrow afternoon at 1300, which is the 27th. They were to be conducted at the Good Sheppard Church on Mt. Elliot. Thousands were expected to attend. Lapaka dropped me off at home and I asked him to pick me up tomorrow at 0800.

I called Louise from the airport when I arrived so she was ready for me when I got home. She had a rum and coke waiting for me and had cooked my favorite meal, Meat loaf, mashed potatoes and gravy, green beans and salad. What a girl! She wanted to know how things went with my sister and me. I told her we were friendly, but I could still feel the chill between us. I told her I was with my Mom when she passed, and that it hurt, it really hurt.

I had lost my father, a brother and a sister, but not one of those prepared me for the loss of my Mother. There is just some unforeseen bond between a Mother and a child. I cannot explain it, probably no one can. She is gone now and I will miss her. And I will think of her often, but now I have to move on.

Lapaka picked me up right on time. Only this time he had different coffee, this one was called KONA KILLER.

Lapaka said, "Taste this."

I did, Christ, you could remove paint with this crap.

Lapaka said, "This is a big seller back in Hawaii."

"Are you sure they don't give this poison away?"

"Hey man, you need to learn to like the finer things in life, like this coffee."

"Yeah right," I said.

Lapaka wanted to know when we should leave for the funeral. I told him I do not go to police funerals. I know I am the big bad cop, however, to be perfectly honest, I get too emotional when I see my police brothers and sisters in caskets. So I just don't go. I will park somewhere and watch the funeral procession, but I will not attend in person. I did once, but never again.

We did just that. Lapaka and I went up on the freeway to wait and watch. And much to our astonishment, we were not the only ones there. Construction workers with hard hats and tool belts, holding American Flags, saluted when the hearses passed by. Boy scouts did the same. Men, women and kids lined the freeway. The women and some of the men had tears in their eyes. The procession was three miles long, escorted by police motorcycles on the ground and helicopters in the air. It was a site to behold. After it passed we knew we had to get busy. First stop, Woodward and 2nd Avenue to locate Doc Hendrix, the homeless man who called with the tip.

Woodward and 2nd Avenue is not the most wonderful place in the world. At one time it was, but not now. Lots of hookers, drug dealers and porno shops, it's also home to the down and out homeless.

People in this neighborhood do not like talking to police officers so we had our hands full. One bearded old guy who was asking for money said he never heard of any Doc. Another refused to answer at all. Several were sleeping on cardboard beds with the ever present shopping carts with all their possessions nearby. I kicked one sleeper on the sole of his shoe, he just grunted, rolled over and went back to sleep. We weren't getting anywhere. Finally I called for a uniform car.

When the uniforms got there I said, "Roust these fuckers up and put them against the wall, we need to talk to them." When everyone was up and alert, I gave them my Hubert Humphrey speech.

"Look you sons of bitches, two police officers have been murdered. We need information. I am not fucking around. I am the guy who gave Vice President Hubert Humphrey a jay walking ticket. If I can arrest him, I am not afraid to book all of you for violating the Green Tomato Act."

One guy said, "What's the Green Tomato Act?"

"That's the law that says you have been growing green tomatoes without a green tomato permit."

"I don't grow green tomatoes."

"Then you will have to explain that to the Green Tomato Judge."

The guy then blurted out, "Doc stays down at 7th Avenue, under the freeway."

"Thank you, I said, you can all go back to sleep now, but you have to quit growing those damn green tomatoes."

The guy who told us where Hendrix was, mumbled, "Fucking coppers, what do they know, I only grow red tomatoes." Even I started laughing over that one.

We went over to 7th Avenue looking for Doc Hendrix. We didn't have any luck. We talked to a couple of more homeless guys who were reluctant to talk to us until Lapaka threatened them with arrest. One guy thought Hendrix was in the VA Hospital, another thought he was in jail, and another thought he was just nuts and in the nut house.

Anyway they hadn't seen him in three or four days.

I asked, "Why do you think he is nuts?"

"Because he keeps mumbling about military vehicles and dead policemen."

Right away, both Lapaka and I connected with the tire print in Callaway County with the killing of Townsend and Jessop. A military style vehicle had to be involved.

We had kept the tire track and the cigarette butt evidence from the public, so there was no way Hendrix could have known about the tire track being military. But he knew what military vehicles were. Bingo, he must know something. But how do we find him? We handed out several cards to these homeless guys hoping they would give one to Hendrix if and when he gets back.

We drove back to the office to check the phone logs and to see how the research into the Townsend and Jessop cases were coming along. There still had been no smoking guns for either officer. There were three calls from Doc Hendrix, but we couldn't find him. All Hendrix said was, "Is Cod Overture in?' When he was told no, he hung up, that was it, nothing else.

We decided we did not need to talk to Myrtle Hemmings, the old lady knocked down by the drugstore assault suspect. We had turned that information over to the assault detail.

We were in our office when Bones walked in.

He said, "I have a couple of items. One, The Friends of Criminal Justice found a house for Lopez and his family. So you need to get him moved. The house is on Greater Mack near Nine Mile Road. Second, a woman from the press wants to talk to you about your progress on the case. Her name is Rolanda Jacobs, she is from the Daily Register. You will have to talk to her."

"Why?"

"Because I said so."

"Okay, when?"

"Now, she is waiting in my office." Lapaka and I headed for Bones' office.

Rolanda Jacobs was an attractive petite brunette, dressed in a blue business suit with matching high heel shoes. She wore her hair in a bun and sported rimless eye glasses She saw us coming and got up to greet us. She was very friendly and professional.

"Hi, I'm Rolanda Jacobs from the Register, you must be Detective Overture, as she shook Lapaka's hand, and I have heard so many good things about you."

"No," Lapaka said, I'm Leo Lapaka, he's Cod Overture," As he pointed at me.

"Oh, I'm sorry, please excuse the blunder." She said.

"No problem, I said, what can we do for you? Is it Mrs. Jacobs?"

"Please call me Rolanda, and no, I am not married."

Well, Lapaka being single, jumped right in, which was okay with me, I was tired of talking about this case anyway. I just let him run with it. He had been around awhile and knew what to say and what not to say.

I left and went down to records to find Redondo. I was going to have her contact Lopez and make arrangements for him and his family to move to the safe house.

Redondo was sitting at her desk pouring over computerized files, I thought to myself, *She must have eye strain by now.*

"Hey Victoria, how are you doing?"

"Pretty good, but I haven't found a thing."

"How far back have you gone?" I asked.

"I started with the latest and am working my way backward."

"Maybe you should go the other way. Start at the oldest cases and work toward the most recent."

She said, "Okay, I'll try it."

I said, "A safe house has been found for the Lopez family. You need to contact Lopez and make arrangements to get him and his family moved. Wilson Tom, from Friends of Law Enforcement has your name and number he will be calling you with all the details. As soon as he calls, get them moved."

"I certainly will," she said.

I went back up to Bones' office to see how Lapaka was doing with the reporter. Bones was there but no Lapaka or reporter.

"Where is Lapaka and the reporter?"

"I think they went to lunch."

"Lunch, wow he sure is a fast worker, they just met."

"Hey, Lapaka is young and single, so is the reporter, they took a liking to each other."

"Boy, they must have."

Shortly after 1300 Lapaka came back to the office, and promptly announced that he was in love. He said he was absolutely smitten.

"Lapaka," I said, "You just met her how could you be smitten?"

"Did you ever hear of love at first sight, that's me?"

"Man get over it, I suppose now you will be in la la land forever."

"Nope, its love, I am taking her to dinner tonight. She is

77

absolutely wonderful."

"Boy, you do have it bad. How could that happen to you so fast?"

"I don't know Cod, all I know is she is the most gorgeous girl I have ever met."

"Okay, okay, can we go to work now? What did you tell her about the case?"

"Nothing but what we have found and done. We talked mostly about us. I didn't give her any case details, just generalities."

"Good," I said.

It was Friday the 28th, I told Lapaka to call it a day. I went down to see Bones but he was already gone. So I said to myself, what the hell, I am going home too, I need some time to think.

ເ✑ CHAPTER ELEVEN ✑ວ

On Saturday morning I called Big Nate and invited him and Leona to a cook out. But he would have to cook. He made the best damn ribs I have ever ate.

"Sure, but, If I cook, you have to buy. Remember I am on a fixed income now."

I agreed, I told him 1400 or 2:00 P.M. to you retirees. I also told him to bring his thinking hat.

I called Lapaka to find out if he survived the night with Rolanda Jacobs. He wasn't home so I called his cell phone. No answer, I left him a message to call me.

An hour later Lapaka called. He said he had a really good time last night. They went to dinner and a movie and then to Rolanda's house.

He said, "I just got home."

"You must be worn out."

"Nah, I'm good."

"Big Nate and Leona are coming over for a cookout. Do you and what's her name want to come?"

"Her name is Rolanda."

"Oh yeah, I forgot."

"I'll call her and get back to you. What time?"

"1400, bring something besides Kona coffee."

"Okay."

We hung up. Ten minutes later Lapaka called back.

"We will be there."

"Great, see you then."

Nate and Leona showed up promptly at 1400. Nate was always

on time. He detested people who were always running late. He could not understand how anyone who knew what time to be somewhere could never get there on time. As a matter of fact he bought his kids watches and told them, "Now you never have an excuse for being late, so don't be."

Leona and Louise went into the kitchen to do whatever it is women do for cook outs. Nate and I went outside and did what men do at cookouts, which is to start a fire and drink. Beer for Nate and a rum and coke for me. And then to bull shit.

Of course Nate wanted to know about the case. I trusted Nate so I told him about the cigarette butts and the tire track. I told him all I could. Then I got to the details about him coming back as a paid consultant.

"What?"

"Look, the Mayor and Chief have approved it. But Bones said I have to sell you and more importantly, we have to sell Leona."

"I don't know if she will go for it Cod."

"Before you make a decision there are a couple of issues you need to know about. You would be a paid consultant, you can't carry a firearm and you have no police power. You think about it and let me know."

"Oh, and by the way, I have this new partner, Leo Lapaka, he's from Hawaii. Did you guys ever cross paths?"

"No I never met him, I heard about him because of the award he received."

"Yesterday Lapaka and I met a writer from the Register, she wanted to know about the case. Lapaka was smitten by her. He took her out last night. I invited them to join us."

As I said that, the doorbell rang. I got up and answered it, Lapaka and Rolanda were standing there. Lapaka had a stupid look on his face. He had a twelve pack in one hand and two pounds of that fucking Kona coffee. He gave me the coffee and started laughing. What the hell I thought. I didn't tell Lapaka this, but I was starting to like Kona coffee.

I invited them in and made all the introductions, Rolanda joined Louise and Leona in the kitchen and Jim followed Nate and me to the patio. The three of us sat and made small talk. Finally I told Lapaka that I had filled Nate in on the details of the investigation, including the cigarette butts and the tire track. And that I asked Nate to be a consultant on the case. Lapaka was all smiles, he told Big Nate that he agreed with the offer and asked him to give it some thought.

After the party was over and everyone left Louise and I sat down and I told her about asking Nate to be a consultant on the case. She was not too happy about it. She did not want me interfering with Leona's retirement plans for Nate.

I asked Louise what she thought about Rolanda.

"I was impressed. She is smart, pretty and knows exactly what she wants from her career and life. She also likes Leo Lapaka a whole lot. They make a nice couple. I don't know how their careers are going to jive though. She in the press, him a cop. How is he going to keep anything confidential from her prying questions? Oh well, that's for them to work out, I'm tired, going to bed."

"Me too."

On Monday morning at 0700 the big white semi with Justin Cunard at the wheel exited the main gates and headed north toward the Johnson Truck Stop. On the previous Saturday, Cunard had a good day peddling stolen military property. He sold six Jeeps, four transmissions and six diesel engines to various businesses throughout the state. He had made $8,000.00 and he wanted to deposit it with Paynter at the truck stop. Then he would find the material that the motor pool needed to repair the main hydraulic systems used for raising and lowering their vehicle lifts.

On the way to the truck stop Cunard stopped at the Wilson Storage Facility. He changed into his postal uniform, picked up his magnetic signs and weapon. Drove to the back of the facility and dropped off the flatbed trailer and hitched up his enclosed Fruehauf. Then he headed to Johnson's.

When Cunard arrived at the truck stop Lavelle Paynter was off for the day, but the secretary knew the combination to the safe and retrieved Cunard's duffle bag. Cunard took the bag out to his truck and counted his money. It was all there. He added the $8,000.00 to the bag. He now had $35,000.00. He returned the duffle bag to the secretary and she deposited it in the safe.

Cunard asked. "How many people have the combination to the safe?"

The secretary said, "Just Mr. Paynter and me."

"Okay." Cunard said, and left.

He drove up to The Place and retrieved the repair equipment he needed and headed back to the motor pool. But again he had to stop at Wilson's and change his clothes, drop off his signs and weapon, and change trailers.

When he arrived at the motor pool one of the two security guards said to the other, "It's Cunard, waive him through. He isn't allowed to be searched. He has been given an open door policy. I sure wish I had his connections."

"Yeah me too." The other security man said.

CHAPTER TWELVE

The three day weekend was gone in a flash. It was Tuesday morning and I was back in my office waiting for Leo Lapaka to show up. I am sure he spent every waking and sleeping minute with his new love, Rolanda Jacobs. However, I wish he would get his ass in here so we could go to work, I thought to myself.

I was interrupted by Victoria Redondo knocking on my door.

"Good morning Cod," she said, with a big smile on her face.

"Well good morning to you too, what makes you so happy?"

"I worked all weekend getting the Lopez family moved to their new place."

"Oh great. How are they coping?"

"Ok I guess. Juan is afraid the killer might find him and his family. I reassured them the best I could."

"I don't blame him for being concerned. The killer did get rid of the only other witness. Frankly, I cannot believe he hasn't already moved his family back to Mexico. We better assign a security detail to him and his family full time. I'll talk to Bones about it."

With that Victoria got up and said she needed to get to work.

About twenty minutes later, Leo Lapaka came in. He was all ga-ga over his new romance. He told me that they had a good time at the cookout and that Rolanda really liked Louise and Leona. He said they really hit it off big.

"Great, but now we have work to do, we need to go talk to Bones about getting security for the Lopez family."

As we got up to leave, Lucy Wales, the bitch of all bitches was coming down the hall.

"Cod I need to talk to you and Leo."

"What do you want Lucy?"

"Look, I know we are not the best of buddies, and I know I come off as a bitch. And I am sorry about our first two meetings. But now I need your help."

Of course my first thought was, *what kind of scam is she trying to run on us?*

"Hang on now, let's all go back in my office and talk."

Once in the office I told Lucy to have a seat.

"Okay Lucy, tell us what are you talking about?"

"I stumbled across some information I don't think I was supposed to know about. I don't think anyone is supposed to know about it."

"What the hell is it?"

"Everyone knows that the Mayor and I are having an affair. His wife found out last week and left him. She took their kids and went out west to see her mother. Then Lance and I went up to his cabin over the weekend."

"He went out to fish and while he was gone I decided to clean the place up. I was looking for cleaning equipment when I came across some files. I read some of them and they seem to indicate he is tied to some kind of Federal surplus property scam."

"Hey, isn't it normal for a city official to try to acquire Federal surplus property."

"The paper work said Jeeps, troop haulers, cranes, portable communication centers, transmissions, and F-15 parts."

"What kind of Jeeps?"

"Hell I don't know, the paper work referred to them as M something Jeeps."

"Why would a city need F-15 parts, I can see a jeep or two, but aircraft parts?"

"Cod, this is not a Jeep or two, this is over 150 Jeeps. Jesus Christ Cod, who needs 150 military jeeps, except the military? Have you ever seen any city employees running around in Jeeps?"

"No I haven't. Have you Leo?"

"Nope."

"Lucy, are you sure it is 150 Jeeps?"

"Yes."

"Have you told anyone else about this?"

"No I haven't. But there is more."

"What?"

"I think it's all stolen."

"What makes you think that?'

"Because the documents I saw indicate a crane was sold to a South African for $50,000. The South African deposited the money in a bank account in the Caymans. I know for a fact that the Mayor has a bank account in the Caymans, he told me about it. He refers to it as his Witch account, I don't know what he meant by that.

"Witch?"

"Yes." Lucy said.

"Do you know who or what Witch means?"

"No I don't."

"Was it his account?"

"Look, he was drunk, he told me about the account and someone or something named Witch, then he shut up, and he never mentioned it again. That's all I know about it."

I thought to myself, $50,000 for a crane. How would a South African even know a crane was for sale here? How could they get it?

"And you may as well hear it all. While I was looking through the paper work, Ellis Walker, the Mayor's Ranch Foremen knocked on the door looking for the Mayor. I asked him what he wanted and he told me that he had found a fenced area on the Mayor's property that was full of military equipment."

"He even saw a man leave in a Jeep. I told him I would tell the Mayor about it. He said okay, if you will take care of it I won't bother him. That seemed to satisfy him. But, I'm scared Cod. The Mayor knows about the military type tire track from the crime scene in Callaway County. I'm not stupid Cod. Military Jeeps and military tire tracks. Could there be a connection?"

"Did you tell the Mayor what the foreman said?"

"Hell no."

"How can we find Walker?"

"At Wilson's ranch in Callaway County."

"Where is this ranch?"

"Its 1000 acres up by Sheep's Crossing."

"How did the Mayor find out about the tire track info Lucy?"

"From the Chief."

"Oh, great, just fucking great."

"Do you have any of the documentation?"

"Yes, I have it in my safety deposit box, to cover my ass."

"How much do you have?"

"Plenty. Lance was gone all day, I copied lots of it. The paper work has approval signatures from others in both city and federal agencies."

"How did you copy it?"

"He's the Mayor. He has a City fax, computer and copy machine in his cabin."

"Will you give it to us?"

"Yes I will."

"Will the Mayor know you copied it?"

"There were so many documents in that room, he will never know anything was touched."

"Did you say transmissions Lucy"? Lapaka asked.

"Yes I did, and there were lots of them."

"Where would all this stuff come from?" I asked.

"According to the paper work it came from military bases."

"When can you get us copies of the paper work?"

"I have to go to my bank to get them. I will meet you somewhere else. I don't want Lance to know I'm anywhere near you."

"Do you know where Ma's restaurant is?"

"Yes."

"Meet us there in an hour. Take my card, it has my cell number on it. If anything goes wrong call us."

"Okay."

"And Lucy, where exactly is this property? Did you say Sheep's Crossing?"

"I don't know exactly where, but yes, it's at a place called "Sheep's Crossing" up in Callaway County."

"Callaway County. That's where Carsey Jackson's body was found." Lapaka blurted out.

"Oh my God." Lucy screamed. "That's where he was found? Cod you have to protect me, that fucking Lance will kill me."

"Take it easy Lucy, just calm down. There is no way he will know, I won't tell him, and I'm sure you won't."

"Okay, Okay." She said.

I looked at Lapaka and said. "Would you call Bowden and find out exactly where "Sheep's Crossing" is?"

"I'm on it."

◟◞ CHAPTER THIRTEEN ◟◞

After Lucy left Lapaka said, "I got Bowden, she said it's off I-75 and the Four Mile Road Exit. She said she would take us in anytime we want."

"But what about transmissions Cod? Could that be the connection between the killer and Townsend and Jessop?"

"Transmissions? How about the name Witch? The tattoo on Townsend's foot, the name on the Mayor's bank account. That cannot be a coincidence. And then Jackson's body being dumped so close to the Mayor's ranch. That's the real mystery. If Townsend and the Mayor are connected, how are they connected, how would they know each other? When the Mayor ordered me back to Homicide, he never said he knew Townsend."

"Yeah, this is really getting eerie. But how would the killer know Townsend and Jessop?" Lapaka said, a rhetorical question at best.

"I don't know, but we need to find out. We already have Redondo researching their cases, what else can we do?"

"Maybe we need to do a comprehensive background on them." Lapaka said.

"You know what Leo? You just might have something there."

I called Bones and told him we need twenty-four hour security for the Lopez family and that we were going to meet Lucy Wales at Ma's for lunch. I didn't tell him why.

"Lunch with Lucy Wales, I thought you two hated her?"

"We do, but she does work for the Mayor, and maybe she wants to make amends."

"Okay, but watch your ass."

Lucy was waiting for us when we got to Ma's. She had taken a booth in the back room. No one else was present. She had three manila envelopes of copied documents.

She said, "This is what I found. Contact me if you need anything else."

That was it. She simply gave us the envelopes and left the restaurant. And she appeared to be scared shitless.

Lapaka and I stayed at Ma's and had lunch. I called Bones and told him that we had some information that he needs to know about. After eating we headed for the office.

When we got to Bones' office the Chief was there. Oh no, I thought. How are we going to explain what we have without the Chief running to the Mayor?

Bones said, "What do you guys have that is so important?"

"Nothing, it was a dead end. We thought it was important, but it was bull shit."

We left and went back to our office. Ten minutes later the Chief left Bones' office.

I called Bones and asked him if he would like to go out for coffee?

He said, "Why?"

"Because we really do have info, but we could not discuss it in front of the Chief, he is a pipe line to the Mayor. And I think it would be better if we were out of the office."

"Okay, where to?"

"Windy's Bar, it will look normal for us to be there."

"Your car or mine?"

"Yours."

"Okay I'll meet you outside."

I called Windy and told him we were coming over to his bar to do some additional research and that we would need to use his back room.

Windy started to freak out. I assured him it was just routine. After all I didn't want him farting in front of all his customers. He finally calmed down and told me we could use his office.

When we got to Windy's there must have been 3000 flowers, candles, and stuffed animals that spanned from the front door half way across the parking lot. It was a citizen's memorial to the two slain officers.

It looked as impressive as the shrine to Princess Diana at Windsor Castle when she passed away. What an outpouring of support for the officers, their families and to police officers everywhere.

When we went into Windy's, Windy was tending bar and bull shitting with some of his customers. When he saw us he said, "What do you think of the shrine?" We all said we were impressed.

Windy told us when the citizens first started leaving the flowers he was going to trash them. However, when he started to gather them up, four bikers rode up and threatened to kick his ass he if touched them.

Two of the bikers girlfriends jumped off the bikes, pinned a Harley-Davidson pin on a stuffed toy of a police officer riding a Harley, laid it at the foot of the other items and said a prayer. Then told Windy, this better be here tomorrow, and rode off.

Windy said he was so scared he considered hiring an off duty officer to watch the shrine so no one would disturb it. But after a couple of days it was obvious no one was going to take anything. He said that people from all walks of life have been coming by at all hours of the day and night. He told us that he has never experienced anything like this in his life.

Windy showed us to his office and left us with fresh coffee and donuts. Donuts, just what cops need.

The killer had been looking for the homeless man named Hendrix for four days. He had acquired the homeless man's name by providing the local winos with free booze and food. They all knew the homeless man with the chrome grocery basket that had two flags attached to it.

The killer picked drunk derelicts as his informants because he knew they would make poor witnesses in the event he was caught. It didn't cost the killer much for Thunderbird Wine and White Castle

Hamburgers. But it paid off handsomely with information on Hendrix.

The killer found out that Hendrix was a retired Navy Medic. That meant Hendrix knew what Military Jeeps looked like. That Hendrix was the only homeless man around who had American and Confederate Flags attached to his grocery cart. And that Hendrix spent his days scrounging through dumpsters looking for things to sell.

The retired homeless Navy Medic was busy picking through the trash dumpsters behind the bars on skid row at Woodward and Fourth Avenue. He didn't hear the semi-truck drive up and park around the corner on Lennox Street.

The killer made his way to the alley behind Woodward and Fourth Avenue. He saw the cart first and knew he was in the right place. Then he saw Hendrix stand up inside a dumpster and toss a broken chair out into the alley. The chair had three legs.

"Hey there," the killer said. "What are you doing?"

When Hendrix looked up and saw the man he knew he was in trouble. This was the same man he saw at Windy's where the two police officers were murdered, this was the same man who forced another man into the back of his semi-truck trailer. This was the same man who had Jeeps in his trailer. This is the same man he had locked eyes with. How the hell did he find me? He thought.

As the killer approached Hendrix, he lit a Cigarette. Hendrix saw the gun and just stood there. What could he do he was trapped inside a trash dumpster?

Hendrix thought to himself. I have the fourth leg of the chair. I can smack this Son-of-Bitch with it.

As the killer got to the dumpster gun in hand, Hendrix swung the chair leg and smacked the killer on the left side of his face. The killer staggered backwards, dropping the cigarette from his mouth, his face bleeding from the blow. Hendrix tried to get out of the dumpster but slipped on the garbage and fell on his face.

The killer ran to the dumpster. As Hendrix was trying to get up, the killer shot him in the back of the head twice. Blood spilled out from the wounds. Brains splattered over the inside of the dumpster. Hendrix slumped forward and died. This man, Hendrix, had fought in two wars for his country. For his efforts he is murdered in a glorified trash can, dying among the garbage and filth.

Gun fire is common place in this neighborhood. No one noticed. No one cared.

The killer made his way back to his semi-truck. He looked at himself in the mirror. Shit, cut face, bruising and swelling near his left eye and his lower lip split open. *How will I explain this?*

"Fuck." The killer said as he was driving away. *I didn't want to kill him here.*

After several miles, the killer stopped and made a call.

"Jason?"

"Yes."

"This is Justin."

"I thought so, what do you want?"

"I found the homeless guy. I took care of him just like you said. Fourth and Woodward, in a dumpster."

"Why there?"

"It was awkward. He fought back. You should see my face, the ass hole smacked me with a chair leg. I had no choice. It was him or me. Do you have any information on the Mexican?"

"No. I don't know anything about a Mexican."

"Too bad, if I fall, we all fall."

"You are not going to fall. How will anyone find out about you?"

My brother is right. How will anyone find me? I can go and come as I please and no one will know. I am never challenged at the gates. Never asked where I am going, never asked what I have. It pays to have friends in high places. Look at all the money I save them. Look at all the money I have. Those dumb fucks, save them a nickel and they will kiss your ass.

Bones said, "Okay spit it out, what have you got that's so damn secret and important?"

"Shit Bones, I don't know where to start."

"How about something novel, like the beginning."

Bones always did have a way with words.

"Well, everybody's friend, Lucy Wales came to see us. It seems the Mayor's wife found out about the affair between Wales and Wilson. So the Mayor's wife split with the kids and went out west to see her mother. Wilson took Wales up to his summer place for the weekend. Wilson went fishing to forget his troubles and Wales decided to clean his cabin."

"While looking for cleaning equipment, Wales stumbled on some information that doesn't look too good for the Mayor. She found documents indicating that the Mayor has been receiving and selling stolen military surplus property. One such item is a crane he sold to South Africa for $50,000, which was deposited in his bank account in the Caymans."

Lapaka said, "While Wales was at the cabin, Wilson's ranch foreman, Ellis Walker, showed up at the cabin looking for Wilson. He said he found a bunch of military property stashed on the Mayor's ranch, and wanted to know if the Mayor knew about it."

"Wales told Walker that she would let the Mayor know. She said that seemed to satisfy the foreman." I said.

"Where does this property come from?"

"Military bases."

"Why does she think the Mayor sold it?"

"Because of the check sent to the Caymans."

"How does she know the Mayor has a bank account in the Caymans?"

"Wales said the Mayor was drunk one night and he told her about it. And you remember the tattoo that was found on Townsend's foot? The star with the word witch?"

"Yes I do."

"Well, Lucy Wales said the Mayor referred to his Cayman account as his WITCH account. There has to be a connection between Townsend and the Mayor. There is no other explanation for the name WITCH."

Bones said, "The Mayor must know Townsend from somewhere, but where? Why didn't he tell us he knew Townsend? What is the Mayor hiding? I am going to have to see the Chief. This case is really getting hairy."

"What does WITCH mean?" Bones asked.

"I don't know, we haven't figured that out yet."

"Hell Bones, this is all hard evidence. Lucy Wales gave us copies of the documents. She copied three manila envelopes full of documents. She gave us the copies today."

"How did she copy them?"

"I asked the same question. The Mayor has a City phone, copier, fax and computer in his cabin. That is where all the work on this crap probably goes on. She used his City copy machine."

While I was filling Bones in on the details, Lapaka was going over some of the documents.

Lapaka interjected, "Bones, Wales said 150 Jeeps, these documents indicate that there was 300 Jeeps. Twenty armored personnel carriers, fifty portable communications centers, F-15 parts, main rotors for helicopters, transmissions, engines and all kinds of miscellaneous military property taken from Military bases and allegedly disposed of through the City Surplus Property Office, but we know that's bull shit."

"And more importantly, I added, remember the jeep tire print we found in Callaway County near the Jackson crime scene? That is apparently not too far from the Mayor's ranch. Could there be a connection between these vehicles and the homicides?"

Bones said, "How are we going to handle this new information?"

"Good question," I answered. "I think we need to....As I was finishing my sentence Lapaka blurted out, "Holy shit, look at this, this says the fucking Chinese were here looking at the troop carriers."

"What?"

"Yeah, look at these documents, they are appointment schedules. China, South Africa, and the Montana Militiamen all had people here looking at the equipment."

Bones said, "This is getting to be one big can of worms. How big is this? Killings, theft, foreign governments and American radical groups. How are we going to cope with this Cod?"

"We need to step back, take a second look at what we have, and try to determine how deep this goes. We are going to have to get the Feds involved now. If this is stolen Military Property, they need to know about it. Which means, the Defense Department Investigators, Base Police and maybe the FBI. But, how could this much stuff be missing and they not know about it?"

"That's simple, someone is on the take." Lapaka said.

Bones said, "I agree. It means we are going to have to put some kind of joint investigative team together. I don't think we can handle this by ourselves. If the military thefts are tied to the homicides we are going to have to incorporate the thefts into our homicide cases. Working with the feds is going to be one big pain in the ass."

"You said a mouthful there," I added.

Lapaka said, "According to the documents, this stuff came from something called the DRMO at military installations. But I don't know what DRMO means, just another military acronym to me. The stuff was signed out to the city. I can't read the signatures, looks like chicken scratching. Probably on purpose. There is a return line on the documents. So maybe the property was supposed to be returned, but what if it wasn't? How would they cover it up? They had to have someone on the inside of DRMO."

"Yeah, if someone inside cleared the books, who would know the difference?"

"But someone there had to see that a lot of the property was missing."

"Hey." Bones said, "Anything can be covered with phony paper work."

"Okay I said, this is my plan of attack. First, we get Big Nate back to do a comprehensive background investigation on all the people we know who are involved with this investigation. From the Mayor and his staff to the two dead officers. Second, we have to contact the feds and get their input. Third, we need a matrix and a time line established. There is no telling how far back this goes or how wide spread it is."

"Why do you want to do a back ground on Townsend and Jessop?" Bones asked.

"These new backgrounds checks are Lapaka's idea and he may be right. You know our backgrounds were not as comprehensive as they are today. At one time you could go to your own doctor for a physical, and a lot of doctors wrote what you told them. I knew a guy who couldn't hear and his doctor passed him. He was found out because he could not hear his training officer's instructions. The Academy did not even pick up on the fact that the guy could not hear. Then they made him a dispatcher, just what we need, a deaf dispatcher."

Lapaka said, "You gotta be shitting me."

"Nope," I said, "True story. I was the guy's training officer."

Bones interjected, "Yeah, you're right, and once your background is done, it's done. There is never a follow up background. Even if you are like Cod and me, we have been around 40 years and we have never had a follow up background. For all you know one of us could be wanted for something."

Lapaka said, "I think some federal agencies are doing follow up financial backgrounds to make sure none of their people are on the take. I do know that when you change police agencies, at least in this state, you have to go through the whole ball of wax. Not by the agency you are trying to go to work for, but by the state licensing agency, which in our case would be POST, no license from POST, no police job. And they are catching some guys who are dirty."

"Okay, Okay, but we're getting off track here. What is your next step?" Bones wanted to know.

I said, "I will get Nate back here to do the backgrounds. Then I will contact the Feds. I'll have Redondo start on a time line and a matrix. Lapaka, I want you to go over the documents Wales gave us with a fine tooth comb. Then get with Redondo and help her with the time line and matrix."

Bones said, "Cod I want you to go with me to fill in the Chief."

"Whoa, Whoa," I said. "We have a problem with the Chief. He is telling the Mayor every step we take. I know this is touchy, but can you avoid telling him? Now that I think of it, the Mayor must have wanted Wales in on the investigation so she could tell him everything we did. That didn't work out, so now he uses the Chief for his information."

"Now wait a minute Cod, you can't expect the Chief not to inform the Mayor, he's the Chief's boss for Christ sake."

"Hey, I just said it was a touchy situation. But now the Mayor may be a suspect in the theft of federal property, if not murder."

"My God, this can't be happening," Bones moaned.

Just as Bones got up to get more coffee his cell phone rang.

"Where Bones asked?" Okay, Cod and Lapaka are with me I will get them on it."

Bones looked at me and said, "Another dead body. This one was found on skid row, two bullet holes to the back of the head, sound familiar? Woodward and Fourth Avenue, male, found in a dumpster. Witnesses, who are homeless, said his name is Hendrix, retired Navy Medic."

"He is the witness we have been trying to find. He called the hot line several times trying to reach me, but we kept missing connections. Shit, another dead witness."

Lapaka asked, "Who knew about him?"

"Bones, did the Chief know about Hendrix?

"The Chief gets a briefing everyday on the status of this case. The Chief gets everything, written reports, phone logs, and press clippings about the case. He looks them over and then sends a recap to Wales, who checks it and then gives it to Porter Homer. Homer assesses the importance of the information, He is the one who decides what the Mayor sees. Homer is the Mayor's Chief of Staff."

"That means BB eyes Homer is right in the middle of this. What is his connection to the Mayor?"

"Nobody knows how they became friends."

"Damn it, that's how they found out about Hendrix."

"Has the Mayor ever shown this much interest in a case before?" I wanted to know.

"I don't think so," Bones said. "But this is an usual case. The Mayor is trying to protect his public image by being involved."

"Yeah, I know, that's what I am afraid of, maybe he is too involved."

"Come on Lapaka," I said, let's get to Woodward and Fourth.

⨌ CHAPTER FOURTEEN ⨌

When we got to the crime scene it was obvious that this was another shit hole of a rundown American neighborhood. Burned out hulks of buildings, that at one time were the glory of the city. Their past, as shining family mansions, once home to manufacturing czars, has long since been replaced by decay, crime and ignorance. Majestic buildings that were a porthole to this cities greatness are now a testament to political failure and apathy.

As I got out of the car I noticed that all the usual suspects were already here. By that I mean the crime scene techs, uniform cops who were guarding the crime scene, the medical examiner's office and the press, which in this case was Lapaka's sweetheart, Rolanda Jacobs from the Register. Just what I needed a Homicide Cop going ga-ga over his girlfriend at a murder scene.

I located the crime scene tech to find out what evidence had been found, if any? His name was Willis Lawrence. Lawrence had been wounded in a shootout several years ago, and damn near died. The perp who shot him was killed by Lawrence's partner during the gun fight. Lawrence was off work for almost a year and when he came back he was sent to the crime scene unit to save his pension.

Lawrence had developed severe psychological issues about working the streets after being shot. So the shrinks suggested that he be taken off the streets for his own good. After that he was considered one of the walking wounded. And most police departments take care of their walking wounded, especially the ones who were shot by ass holes.

Lawrence gave Lapaka and me the high sign, which meant he was done with the crime scene and it was okay for us to go tromping around in it.

I asked Lawrence, "Find anything of use?"

"Oh yeah," he said. "Two bullet holes to the back of the head, execution style, he was shot in the dumpster he was found in. And I found a cigarette butt with the initials LZS on it." Lawrence held up the bag so I could see the cigarette butt.

How did this asshole find Hendrix when we couldn't? I thought to myself.

"I also found a chair leg with blood on it. I will run tests to see if it is the victims."

Lapaka didn't hang around to hear the answer, he spotted Rolanda Jacobs talking to another crime scene tech and he went over to make sure she wasn't getting too much information. He found out that Jacobs was not getting anything from the tech, which was a good thing. It didn't make Jacobs happy though.

I said, "As you know similar cigarette butts have been found at the other crime scenes. The killer knows that a DNA test is worthless because his DNA is not in the system, that's why he leaves the butts, he is openly challenging us. I am beginning to think that he must feel he has someone who will protect him, or he has one great cover."

"Maybe he has both." Lawrence said.

"Good point, I'll remember that." I said.

I walked over to Lapaka and Jacobs. I said my hellos to Jacobs and asked Lapaka if he was done talking to her. I needed him to help me round up one of homeless guys who could show us where Hendrix spent his nights.

I should have kept my mouth shut. Jacobs, who is a typical nosey reporter asked, "Can I go along?"

"No," I said, "This is a criminal investigation going on here, we can't show favorites."

I wanted to inventory Hendrix's belongings, which really meant I wanted to search them without a warrant. He was a witness not a suspect, he was dead, so his property had to be protected. And we didn't know if Hendrix had any next of kin.

We found one homeless guy who wanted to know if we were "The Green Tomato Cops?"

I couldn't keep a straight face, I busted out laughing. He wanted to know what the hell was so funny? But I was laughing so hard I couldn't answer him, Lapaka had to. I thought, man word sure gets around down here.

But he volunteered to take us to where Hendrix had his night spot. It was located under the freeway overpass at Woodward and Second Avenue. The homeless man, known as Corncob, told us that because Hendrix was a veteran, no one would bother his property. Even the homeless have respect, and value for veterans.

Hendrix lived in a large wooden crate, at one time it must have been used to store furniture. It was also obvious that he was a very neat individual, everything had a place. Lapaka commented that it must have been his military background that made him so neat. He even furnished the place. He used orange crates for end tables and candles for light.

But the most interesting thing was a cardboard box filing system.

I opened the box and found an alphabetized row of files. This guy must have kept every piece of paper he was ever given. I looked in the "O-File," and found my business card. I thought it must have been one of the cards we had given to the homeless men during the green tomato gig.

The back of the card had writing on it. "Windy's Bar, Semi Truck, Jeep, Gunshots." I showed the card to Lapaka.

"What the hell does that mean Cod? Was Hendrix at Windy's the day of the killings? Was the killer driving a Semi Truck? If he did not see the shooting he must have at least heard the gunshots that killed Townsend and Jessop."

"Well Leo, Maybe the Jeeps were on the Semi-Truck Hendrix saw. And apparently he heard the gun shots."

I called for some uniform cops to meet us at Hendrix's and had them gather up everything in the box that Hendrix used for his house.

We hung around Woodward and Second Avenue for a while talking to the other homeless people to find out if Hendrix had ever mentioned anything about the two cop killings. But we ran into a brick wall.

We were getting nowhere fast, finally one guy said, "Once in a while I would hear Hendrix mumbling to himself about cops and jeeps, especially when he was on T-Bird, but that was it. He never really talked to any of us, he was a real loner."

As we were leaving Lapaka asked, "What is T-Bird?"

I said, "Christ, have you lived a sheltered life or what? It's wine, Thunderbird, probably a dollar a gallon. Taste a lot like your Kona Coffee."

"Screw you Overture, Kona is great coffee. But that wine must be like the crap my uncles in Hawaii drink."

"Here are the car keys, you drive, let's go back to the crime scene."

When we got there Rolanda Jacobs was hanging around trying to glean every scrap of information she could get. When Rolanda saw us drive up she wanted to know what the white thing was in the clear plastic bag that Lawrence had shown me. I told her it was the suspect's brain matter, that shut her up.

It was 2100 hours when we left the crime scene, I told Lapaka he could get a ride with his Girlfriend, I was going home.

Another tragedy I thought to myself, a retired military man who meets his end in a damn garbage can.

The next morning I called Nate. Big Nate answered the phone and said, "The answer is no Cod."

"How the hell did you know it was me?"

"I didn't, Leona did, woman's intuition. She told me last night you would be calling."

"She been talking to Louise?"

"Fuck, I don't know, but they have been friends for a long time."

"Look Black Thunder, I need your help. Will you at least hear me out?"

"Okay, but it will cost you lunch at MA'S."

"10-4, what time?"

"I can be there at 1400."

"Okay you're on."

When I got to MA'S Big Nate was waiting at our favorite table in the back room. MA always had a back room saved for cops. Nate was sitting there with a shit eating grin on his face.

I said, "What the hell are you smiling at?"

"You, you helpless honky. Gotta have Big Nate's help huh?"

"Damn right, I am working on four killings. I need something. Nate, you are not going to believe what I am going to tell you."

I gave Nate a forty-five minute update on this case. I told him everything I could remember. Including the WITCH tattoo found on Townsend's foot and the Mayor's WITCH account in the Caymans, as well as the stolen military equipment.

I said, "Nate, Townsend and Mayor Wilson have to be connected in some way. But the Mayor never mentioned the fact that he knew Townsend. Why would he hide knowing a police officer?"

"I can't imagine."

"I also think someone in the Mayor's office is tipping off the killer. How would the killer have known about Hendrix if someone did not tip him off?"

"Good theory," He said. "But how do you know the killer is getting any information from anyone? Maybe he found Hendrix on his own. If this guy Hendrix saw the killer, maybe the killer saw Hendrix. How hard would it be to find a homeless guy? They only stay in certain places."

"You're right about that."

"But, anyway I will do it."

"Do what?"

"Whatever you want."

"Don't you have to talk to Leona about it?"

"Nah, she said it was okay with her last night."

"You big prick, why didn't you call me?"

"I told you, she said you would call me, besides I wanted a free lunch."

"Are you sure you are not a con man in disguise.

All he did was sit there and laugh like a fucking Hyena. Then I started laughing like an idiot. Everyone in MA'S must have thought we were nuts.

I told Nate that we wanted him to do a comprehensive background check on everyone involved with this case, from the Mayor on down.

I asked him to meet me in our old office the next day at 0800 sharp. I needed to have him finger printed, issued Police ID cards, and computer clearance pass words. Nate also had to go to the Personnel Department as well as the Business Office to sign all the necessary Contractual Agreements. He nodded, smiled and said, "I will be there."

ᘓᕲ CHAPTER FIFTEEN ᕲᘓ

The next morning Lapaka, Bones and I were already in my office when Big Nate showed up. Everyone in Homicide came to our office to greet him. Big Nate was always very popular with the other investigators.

That afternoon when Nate was done with all the bureaucratic bullshit, I took him to meet Victoria Redondo. I explained to Nate what Victoria was doing concerning the case file searches on Townsend and Jessop. I wanted Redondo and Nate to work together on the files and the backgrounds. I also asked them to finish the time line that Redondo had started.

I reasoned that Redondo was a full time officer and could be the front person for Nate if he had any trouble getting the information we needed on the backgrounds. A bigger problem was how to keep the Mayor from finding out his background and that of his staff was being investigated.

After getting Nate settled in with Redondo, Lapaka and I went in to see Bones about how we were going to keep the Mayor's background check confidential.

"That's a good question," Bones said. "No one in the Mayor's Office has NCIC authorization, so he will not be able to find out that way. We will have to do it secretly of course. And I mean hush, hush."

"How are you going to keep the Chief out of the loop?" I asked.

"I can't, he has to be advised. We cannot investigate the Mayor and his staff without telling the Chief. I have no choice in the matter, he is the Chief. I'll set up a meeting with him as soon as I can, and I want both of you at the meeting."

"We need to know why the Mayor didn't tell us he knew Townsend. How are we going to get the Mayor in here for an interview?" I asked.

Bones said, "I don't know, I'll have to run that by the Chief."

"Okay. Well I guess we had better call the Feds and fill them in."

I called the Department of Defense Criminal Investigations Office at the Federal Court House. And as you can surmise, it was as if I wanted to talk to the Pope. Talk about the run around. Finally I got a low level secretary who connected me with some guy who sounded like I woke him up.

I identified myself. He said he was Special Agent JR Benoit and wanted to know how he could help me.

"I don't know that you can help me, but I am pretty sure I can help you."

"Yeah, how so?" Benoit wanted to know.

"My partner and I are working a series of homicides. During our investigation we have uncovered a considerable amount of Military Surplus Property that we think is stolen and we are pretty sure is connected to our homicides."

"How do you know, its stolen military property and how do you know the deaths are homicides?"

"Two bullet holes to the back of each head. And we think the Military Property is on some acreage of land up north. Is that enough info for you?"

"What are we talking about here Detective, ammo boxes, MRI'S or combat boots."

"Look, Junior GMAN, do you want the fucking info or are you going to interrogate me?"

"You local yokels are all alike, you get all excited whenever you hear something has been stolen from the military, like someone was going to bomb a building or something."

"Excuse me! Local yokel! As I recall we did have a few bombings recently, or were you asleep like the rest of the Federal Agencies when that happened?"

Benoit responded, "Okay, okay what do you think is worth reporting to me?"

"How about Jeeps, portable communications trailers, armored personnel carriers, F-15 parts, helicopter rotor systems, a crane that has already been sold to South Africa. Not to mention untold numbers of engines and transmissions."

There was a hushed silence on the other end of the phone. All I could hear was heavy breathing from the GMAN.

"Jesus Christ" he finally said, "You can't be serious, can you?"

"Oh yeah, I'm very serious, and we have the documentation. Now are you interested in a meeting?"

"Damn right I am. Where and When?"

"My office tomorrow at 0800, is that okay?"

"I will be there with my boss."

"Okay, Police Headquarters, Homicide Investigations, ask for me or Detective Leo Lapaka."

"Ah, what was your name again?"

"Cod Overture, Overture, like a Symphonic song. Write it down."

"See you tomorrow Detective Overture."

I thought to myself, The Feds, everyone has to have a damn title. Why can't we just go by our names?

After talking to Benoit, Lapaka and I went to see Bones. We needed to fill him in on the meeting with the Feds. I also wanted to let him know that Big Nate and Redondo would be there too. I wanted to ask Bones to attend as well.

When we got to Bones' office he was gone. His secretary, Haley Staten, said he was in the Chief's Office and would be back in about an hour.

"Thanks," I said. "Haley would you have him call us when he gets back, it really is important."

"Of course," she said.

Haley Staten was a pretty brunette who had been on the job several years. She had been working for Bones ever since she started on the department. First in Organized Crime, and when Bones transferred to Homicide he brought Haley with him. All the cops called Haley, Twin Peaks, in private of course, because of her shape. No one would mess with her, however, because she was married to an Internal Affairs Lieutenant. And believe me, her husband kept a close eye on her and he hated her nick name.

When we got back to our office, Haley called.

"Cod, Bones wants you and Lapaka in the Chiefs Office ASAP."

"Okay we are on our way."

The Chief's Office was on the fifth floor of Police Headquarters. He had a corner office that overlooked most of downtown. It was lavishly furnished with an oak desk, and built in book cases lining the two remaining walls. One of the walls was his "I love me wall" with all his commendations, citations and photographs of him and dignitaries. Nothing wrong with that, I have my own I love me wall, in the front bedroom of my home. Only with no photographs of dignitaries. My dignitaries are my wife, kids and grandkids.

There was a food cart in the corner with coffee and donuts. No shit. Donuts! Cops seem to be attracted to donuts and coffee. Now all we needed was some of Lapaka's paint remover KONA Coffee.

The Chief didn't look too happy, but he invited us to sit down and offered us coffee and donuts. I took the coffee but declined the donut. Lapaka took both.

Bones talked first. "I have given the Chief a complete rundown on the facts of this case including the information about the WITCH tattoo and the WITCH account. The Chief has assured me that he will back this investigation no matter where it goes or who it takes down."

Bones looked at the Chief and said, "Chief do you have anything to add?"

"Yes I do. These are very serious allegations against a man with a lot of political clout. I have to say, if this information is accurate, and I don't have any reason to believe that it isn't, then we have a major undertaking on our hands. As far as interviewing the Mayor, well I will have to mull that around with our legal eagles. With that in mind, we will have to come up with a plan that will keep the Mayor advised, but with information that is not accurate."

"Bones you and I will decide what information the Mayor's staff gets. Which means, I will be in the loop at all times and on everything that goes on. Next, I want the investigative team moved to an undisclosed location that will be known only by those assigned to the team."

"Chief if I may interrupt? The Feds are coming over for a meeting in the morning, they are going to be knee deep in this. Is it okay to ask them if they have space for a joint task force?"

"That's a damn good idea Cod, that way you would be segregated from City Hall and Headquarters. You have my okay to make that happen. If the Feds need any financial help, I can get that. But they probably have more money that they know what to do with anyway."

"I have one more thing," the Chief said. "Who is on the team with Cod and Lapaka?"

Bones said, "Big Nate is back for the backgrounds I told you about, and Victoria Redondo, the rookie is doing the case file and phone log research."

"Why are you using a rookie?" The Chief asked.

"She was assigned to the case because we needed a Spanish speaking officer to help with the Lopez family and their relocation. She was the only one on duty at the time who spoke Spanish. And, by the way, she is really doing a good job."

"Lucky break for her. Okay, that suits me. You guys decide what you need in the way of hardware and supplies. Bones, get them lap tops, I don't want the computer people having to put in a hard wire system anywhere, that will only raise flags."

"Okay boss."

"Well I guess that's it for now, Cod, I want to talk to you." The Chief said.

Lapaka and Bones got up and left.

"Cod, you and I have been around a long time. I want you to know that I have never forgotten what you did for me when I was a young cop walking around in my underwear. That is also the reason I wouldn't fire you over your confrontation with the Mayor. Believe me, I will back you to the hilt on this. However, I am loyal to the Mayor, I have always felt a person should protect their boss, but not if the boss is dirty, that changes things. That's all I wanted to say."

"Thanks Chief, all of us will need your support before this is over." With that I got up and left.

ᘓᕲ CHAPTER SIXTEEN ᕙᘔ

The next morning at 0800 Special Agent JR Benoit and two other individuals were escorted to our office in Homicide. Special Agent Benoit introduced himself, as well as his boss, Special Agent in Charge, Isabel Connor and Special Agent Jared Bellamy, who was with the USAF's Office of Special Investigations.

I introduced myself as the Lead Investigator, Leo Lapaka as Second Lead Investigator, Nate Randal as our Back Ground Coordinator, Victoria Redondo as our team Research Analyst, and Bones as our Supervisor in Charge. Bones, Lapaka and Nate looked at me like I was crazy. We never used titles, but what I was doing was giving the Feds a little of their own bureaucratic medicine. Redondo just sat there and smiled, she was a rookie she didn't know what the hell I was doing.

We were all sitting around a large round table in the middle of the briefing room. Everyone looked uncomfortable and nervous because we didn't know each other. I also suspected that there might have been some jurisdictional jealousy involved. Federal investigative authorities do not like to share information with local jurisdictions, at least that has been my experience.

Finally to break the ice I suggested that we re-introduce ourselves and give a synopsis of our backgrounds. I thought that would put everyone at ease. Prior to the introductions I offered all the participants coffee or tea. Benoit and Bellamy took coffee and Connor wanted tea.

Benoit started the introductions, "I am from Lansing, Michigan and my parents are French-Canadians from Quebec, Canada. I have been with DCIS about ten years. I have done tours at Quantico, Mare Island and Ft. Knox in Kentucky."

I told him that my mother was from Newfoundland, Canada, so we had something in common.

Connor was next, she said, "I am from a Phoenix, Arizona suburb called Gilbert. I have been with DCIS about five years. I came over to DCIS from The Naval Investigative Service to get a promotion. I have ten years of Federal Service."

"How about you Jared?"

"Oh me. I'm from Little Rock, Arkansas, I have been in the Air Force ten years but I am getting out next January to take a job with the Little Rock Police Department. I've already been hired by them. I am trying to get an early out to take the job. The Air Force has an early out program for people who go into public safety jobs in the civilian community. If I get that, I will be out in about six weeks."

"Not much time to help us out then." I said.

"Yeah, maybe not." He said.

I said, "While we are waiting for the coffee, let me start by explaining what some of the issues are and to let you know that some of the suspects involved in this case are politically connected, not just here, but in Washington D. C. So it will be necessary for all of us to maintain the utmost secrecy on our information."

With that I asked Lapaka to explain the issues about the case.

Leo started, "This case involves at least four homicides and an untold amount of stolen Military Property. We have documentation that indicates 300 Jeeps, 50 Portable Communications Centers and 20 operational Armored Troop Carriers, F-15 parts, Helicopter Rotor Systems as well as an unlimited supply of engines and transmissions that have been stolen from Military Bases."

"We know that a crane was sold to South Africa for $50,000 and that money went into a personal checking account in the Caymans. We also have documentation that the Chinese Government as well as one or two American Militant Organizations had representatives here looking at the Armored Troop Carriers."

The Federal Agents just sat there in stunned silence. They could not believe what they were hearing.

Finally Isabel Connor said, "Special Agent Benoit told me that you had information concerning the alleged theft of military property. But he didn't tell me it was this extensive."

"I didn't tell Agent Benoit the amount of the thefts, because I was not sure of the numbers. But using the Military Documents, we figure it is in the neighborhood of $300,000,000 in Federal acquisition costs. And if the property was sold for just ten cents on the dollar that is $30,000,000. Quite a chunk of change."

Connor then asked, "What evidence do you have that we could look at to determine if the property in question was in fact stolen? That's why I asked Special Agent Bellamy from the Military Police to attend so that he can look at the documentation to see if the documents are authentic. So if you have them may we see them?"

Boy, this chick really had the Federal bull shit line down pat. She even looked like a Fed, two piece business suit, white blouse, nylons and high heels. The only thing missing was a tie.

I asked Lapaka to show the documents to Bellamy.

After looking at the documents for several minutes, Bellamy said, "This property came from the DRMO's at several different Military Bases. DRMO is the Defense Reutilization Maintenance Office. Each base has a DRMO Office. They handle all the military surplus property at a given base."

"The concept was for communities to borrow useable surplus property from the military. As an example, Fire Trucks could be loaned to small communities for emergencies. When the emergencies were over the communities would have to return the equipment. But over time it got too costly for the military to maintain paperwork and to shuttle the equipment. So the Military decided that the communities could keep the equipment, when it was no longer needed by the community, the community could sell the property and keep the money."

"Once the property was sold, the community had to notify the DRMO who the property was sold to so the DRMO could clear their books. That does not seem to be happening in this case. Apparently phony paper work is being returned to DRMO indicating that the property was sold. This paper work says that the Jeeps are Model MI51's. That model Jeep is not even supposed to be on the road. They were supposed to be destroyed on orders from the USDOT because they were deemed unsafe."

"This really is theft of Federal Property. If the property is not legally sold by the Cities they are required to return the property. Cities do not have "Carte Blanche" to do what they want with this property. There are Federal Guide Lines that are not being followed. Are you sure the City is getting the property?"

"Well not exactly," I said.

"It looks like the DRMO's are doing what they are supposed to do. But what is not happening is that the property is not being disposed of in accordance with State Law and Federal Guidelines. The DRMO's are getting paper work back that says the property was disposed of legally and, as we now know, it isn't." Lapaka said.

"Someone at DRMO must be involved," Redondo said. That was the first peep I heard out of her at any of the meetings.

"Not necessarily so." Bellamy said. "If the city is returning the paper work indicating that they did in fact sell the property, the DRMO'S have no way to know if the property was sold or not. There is no follow up by the DRMOS."

Lapaka added, "And it looks like someone at the City Surplus Property Office could be involved."

"That could be true also."

Isabel Connors asked, "How is this property tied to your homicides?"

Bones said. "Let me answer that Cod."

"We have reason to believe that whoever committed these homicides is the same individual who is stealing the Military property. We have found Jeep tire prints at a crime scene in Callaway County, and we believe that another victim, who was a homeless veteran, by the name of Hendrix, a retired Navy Medic, saw a Jeep or military vehicle at the scene of the Townsend and Jessop killings. He wrote on the back of one of Cod's business cards, "Windy's, MI51 Jeeps and Semi truck, Gunshots."

"Windy's is the bar where Townsend and Jessop were murdered. We believe Hendrix may have seen something at Windy's that got his attention, something other than the killings, probably the Jeep he wrote about on Cod's business card."

I added, "Homicides are committed for several reasons, love, money or to conceal another crime. This case involves two of those issues, money and to conceal the crime that is creating the money."

"Where did you get the documentation?"

"The documentation came from a witness who stumbled onto it by mistake."

"Who is it?"

"We are keeping that information confidential to protect the witness."

Bellamy said, "You mentioned earlier that you were not sure if the City was getting the property, if they aren't where is it?"

"We are not sure, we think is it is stored somewhere in the Northern part of the state."

"Who owns the land?"

"We are not sure of that either. We are still in the process of searching property records."

Jared Bellamy said, "If this property if being stored somewhere up north, there is no way the City could be in possession of the property. Therefore it is stolen."

Benoit asked, "How did the suspect know about Hendrix?"

"We don't know, we haven't figured that out yet." Bones answered.

Big Nate said, "I believe if Hendrix saw the killer, then maybe the killer saw Hendrix. Hendrix would not have been hard to find. Maybe the killer found Hendrix on his own."

I interjected, "Which brings us to another problem. We are considering moving our office to segregate us from the City Hall. If we create a Task Force, would you have space for us at your office?"

Connor said, "I am not sure we should join forces. That constitutes a lot of problems. A couple off the top of my head are, liability, report formats, prosecution and who would be in charge. But I'll run it by my boss and get back with you."

I wondered to myself. Do the Feds have to make a mountain out of every damn mole hill?

I said, "I really don't see a problem. We both have issues here. Yours, the Military Property, ours the homicides tied to the Military Property. Couldn't we have joint responsibility? If we work as a team we could help solve each other's problems."

"I still have to run it by my boss."

Before the agents left I had Redondo copy all of the documents and give Benoit the copies.

CHAPTER SEVENTEEN

The next morning I was going over a plan of attack, this case was getting so involved I had to have a plan. Something I have never done in my career. But I never had a case like this before. I had to have a plan or I would forget where the hell I was or what the hell I was doing.

My phone rang, "Couple of out of town deputies to see you the operator said."

"From Callaway County?"

I heard the operator ask, "Are you from Callaway County?"

I heard the reply, "Yes."

That voice, it had to be Deputy Bowden.

"Is one of them female and as big as King Kong?"

"Yes sir," said the operator.

"Send them up."

"Okay."

Two minutes later Bowden filled my office doorway with her huge frame. Behind her was Deputy Cocran.

"Hi Cod." She said, her voice rattling the office windows.

"Hi Bowden, Hi Cocran what brings you two to the big city, lose your way?"

"Oh no, we have some info for you on the crime scene, we were coming down so I wanted to give it to you personally, besides Cocran here wants to get an application for your department. I told him that he's nuts but he insists on trying."

"Smart boy." I said. "Hang on I'll call personnel for you Cocran."

I called Donna Douglas in personnel.

"Donna? Cod here. Remember the kid I told you about from Callaway County? Well he's here. Is it okay if I send him down? Thanks, I'll send him right down."

"Cocran, take the elevator to the second floor. Exit the elevator to the right. Fourth door on the left, Donna Douglas, she'll be waiting for you."

"Thanks Cod." Cocran headed for the elevator.

"What's the info Carole?"

"Remember the two kids who found Jackson's body, Jerome Richards and Judy Carlson?"

"Yes, never met them but I remember two college kids found the body."

"Well, they didn't tell the whole truth about what really happened."

"What do you mean?"

"They were out in the woods, they said hiking, when they heard a commotion. They said it sounded like doors banging and then they heard an engine start. They thought they had been caught by Judy's father. He never has liked Jerome."

"When they got up they saw a couple of guys dumping a body. At least they think it was two guys. The suspects were talking to each other, but the kids only saw one suspect, and they didn't give a very good description of him. They did hear the names Justin and Jason. One of the suspects told the other one to get in the Jeep. So that fits with the tire print you found, you know, the Jeep tire print."

"Yeah I got it."

"Fortunately, the perps didn't see them. They were afraid to say anything at the time because they didn't want Judy's Dad to find out they were together, that's why they said they were hiking. But they were blowing off to friends, and word got back to me, just as I told you it would. So I confronted them."

"Jerome Richards admitted he ripped the plastic off of the body. But he said that was all he did. He also said when Judy saw the blown up head she screamed and ran like hell. He had to chase her down because she was running in the opposite direction of where they parked. That must have been funnier than hell."

"Did you get a description from them?"

"Yes, but it's not very good. I taped it and brought you the tape."

"Thanks, Bowden, I appreciate that, can you give me a recap of the description?"

"Yeah, the one they saw was a male, with white hair, 5-10, 170 Lbs. They don't think they could identify him. As I said they did not see the other suspect."

"You said they heard two guys talking but only saw one?"

"Yes. But something else, they both said it sounded like the two men had the same voice. They thought the two might be brothers."

"I guess that could be a possibility. I'll have to think about that. So what's the deal with Cocran, why does he want to leave Callaway County?"

"He's young, and ambitious. Not much going on in Callaway County, he wants to be where the action is."

"Yeah, I can understand that, I know it's hard to believe, but I was young once."

"Oh, come on now, you don't look that old. How old are you?"

"I started when I was 22, I have been at it 43 years, you figure it out. When I started they called me "Kid," now they call me "Old Timer.""

"Do you ever think about retiring?"

"Every once in a while I think about it. My old partner retired, but he is back as a consultant on this case. Maybe after this case is over I will give it some more thought."

"Hey, I can ask the Sheriff to give you the job running the jail. We need a Jail Commander."

"No thanks. I like it up there, but not that much. I'm a big city guy."

"I'm glad you came by, I was planning on calling you about Sheep's Crossing, remember Lapaka called you about it a couple of days ago. Let's see, where the hell are my notes? It's supposed to be near 1-75 and Four Mile Road, is that right?

"Yeah that's right." Bowden said.

"We have information that there is some military equipment stashed up there on our Mayor's ranch. And please keep quiet about the Mayor being involved in this, we have not interviewed him yet. He owns 1000 acres up there around Sheep's Crossing. Would you try to find it for us? It will save us a trip."

"What kind of military stuff?"

"All kinds, Jeeps, trucks, engines, you name it and it's supposed to be up there."

"If it's up there we'll find it, and when we do I'll call you."

"Thanks that will be a big help."

"I'll get on it as soon as we get back home."

I woke up at 0600, it was Monday morning. I was awakened by the sun peeking through the windows and the pleasant smell of freshly brewed coffee. It was the Kona Coffee Lapaka had brought us. I also smelled something else. Louise was up making cinnamon toast. I couldn't resist it. I jumped out of bed and headed for the kitchen.

"Good morning lover." I said to Louise as I hugged her from behind, kissed her on the neck and squeezed both of her breasts. "Hmmm, nice I said."

"All you get now is toast and coffee, you can have chocolate cake tonight." She said.

"I'm ready." I said.

Chocolate cake was our code words for sex. Several years ago when our kids were little, Louise and I were talking about our chocolate cake code words. The kids overheard us and wanted to know if they could have some chocolate cake. I busted out laughing and told them I had eaten it all. Louise's face got red as hell and she slapped me. And, she made me go buy the kids real chocolate cake.

120

After gulping down fresh coffee and cinnamon toast it was time to shower and get ready for work. Lapaka would be here any minute.

The doorbell rang, it was Lapaka. I kissed Louise goodbye and left.

"It's a new day Lapaka, maybe we'll get somewhere this week." I said on the way to the office.

"Who knows?"

"The Shadow knows," I said jokingly, referring to an old Radio Show my brother, sister and I used to listen to as kids.

"Who the hell is the Shadow?" Lapaka asked.

After a lengthy explanation of the Shadow, Inner Sanctum and other Radio Shows from years gone by we arrived at the office.

Lapaka laughed and wanted to know if I was around when the Telegraph was invented.

I said, close but not that close.

I had two phone messages waiting for me when we got to the office. One from Windy Benefield and one from Agent Connors. Benefield's said urgent.

I called Windy first. He was all freaked out.

Windy said, "I haven't seen Lopez in three days. I called him but he doesn't answer his phone."

"Okay, Okay simmer down. There is probably a simple answer. Maybe his wife had her baby and he and the kids are at the hospital." I said.

But I knew something was wrong. Lopez would not have left on his own. At least I didn't think he would. Something or someone got to him. Only a few people know where he lives. Redondo, the security detail and me. Even Wilson Tom of Friends of Criminal Justice doesn't know where he lives. Safe house addresses are always coded.

I called Redondo.

"Redondo this is Cod."

"Yeah Cod what's up?"

121

"Windy has not heard from Lopez for three days. Go over to the safe house and find out if he is there. Get back with me right away."

"Okay, I'm on it. Oh, and by the way, Big Nate and I are going to start the backgrounds today. We are going to start with Townsend."

"Okay, see what you can dig up."

We hung up. Then I realized if Lopez had left, it must have been his wife wanting to get back to Mexico to protect her kids. He is the only living witness. If he took his family back to Mexico we're out of luck. We will never find him. But what can he offer anyway? He did not see the shooters face. Maybe we won't need him after all.

Then I called Connors. I had to go through the same telephone bureaucracy as before. Finally I got Connors.

"Good Morning Detective," She said. "I have good news. My boss wants us involved in the Task Force. He also said we would give you office space. He feels if we are close it will make working together easier. It will also make the exchange of information less cumbersome."

"Hey that's great news. How soon can we move in?"

"Today is Monday, how about Wednesday?"

"Wednesday will be fine. I will call you Tuesday to finalize the move."

"Okay, see you Wednesday."

An hour later Redondo called me.

"Bad news Cod. Lopez has packed all his families clothes and some of their belongings and left."

"How did they leave without the security team knowing?"

"The security team told me they went to lunch and were gone about an hour. Lopez must have left with his family while the security team was eating. I talked to a neighbor and she said a cab showed up and the family next door, meaning the Lopez family, loaded up and left. The cab had Mexican writing on it."

"Okay, when you get back, write it up and then try to find the cab company."

I called Bones and gave him the information about the Lopez family.

He was livid, I have never heard him so pissed off before. I just hung up, I didn't want to hear any more of his ranting.

◌ CHAPTER EIGHTEEN ◌

Prior to moving in with the FEDS we decided to have a joint meeting with the Federal Agencies. It was important for us to know what kind of restrictions the Feds might have concerning our participation.

On the Tuesday prior to the move, Bones, Lapaka and I met with the Federal Agents to hash out the details of the Task Force.

Right from the start there were problems. A lawyer from The US Attorney's Office was present. They demanded every bit of information turned over to them for examination and approval. And every aspect of the investigation had to be approved by the US Attorney's Office. He also said that the US Attorney's Office would not share any of its information with us.

This particular US Attorney had a reputation as being a "Micro Manager." I felt sorry for the Federal Investigators. They could not do anything without the US Attorneys permission.

During the meeting, the FBI opted out of the investigation because, they said, not our jurisdiction. But I suspected it was due to the US Attorneys Micro Managing.

Bones promptly asked the US Attorney, "What do you mean you do not share information?"

"Just what I said," was the Attorneys response.

"So you want our help with information, but we don't get your information."

"That's about it," was the reply.

Bones said, "We will not agree to that. We, in this agency do not get anyone's permission to conduct an investigation or interview. We do not work for the US Attorney's Office. What kind of bull shit is this anyway? We can't interview someone unless you approve it. If that is going to be the case we will not participate."

The US Attorney looked stunned. You could tell he had never been talked to like that by anyone. Of course he had never run up against Bones before. I just sat there with a smug smile on my face and glad that Bones was there to support us.

The US Attorney backed down and said the rules would only apply to the Federal Investigators. Then he said. "Don't expect any help from us on your State prosecutions."

What a fucking prick I thought.

And then Bones said. "You take your Task Force and shove it up your ass, we are out of here."

You talk about stunned looks. They were all in shock.

Well, I guess that ended our Task Force days.

As we were leaving Connors asked me to call her when things cooled off. I told her I would.

Then I figured it out. DCIS agreed to a joint investigation because our agency could get around the US Attorney's rules. Could DCIS be that devious? Of course they could. They are the FEDS.

Jared Bellamy was at the meeting with his new partner Sonya Harris, a striking blue-eyed blond who was a career Military Investigator. She had been in the Air Force Special Investigations Unit for twelve years. Her father was a retired US Border Patrol Agent. Her mother a retired educator.

Bellamy brought Harris over to introduce her to our team.

Bellamy said, "Shortly after I reported the missing Military Equipment to my boss he assigned Harris as the lead investigator for our role in the investigation."

Harris who had not said anything up to this point finally said. "The US Attorney did not mention this but our Base Commander is conducting a press conference on the theft of the Military Property as we speak. It will hit the papers tomorrow morning."

"What" I screamed. I couldn't believe my ears. "This is going to fuck up the whole case."

Harris said, "How do you tell a Two Star General he is making a mistake? You can't. We are really sorry, but we have to put up with this all the time."

"I hope there is not too much damage to our homicide investigations," I said.

I was upset that the Base Commander had decided to call a press conference concerning the missing military equipment. I reasoned that he was covering his own ass and at the same time looking for a scapegoat. Military brass are experts at finding scapegoats to point the finger at. After all, why should a general officer take the heat, when an enlisted non-com can be blamed?

When we got back to our office Redondo was waiting for us. She found the cab company.

Redondo said, "The cab company is run by a Mexican family that caters to Hispanics. The driver told me he picked up the Lopez family and took them to the Greyhound Bus Station. He did not know where they were going. They had six bags with them. It looks to me like they went back to Mexico."

"Our only eye witness and he's gone. What a mess. We will never find him, but you know what? The killer won't either." I said.

The next day I called Connors, only this time I had her direct line.

"Hi Cod," she said. "I'm sorry about yesterday's meeting. But the AG's Office can really be ball busters, they even bust my balls and I don't have any to bust."

"Well that guy was really an asshole. Does he treat criminals that way?"

"The US Attorney who runs the office is a political appointee and a real micro manager. Nothing goes on without his approval. You don't understand what a problem that causes. Getting approval from those jerks on everything we do."

"Well you got a taste of the real police when Bones let loose on him."

"Yeah, we would get suspended if we talked to an AG like that."

"You know what? Those dip shits need a dressing down. They

don't walk on water."

Then Connors said, "I have thought of a way that we can continue this case as a team. What if we bypass the AG's Office and go for State prosecution? We never put people in jail anyway. All we do is fine people. We could assist you and use the State's Attorneys for help. We would just ignore the AG's Office. One thing the AG cannot do is tell us who we can work with."

"Will your boss go for it? I know Bones will."

"He already told me to go for it."

"How about the Air Force?"

"I will call Sonya Harris and get her onboard. We can get her and Bellamy put on temporary assignment to our office, no problem. I know for a fact the Base Commander will go for it. He hates the AG."

"Okay, let's do it."

"I'll get back with you."

"Okay, I'll start making plans." I called it a day and headed home.

The next morning I was scouring the morning paper looking for the General's press release. Which really was not a problem for me. I have been reading the morning newspaper ever since I can remember, just as my father had done, and his father before him. My father was such an avid newspaper reader that he even read the damn classified ads. I couldn't imagine why he did that, because he never bought anything from those ads.

I suppose reading the morning paper will soon come to an end because of the internet. Another American tradition that will fall by the wayside.

I found the press release on page three of the second section of the paper. The heading of the article read. "Military Property Reported Missing." When I read the article I could not believe my eyes. It read, "A few jeeps and some airplane parts are missing. The Base Police, and Defense Department are conducting a joint investigation." That was it.

No details, no cost, no reason, no nothing. I thought to myself, Wow, the General's PR guys did a great job of minimizing their own boss's press release.

Even more interesting was there was no mention of the homicides being tied to the military property. Hell, our department was not even mentioned. Good for the General, but better for our investigation.

I hoped that not too many people would notice the article, especially the suspect. But I also knew that if I read it others would too. And I was afraid one of them would be Rolanda Jacobs from the Register. She always seemed to turn up at the most inopportune times. I suspected she was on to the connection between the Military Property and the homicides. She knew that Doc Hendrix, the murdered homeless vet, was retired military and that we had an unusual interest in his case. I also knew she wasn't stupid, she would figure it out.

Lapaka told me that during one of their trysts, she asked him, "If you and Overture are supposed to be looking for cop killers why are you given other homicides to investigate?"

Lapaka told me he made up some cock and bull story to appease her, but he didn't think she believed him.

I told Lapaka, just be sure you don't have a slip of the tongue in a weak moment. "No pun intended."

I got to my office two hours late, unusual for me, and of course Big Nate was in my office waiting. And he promptly asked, "Do I have to buy you a watch like I did my kids so you will get to work on time?"

"Shut up you big ape." I said.

He handed me a message from Isabel Connors.

I returned her call and she told me, "Sonya Harris and Jared Bellamy will be assigned to temporary duty to my office Monday morning. It is a go."

"Good deal," I said.

I went in to talk to Bones about Lopez and the new plan suggested by Connors. Bones was still pissed off about Lopez eluding the security team. But there was nothing he could do about it. Lopez was gone. We had to face facts. We would have to solve this without Lopez.

Bones was okay with the new plan that excluded the Federal Prosecutors. Bones said, "I have one suggestion. "I don't want you using Federal Offices. There is an empty office over on Palm Lane. You know, the place they call Palm Springs?"

Cops, we have nick names for everything. "Yeah I know it."

"Move in there, the rent is paid for another year. The Narcs moved out last month."

Bones might have said suggestion, but what he meant was, do it.

So we did. Palm Street, better known to us as Palm Springs, became our new home, at least for now.

After we moved into Palm Springs I called Connors and invited her and her team to meeting in our new offices. I ordered pizza and cokes for the meeting, courtesy of the City.

During the meeting we hashed around a dozen or so ideas on how to proceed.

What do we have?

Two dead police officers, one dead bartender, one dead Navy veteran and some partially smoked cigarettes with the initials LZS that tie the killings together. DNA, but no match in the DNA database. We have fragmented bullets, probably 38 Caliber. Only hearsay from Mrs. Jackson, whose information came from her husband. And they are both dead.

We have absolutely no probable cause to do anything.

Our only witness to the Townsend and Jessop killings has fled, but he could not identify the shooter. So he was not much use anyway. And of course the theft of military property that is somehow connected to the homicides.

We did make some decisions that everyone could live with. The Air Force Agents would start putting pressure on the DRMO workers and supervisors. We would start a stake out of the transmission shop at 4000 Chalmers. And Big Nate would try to track down LZS cigarettes.

And I made the decision to advise Isabel Connors about the

WITCH tattoo and the WITCH account that belonged to the Mayor. Even though the Chief said keep it under wraps, I had to tell her, she was our investigative partner; she had the right to know. She agreed to keep it to herself.

I called the Motor Pool and talked to Wayne Holmes, who every one called Sherlock. Which later was changed to "No Shit Sherlock," because every time he was told something he said, "No Shit."

Because the case involved the murder of two police officers, Sherlock knew I had an open check book.

"What do you need Cod?" Sherlock asked.

"Sherlock, I need a large van. Double back doors with sliding doors on the passenger side only. Outfitted like an electrical contractors truck. It has to have enough room inside for four people, cameras and taping equipment. Also a blind for electrical tools and wires. I want you to paint "Libby's Electrical Contractors" on both sides.

"What about phone numbers and an address?"

"Yeah, I will have to have dummy numbers set up. I will call you back with that info. How long will it take?"

"Give me a week, and don't forget the numbers."

"Okay, thanks Sherlock."

That afternoon I called Sherlock with the dummy numbers.

Four days later Sherlock called me and told me the van was ready.

Sherlock was a genius when it came to outfitting vehicles.

The next day I took the van to the Sheriff's Office to have Oscar Smith equip the van with the monitoring devices. He volunteered to join us at the stakeout to get us off on the right foot.

I gladly accepted, we needed all the help we could get.

ᐸᕐᐳ CHAPTER NINETEEN ᕐᐸᕐᐳ

We decided to start the stakeout of the Jackson's former transmission shop as soon as we found a suitable location from which to observe the comings and goings from the shop. We located an empty store front across the street from the transmission shop, but down three doors. Redondo tracked down the owner who gave us permission to use the facility. Not the best observation point, but it would have to do.

We started the stakeout at 0700 on Monday morning. Lapaka and Redondo were dressed as electrical workers and carried supplies into and out of the fake store front. Connors, Smith and myself dressed as laborers but stayed in the van to do the monitoring. We knew that sooner or later we would have to trade off with Lapaka and Redondo because of the boredom involved with stakeouts.

The 4000 block of Concord was a mixed use neighborhood. The transmission shop, a starving art studio, and a local restaurant. There was a bank on the corner. We were between the art studio and a former dime store.

We had been at the stakeout about two hours when a young woman, who introduced herself as Jenifer White, approached Redondo and Lapaka about getting an electrical estimate on the abandoned dime store. She told them she was going to open a beauty salon in the front of the old dime store building and needed the electrical system updated.

Redondo and Lapaka didn't know shit about electrical work. They were speechless. All they could say was call the number on the van. After that, I knew our cover was working. We spent two weeks on the stakeout and got absolutely zero. No delivery trucks, no semis, no nothing. Just the normal automobile traffic.

Bellamy and Harris were not having any better luck with the Military DRMO supervisors or employees. The DRMO personnel worked for the Military, but they were civilians and not subject to the Uniform Code of Military Justice. Once they were read the Miranda Warnings they refused to talk without attorneys.

As we were making no headway with the stakeout we decided to confront the owner of the transmission shop head on. What did we have to lose? We weren't getting anywhere as it was.

Lapaka and I entered the shop looking for someone to talk to. We heard a woman's voice say, "Can I help you guys?" I heard the voice but I didn't see anyone.

I said, "Where are you."

"I'm down here."

She was a little person. She came out from behind the counter. She was about 3' 6" tall and about 40 pounds, very attractive with nice proportions, just tiny. She apparently had a viewing window down at her level so she could see people entering her business.

I introduced myself and Lapaka and we presented her with our badges and ID cards.

She said she was Margaret Vestel, the owner, and wanted to know what we wanted.

I told her about the stolen transmissions.

She said, "I don't know what you are talking about. The only transmissions I have bought, I bought from a City employee. But I haven't seen him in about a month."

"What did he look like?"

"White guy, 5' 10," 160 pounds, grey hair, about sixty years old. He was wearing a City uniform with the City Logo. His truck had City Logos on the door. It was a white semi, with a white trailer."

"That's the problem. He is not a City employee. We believe he was dealing in stolen transmissions."

"No way, that old man. He is like a grandfather. You guys are barking up the wrong tree."

"Well in any event we need to look at your inventory."

"Ha!, you want to look at my inventory, get a fucking search warrant. And don't come back until you do. You cops are always looking for a patsy. Well I'm not it. Now get out of my shop. Instead of bothering little people why don't you go catch the guys who killed your two cop buddies?"

As we left, Lapaka said, "That went well. Feisty little shit isn't she?"

"You got that right, but it was worth a shot."

"Now what do we do?"

I don't know. We can't get a warrant because we have no probable cause. We can't even try; we would be laughed out of court."

As we were getting in our car I saw a black semi-truck loaded with crushed automobiles. It turned left off of Concord onto West Southern Avenue. I decided to follow it.

"Lapaka," I said. "Look at that black semi. It's loaded with smashed cars. What the hell is wrong with us? Why didn't we think of it? We can't see the forest for the trees. Have we been blinded by the killings? This is not the only transmission shop in town. We need to check all of them. And how about the wrecking yards and shops down on Southern Avenue. That's where that truck is going. He wants to sell his junked cars."

"You're right Cod, whoever we are looking for has to be selling his loot somewhere. Where else would be better, but wrecking yard row?"

"I'm going to call Connors and set up a couple of teams to canvass the Southern Avenue wrecking yards. I am going to suggest that we put one of our team members with one of hers and let the teams go at it."

We met at Ma's the next morning at 0600. Over breakfast we decided to team Sonya Harris with Leo Lapaka and Victoria Redondo with Jared Bellamy. I would accompany Redondo and Bellamy and Connors would be with Harris and Lapaka. Our plan was for Harris, Lapaka and Connors to canvas the North side of Southern Avenue, while Redondo, Bellamy and I would canvas the South side of Southern Avenue. I arranged to have two uniform officers to assist us. One of them had a police dog.

We also had state statutes to back us up. Per the statute, an owner of any car wrecking or dismantling business, junk yard, metal scrap yard or pawn shop must on demand, by a police officer, surrender any and all records to that police officer for inspection. I issued copies of the statute to all the parties involved in the canvas.

We started at 8:00 A.M. And wouldn't you know it. The first damn stop for Harris, Lapaka and Connors was Grants Auto Wrecking. The man behind the counter saw the guns and badges and ran like hell. He was caught two blocks away by the police dog. Who, by the way took a big chunk out of this guy's ass. This idiot was wanted in Blue Lick, Kentucky for burglary and auto theft. Blue Lick, Kentucky, where in the hell is that? It figures, an auto thief working at an auto wrecking yard.

Across the street, Redondo, Bellamy and I were having our own problems with these jack offs. We stopped at Bernie's Scrap Iron and presented the owner, Bernard Lowenstien, with our police identification and the state statute. He refused to cooperate. At which time I called the two uniform officers and had them block the driveways of all in and out traffic and shut Bernie's Scrap Iron down.

After the yard was shut down and five semi-trucks could not enter, Lowenstien, had a change of heart and agreed to talk to us. He admitted that he had been buying scrap iron and not reporting it as required by state statute.

But he said, "I have been buying it from the US Post Office, so I thought it was okay."

"The Post Office?" Bellamy said.

"Yeah the Post Office. The guy was driving a Post Office Semi and he had a Post Office shirt on."

"Did he show you any Post Office Identification?"

"No he didn't. But who would come in here and pretend to be a postal worker? He had the truck and the uniform. So I thought it was okay."

"What did he look like?"

"He is 5'10" or eleven, 160 to 180 pounds, gray hair, blue eyes. About 65 years old. Dressed in mail man clothes."

"Do you know who he was?"

"No I don't."

"Does that security camera up there in the corner work?"

"Yeah it does."

"We are going to need the tapes." And Bernie, I think you have been had. Now if you want your yard reopened, get the damn records out here as well as the security tapes."

"I don't have any records on those transactions. But I think I still have the tapes. To save money I reuse the tapes, so what you want may not be on them."

"If you want your yard opened before the next century you had better come up with the sales records."

Bernie told his secretary to dig up the tapes and make copies of the sales slips.

Bernie's secretary was gone about ten minutes when she returned with the sales slips and video tapes. The sales slips indicated that Bernie paid $2500.00 for 2000 lbs. of copper. The sales slips were made out to cash. Bernie Lowenstien knew what he was doing. The copper was worth twice that. And we could not trace who he bought the copper from.

Bernie's secretary really looked nervous. She kept looking at me as if she had something to say. But I figured she was afraid to talk in front of Bernie.

"Bernie," I said, "You know you have violated State Law. You are supposed to report who you buy scrap copper from, with an address and account number. You did not do that on these sales slips."

"I know, I know, I was cutting corners. Things have been tough. I am just trying to make an honest dollar."

"But Bernie, what is honest about this deal?"

Bernie said I am going to call my lawyer."

"Good Idea," I said.

"Here is my card, when the mail man comes back, get a damn

plate number and some kind of ID from him. Make up some bull shit story about your annual audit by the state is coming up and you need to cover your ass."

I also gave my card to the nervous secretary, and said, "Please call anytime if you think of anything that will help us."

"What is going to happen about the records?"

"Nothing if you cooperate."

"Hey, you got my full cooperation. Will you open my yard now?"

"Do we have a real deal Bernie, or are you going to blow us off to your lawyer as soon as we leave?"

"No sir, you have my word." Then we shook hands. I called off the uniform cops.

After leaving Bernie's I called Connors and asked if they were done? If so I wanted all of us to meet at Ma's for a de-briefing. We got to Ma's about 1900.

We all had coffee and sandwiches. We filled each other in on what each group had accomplished for the day. I asked Connors if she knew any Postal Inspectors. She said she knew Joseph P. Windom, who she would call and find out if they felt they should be involved.

The next morning Connors called me and advised me that the Postal Inspectors did not want to get involved, they would be satisfied if Connors would just keep them informed about the case. I gave a silent thank you. We did not need any more Federal Agents involved.

"The rest of the week was spent chasing down junk and trash yards, which gave us, nada, nothing, zilch. These people were making money off of the stolen property and were not going to tell us squat. And we still did not have enough probable cause for any search warrants.

Friday afternoon I received a call from a female named Charlee Lagret. "I said who?"

The caller said, "Charlee Lagret, Bernie Lowenstien's secretary."

"Oh," I said. "What can I do for you?"

"Bernie lied to you. That old guy selling junk to Bernie has an open account here. He doesn't always take all his money. He leaves it here and comes and draws money out whenever he needs it. Like a bank account. Bernie screws him cross eyed with his price. But the guy does not seem to mind. It really is an unusual situation. I just thought you should know about it."

"How much does he have on the books?"

"About $6000.00."

"Can you get us a copy of the account?"

"No, Bernie keeps it in his head, no paper trail."

"Thank you Ms. Lagret, I appreciate the information."

"But please, don't tell Bernie I told you."

"Don't worry I won't, but if you don't have any documentation I'm afraid we can't use it."

After Charlee Lagret hung up, I had another call. It was Bowden.

"Hi Carole." I said, "What's up?"

"I found the Mayor's property. I searched for about two days but I finally found it. There is a small fenced area, about twenty acres, that contains military equipment. I took pictures of it for you."

"Great, do you know any judges named Barney that will give us a search warrant?"

"Shut up Overture, I know it's a hick county, you don't have to remind me. But yes, I know a judge; his name is "Billy Bob.""

"Are you serious?" And then I started laughing, I couldn't keep it in.

"Are you laughing Overture.?

Yes I am, but I can't help it. I'll try to get up there Monday to do the paper work."

"Okay, see you then."

Before leaving for the night I tried the tapes Bernie had given us, they were blank. That ass hole lied to us. But what could I do about it? I could do one thing. I would turn it over to the Scrap Metal Detail. They will fix his lying ass. They will audit every damn receipt he has. There is always more than one way to skin a cat.

ᑦᑐ CHAPTER TWENTY ᑐᐠ

The killer parked the semi-truck at the Patagonia River Cutoff Rest Area. The killer was waiting for his niece, Myrna. She was his niece by marriage to her aunt. He didn't like her, but he liked the sex she provided. She was such a bitch. Always wanting more money to support her habit. If she wasn't so good in bed he would cut her off. She looked worse every time he saw her. How old is she now? He asked himself, thirty, thirty five. How could someone that young be so screwed up he wondered?

He decided to call his brother while he waited.

"Hi Jason, it's me Justin."

"What are you doing Justin?"

"I'm waiting for Myrna."

"Why do you keep seeing that dope using pig?"

"I don't know, I hate the bitch myself. You should see her. Skinny, half her teeth are gone and she has sores all over her face."

"Then why do you see her?"

"Because she is good in bed and gives good blow jobs."

"You dumb ass, you are going to get AIDS. You are not careful enough. Always taking chances."

He had talked about two minutes when the white Chevrolet Caprice pulled in behind the truck. The tall skinny blond woman exited her car and made her way to the truck. She had sores on her face and half of her teeth were gone. He did not hear her approach the truck. He was in half sentence when she opened the door, startling him; he slammed his cell phone shut when he saw her.

"Hi Uncle, who were you talking to?" She said as she climbed aboard the large Mack Truck Tractor.

"I haven't been talking to anyone."

"You just closed your phone I thought I heard you talking."

"I said I wasn't talking to anyone."

"Okay uncle, don't be so fucking touchy."

Even though her Aunt Agnes had divorced him years ago, she still called him Uncle.

Myrna's Aunt Agnes went to work for Justin in his junk yard and ended up having an affair with him that led to her divorce from Jason, Justin's brother. Justin and Agnes married shortly thereafter. But that ended in divorce too.

Justin had caught Myrna stealing money from his wallet. Myrna confessed to him that she was hooked on Heroin. They made a bargain. He would not tell her aunt, but in return he wanted her help in some of his criminal activities, for which he would pay her. Myrna agreed to the bargain, because she wanted money to support her habit. It worked well for both of them.

"How have you been Myrna?"

"Not too good. It's been tough. I lost the kids to the State. I can't find a job because of my habit and I have no other support. If it wasn't for Aunt Agnes I would be on the street. Look at me, sores all over my face, half of my teeth are gone, who is going to give me a job. Food stamps are not enough to survive on. I need more money uncle."

"What are you talking about, I give you money all the time. What do you do with it?"

"You've only been giving me money for about three years, ever since we started meeting again, and besides money doesn't go far."

"Enough about your money problems. How's Agnes?"

"Agnes, Agnes, that's all you ever say. You fucking ass hole, you only think of yourself or Agnes. What about me?"

"Answer my question about Agnes."

"She is still down and out. She has never accepted Victor's death."

"It's time she got over it, it's been over twenty years."

"She's a mother, she will never get over it. She still blames you."

"What are you talking about? Why does she blame me? I didn't kill him. All I did was set up the burglary, I didn't pull the trigger. If you wouldn't have backed out he would still be alive."

"She knows all about it Uncle. I don't know how, but she knows all the details of Victor's death."

Then it dawned on him, why so many years ago, he had been caught robbing the Gaylord Bank. Agnes had alerted the police to get even with him for Victor's death. The cops must have told her that I was responsible for Victor's death. That's why she turned on me, that fucking whore.

"Your nuts, your whole fucking family is nuts. He was stupid, he should have run. Get the fuck out of my truck."

"This isn't your truck Uncle. Besides, I know what you have been doing. It hit the papers this morning."

"What the hell are you talking about?"

"You should start reading the papers Uncle Justin. The stolen military property. It was in the paper this morning. You always dealt in stolen property. You are the one who told me you had access to the bases. It has to be you. You were a junk man remember?"

"What, what's in the papers?"

"How someone has been stealing Military Property from the bases."

"It isn't me."

"Uncle, I am not a fool. I may be a lot of things but I am not stupid. Where do you get your money? You can't work. How come you are always in a Semi Truck? You can't own one."

"What do you want?"

"I want $100,000 or I'm going to the police about Victor's death and the Military Bases."

"I don't have anything close to that. Besides, there are other people to consider."

"What other people?"

"That's none of your business. What will it take to shut you up?"

"I told you $100,000."

"That is out of the question."

"How much do you have access too?"

"I don't know, I have it stashed all over the state."

"How much do you have on you?"

"I have about $20,000 inside the trailer. It's in an ammo storage container."

"Let's go get it."

"First things first. I want some service."

"The money first Uncle, I don't trust you."

"Okay, I have to get it out of the trailer, come on."

When they entered the back of the trailer she said, "I knew I was right. Look at the Jeeps."

He unlocked the ammo storage building and they went in.

As they entered Myrna said, "What's all this dark red stuff, paint?"

She was dead before she hit the floor. Two bullet holes to the back of her head. One exited over her right eye carrying brain matter with it. The other shattered her lower jaw taking out some of her remaining teeth.

"Stupid bitch. She would have fucked up everything."

He closed the ammo container door and locked it. He exited the trailer and climbed into the truck and headed east. Where I am going to dump this bitch's body he wondered?

He stopped alongside the Patagonia River. He exited the semi to check his truck tires, which was a ruse; he was really looking for witnesses. No one in sight. He entered the trailer and retrieved his niece's body from the ammo container. What a mess she made of things with her big mouth he thought. He drug her body through the trailer, the body dripping blood along the trailer floor. He looked for witnesses one more time before exiting the trailer with Myrna's limp, dead body.

He carried her to the edge of the river and tossed her body down the embankment. He threw his cigarette after her. For someone so skinny she sure was heavy, must be what is meant by dead weight, as he laughed at his thought. He returned to the truck and headed to the Johnson Truck Stop to clean his blood laden truck trailer and ammo container.

He parked in the rear of the truck stop near the water and air hoses. It took Myrna's killer four hours to clean the blood and brains from the trailer and ammo container. Then he headed to his house. But first, the storage facility, to change and stash his weapon.

When he reached his house the guard on duty knew it was Justin Cunard in the big white semi and waved him through the gates. He parked and went to his motor pool office to fill in his daily work log. Then he went to his room. Another day he did not have to eat their slop.

He woke in a panic. The car, he said to himself, I forgot about her fucking car. I can't leave now. I will have to take care of it in the morning.

At 0600 the morning after Myrna's body had been dumped down the embankment of the Patagonia, three kayakers, Bill Bushy, John Clifford and Bob Moses, were paddling along the river. Moses was in the lead kayak, Bushy and Clifford were following in single file. The three of them had been kayaking the Patagonia River for ten years. They knew every bend, every fallen tree, every sunken log and every ripple of this River.

Moses was the first to see the dead body. Moses signaled to Bushy and Clifford and pointed to the shore line. When they saw the body they knew something was amiss. The kayakers slowed to investigate. They discovered a female body, blond, skinny, and covered with blood. Parts of her face and lower jaw missing. The body covered with flies with the stench of death filling the air.

The Patagonia River, a pristine water way. Home to Blue Herons, White Egrets, Beavers, Turtles, White Tail Deer and Brown Bear. The banks littered with drift wood that over time had been shaped like living creatures. Majestic Weeping Willows cascading their branches over the river to form a tunnel of trees. The slowly flowing river drifting to the great lake beyond. It had now become tainted with the dead woman's body. It would never be the same for the three kayakers. They would remember this forever.

Moses used his cell phone to call the police and the three of them waited by the roadside to direct the officers to the body.

The first officer on the scene was a fifteen year veteran who immediately secured the crime scene and then interviewed the three kayakers. The officer then called for the Evidence Collection Unit and Homicide Detectives.

When the Evidence Unit arrived they did the normal job of searching the entire area for evidence. Yellow evidence tape and numbered flags used to mark possible evidence dotted the entire landscape. This unit was good, they left nothing to chance.

When Lapaka and I arrived, Lawrence, the Senior Evidence Tech at the scene, was busy looking over the body. Dead about 12 hours. Small amounts of blood pooling, rigor mortis already setting in. Two holes in the back of her head. No exit wound he could see, half of her lower jaw was gone. But no brain matter or skull fragments lying around and not a whole lot of blood. Most probably killed somewhere else and dumped here. From the looks of the underbrush, she must have been tossed from above and rolled to the river bank.

He thought to himself, this is just like the other recent homicides. The body in Callaway County, the homeless guy in the dumpster. I wonder if they are all connected to Townsend and Jessop? If I find one of those damn cigarette butts with LZS on it, I will know they are connected.

He didn't have to look long or hard. There it was, stuck to the back of the dead woman's right pant leg. Big as life. Only this time the whole name was present . Who in the fuck makes a cigarette named KILZS? He wondered. Such an appropriate name. They kill you if you smoke them and now they are evidence in killings.

Lawrence told me. "I found a cigarette with a whole name. Would you believe it? KILZS cigarettes. I also found car keys in her right front pants pocket. They are for a Chevrolet."

Lapaka interviewed the three kayakers and gleaned all he could from them. They had found the body and had not disturbed it. They could not add anything else to the investigation so they were allowed to leave and continue on their journey down the river.

Lapaka did learn that these three kayakers were the founding members of "Green Kayakers for America" a non-profit organization that sponsors youth kayaking clubs.

ᑫᔕ CHAPTER TWENTY-ONE ᕪᔓ

Raul Amos was a young rookie State police officer. He had been on his own for two weeks when he noticed the white Chevrolet Caprice in the rest area. It was illegally parked in Semi-Truck parking only area. How stupid could this person be he thought? It was parked right under the "Semi-Truck Parking Only" sign.

He exited his patrol car to check the vehicle. He found the doors locked. He returned to his patrol car to get his "Slim Jim." A tool designed to open locked car doors by sliding the tool between the window and door frame and catching the locking mechanism, and with an upward motion unlocking the door. He had excelled in the "Slim Jim" class in the State Police Academy. He used the tool deftly and had the door of the illegally parked Chevrolet unlocked in seconds.

The Officer found a white purse lying on the right front seat. In the purse was a pink wallet that contained several pieces of identification including a driver's license, social security card, as well as a food stamp card. He also found a baggie of Crystal Methamphetamine; at least that's what he thought it was. The baggie also had three cigarettes in it.

Why would a woman leave her purse in a locked car he thought? Women don't do that. And the dope, what about the dope? A doper wouldn't leave their stash. Did she meet someone? Was she buying more dope? Was she selling dope? Was she ripped off? Was she kidnapped? Was she dead? So many questions with no answers he thought to himself.

The purse belonged to Myrna Dobson, address 2925 Rymal. The Driver's License photo was of a White Blond Female. She was in her late thirties. He ran the name in NCIC, no wants, but a history of drug arrests.

The officer inventoried the vehicle, called for a tow truck and had the vehicle impounded. After the vehicle was towed, he headed to his office.

As the Patrolman got to the Patagonia River Cutoff he noticed all the police cars and activity. He stopped to assist.

He exited his car and approached two men in civilian dress with guns and badges attached to their belts.

"Hi," He said. "I'm Patrolman Raul Amos. What's going on, need any help?"

"I'm Leo Lapaka, he's Cod Overture. We are processing a crime scene. A dead female's body was dumped here. It was found by three kayakers. She was a blond, real skinny. Two bullet holes in the back of the head."

"Did you say blond?"

"Yeah she's a blond."

"I just impounded a white Chevrolet Caprice back at the rest area. I found a purse in the car with a Driver's License. The photo is a white blond female, her name is Myrna Dobson. I have it in my car if you want to look at it. I also found a bag of Crystal Meth, at least I think its Meth. There were cigarettes in with the meth. Maybe you guys could look at it and see what you think."

"Oh yeah, we want to look at it."

The Patrolman retrieved the purse from his car and handed it to Lapaka. He handed the baggie to Overture.

Lapaka searched the purse and found the wallet and license. He looked at the photo and said. "It could be the victim, but half of her face is gone. Where did her car go?"

"It went to Arts Enco on the Benson Highway."

"Arts? I've known him since I was a young rookie." Cod interjected.

"Find anything else of importance in the car?"

"No sir, just the purse. There was trash all over the floor, cigarette butts and papers but nothing important. I did run her name, no wants, but a history of drug busts. There is a next of kin's name and address in the wallet, a woman named Agnes Cunard. I was going to call her about the car and the owner, but I guess you guys will want to do it."

"Yeah, we will take care of it and let you know."

Overture was looking at the baggie of rocks. But it wasn't the rocks that caught his attention. It was the cigarettes. They were KILZS Cigarettes. "Holy shit," he said out loud.

"What," Lapaka asked?

"Look, the cigarettes, they are KILZS. This victim must have known the killer, she has the same kind of cigarettes. And you're right Amos this is Meth. But the important thing here is the cigarettes. This brand of cigarette has been found at the last four murder scenes. You have given us some very important leads concerning four homicides Amos. I want to let your boss know how you have helped us, what is his name?"

"Thanks, his name is Sergeant Harry Moore, State Police Barracks, Livonia."

"We will have to keep the purse for evidence. I'll get you a receipt. One more thing, will you notify Art and let him know we will be by?"

"I Sure will. If you don't need my help I'll get out of your way."

"Hey, you haven't been in our way. You have given us a ton of help, thanks again. If we can ever be of assistance to you call us. Here's my card. Call anytime." Overture told him.

As Patrolman Amos drove off, Lapaka said, "Thank God for nosey young cops."

"Amen to that," Overture said. "By the way, were we ever that young?"

"I don't know about you, but I was."

"Real funny, Lapaka."

"Well, we're done here, let's go to Arts and search the victim's car." Lapaka said.

"Okay."

Justin Cunard left his house and decided to have breakfast before hitting the road. After eating he went to the motor pool and entered the big semi-truck. He fired up the truck and started for the main gates. He was waved through the large gates at 0700. He was headed to the rest area to get Myrna's car. He was supposed to be going to get a load of cement blocks for his bosses so they could finish their perimeter wall. But that had to wait. He had to get the car.

When the big semi entered the rest area, Justin saw the State Cop searching Myrna's car. He knew he was too late. "Shit," he said to himself. He parked the semi-truck and waved to the officer, as if nothing had happened, and went into the rest area men's room. When he was finished he left the men's room and saw the tow truck. Arts Enco, 3500 Benson Highway. He would have to deal with this later. But how? The tow company must have a State Police Contract. They can't get rid of that car without police permission. What the fuck am I going to do? He wondered.

Justin sat behind the steering wheel of the semi-truck, acting as if he was doing paper work. All the while keeping an eye on the State police officer. He noticed the white purse in the officer's hands. He thought, now they will know who she is. He panicked. I have to call my brother, he said to himself.

"Jason, its Justin."

"Yeah, what can I do for you?"

"I killed Myrna."

"What?"

"I killed Myrna last night and dumped her in the Patagonia River. She figured out I was stealing from the bases. And she knew about an old homicide I caused. She threatened to go to the police if I didn't give her $100,000. How was I going to do that?"

"I don't know, but what homicide are you talking about?"

"You don't need to know about it."

"Okay, but I can't help you if I don't know all the facts."

"It was a long time ago. I was responsible for a burglary that got Victor killed. I planned to burglarize the Three Points Gun Shop with Victor and Myrna. Myrna didn't show up to help. Victor was left alone and got killed. I hauled ass because I did not want to be tied to it."

"When the police showed up to tell Agnes, Victor was killed

149

committing a burglary, they told her I was involved but they could not prove it. She knew it was my fault. I thought I had convinced her it was all a mistake. But now I know who tipped off the police about the Gaylord Bank robbery. It was Agnes. That's how she got even with me."

"Yeah, I guess she got even. How long has it been? Twenty-two years."

"Yes. Anyway, Myrna is out of my hair. But I forgot about her car and when I went back to get it the cops were having it towed."

"You fucking idiot. You really screwed up this time. If they find Agnes, they will find you. You blew your cover you nitwit."

"I told you not to cuss me out and call me names. Just like when we were kids, calling me names and cussing at me."

"You dumb ass, what are you going to do, kill me too?"

"I just might, I just fucking well might, good bye you ass hole." And he hung up on Jason.

Then he thought, *I might have to kill Agnes.*

We got to Arts about 1300. Art Langford had owned his gas station and towing company about 25 years and was well known by all the local, county and state police. He was tall and skinny with flaming red hair. No one called him "Red," because he hated his hair and he had a bad temper. He blamed his mother for his hair, she was a red head too, and he hated her for it. He was always the brunt of jokes in school. All the other kids called him "Woody Woodpecker" after the cartoon character.

When I got out of the car I noticed that the front door of the garage was open and I heard a banging noise coming from inside, I knew it had to be Red, he was too cheap to hire any help.

I yelled, "Hey Red, you in there?"

"Who the fuck is calling me Red?" He screamed.

"I am, you red headed woodpecker."

"Goddamn it Overture, you are the only one who can get away

with calling me that. Where the hell have you been keeping yourself, and how the hell have you been?"

"Hey, I'm great. I want you to meet my new partner, Leo Lapaka."

"Hi Leo, you are welcome here, but don't ever call me Red."

"Okay Red, I won't call you Red."

"Well Cod, I see you have him trained already."

"Take it easy Art, he's just kidding."

"Come on in, my wife just made some fresh coffee. Some new brand called KONA."

"You have to be shitting me, KONA, my God, Lapaka will love you. He drinks that stuff."

"Well at least your wife has good taste." Lapaka said.

"What do you two flat feet want?"

Lapaka said, "Flat feet? Where did that come from?"

"How long have you been a cop Lapaka?" Art asked.

"About five years."

"Flat foot is an old nick name for cops who walked the beats. You know, so much walking their feet got flat."

"Never heard it." Lapaka said.

"I suppose you never heard, "Brass buttons, blue coat, can't catch a nanny goat."

"Nope, never heard that either."

"How about?" "Does your dad work? No. He's a cop."

"I never heard that one either."

"Christ, Overture you need to educate this boy."

Lapaka said, "What can I say Art, I'm Hawaiian. I just got out of the outrigger."

When we went into Art's house, his wife Carolyn poured us

Kona coffee that smelled like kerosene, and then served us cheese cake. Carolyn was a small dark headed girl. She had a "Steal Magnolia" hairdo straight out of the hills of Tennessee where she was raised. And she painted her blue jeans on. I never could figure out how she got into those tight blue jeans. But she was always pleasant and very dedicated to Art.

Art Langford lived in a double wide house trailer behind his gas station/towing company building. He did live in a single wide until he got married and his wife insisted that they get a bigger house, so he bought her a double wide manufactured home. As cheap as he was I'm sure it about killed him. But he was good to law enforcement officers. He always had time to fix cops private cars. And if your personal car broke down, Art would tow it free. He never charged the police for anything. And he never expected any favors.

Langford's wife Carolyn had a son before she married Art But that didn't bother Art, he took the kid in like he was his own. Art did discipline the kid, and the kid had to work around Art's shop. He didn't get a free ride because of his mother. And someday, Art once told me, the kid will get the place. Art had no other family, his parents had passed away and he had no siblings, so all his energy went to his business, wife and stepson.

During our coffee with Art and his wife, we explained the homicides and that we needed to search the Chevrolet Caprice that he had towed earlier in the day. He told us it was out in back, but there were no keys for the trunk so he would have to pop it for us. The owner was a homicide victim so I figured we could legally inventory the car.

After finishing our coffee and catching up with each other over the years, we went out to search the car. We first searched the interior and found piles of paper, empty food cartons, discarded empty KILZS cigarette packs, and a few receipts form Johnson's Truck Stop for food, gas and a room. I wondered, *Why would she need a room at Johnsons?* The young state cop said she had an NCIC history of drug arrests, so maybe she was doing truck drivers. I said to myself, we will have to look into that later.

Art Langford popped the trunk. Inside was the normal stuff. Spare tire, car jack that was just lying there loose, out of its storage place, and a brown leather briefcase that was unlatched, with part of the contents spilled on the trunk floor. Lapaka picked up the briefcase and started sorting through the contents.

I picked up the papers that had spilled onto the trunk floor and discovered a sealed manila envelope addressed to Mrs. Agnes Cunard. The envelope said, "Upon my death, please deliver to Agnes Cunard, 2901 East Forgeus." Signed, Myrna Dobson." The envelope was large and bulky. What a coincidence I thought. We are going to see Mrs. Cunard later in the afternoon. We will give her the envelope and maybe she will fill us in on the contents.

After searching the car, we did the necessary inventory sheet, shot the bull with Art for a while and then we headed to the Cunard residence before it got too late.

✐ CHAPTER TWENTY-TWO ✐

Lapaka and I arrived at Agnes Cunard's house at 2901 East Forgeus at 1400. The apartment complex was called Eden's Paradise, what a fucking joke. It might have been Paradise at one time but now it was a rundown complex of six two story brown stucco buildings. It looked like it belonged in a war zone. Shit, this probably is a war zone. Graffiti on the walls, abandoned cars in the driveway, drapes blowing out of unscreened windows, busted shutters hanging on with one nail and basketball backboards with no hoops. How do you play basketball with no hoops?

Two uniform cars were parked across the street, hood to trunk, like two horses swatting flies off each other. As we approached the cars I recognized one of the cops. It was Richard Spalla. Spalla was in the old ID section when I came on the department. He is the one who fingerprinted me. ID is now known as the Evidence Collection Unit.

Several years ago Spalla pissed off the Chief of Police and was sent back to the Uniform Division and put in my squad. We were on the graveyard shift for three years working side by side beats. That's when we became friends.

On one of our shifts, while we were bull shitting, Spalla told me all about his run in with the Chief. That Chief is now gone, he left for another job in Florida.

Spalla told me that the Chiefs Press Liaison Officer, Sinclair Adams, was drunk driving one night and ran over several mail boxes before hitting a fire hydrant. When the beat cop arrived at the scene the driver was gone.

Spalla was the ID officer on duty that night. When he got to the scene he recognized the car and he knew right away who it belonged to. Spalla called for a Sergeant to give him the details so they could go get Adams and charge him with leaving the scene of an accident. Everybody hated Adams because he was such a suck ass, and screwed over several of his fellow officers. Spalla figured this was a good time to get even for all of Adams' bullshit.

The Sergeant that showed up that night is now Chief Larry Flint, well Flint was scared to death, no way he was going to arrest Adams. Spalla said he and Flint went round and round. Finally, Flint called the Shift Commander, who then called the Chief and got him out of bed. The Chief quashed it. No report, no ticket, no nothing. Two weeks later Spalla was in uniform. So much for equal justice. And Sinclair Adams, nothing happened to him. He just kept on walking around the office with a shit eating smile on his face sucking up to the brass.

I had always heard a rumor that Sinclair Adams had photographs of certain individuals in compromising positions, and he promised to publish them if he ever got in trouble. Apparently, it was not a rumor.

When Spalla saw me coming he jumped out of his car and gave me a big hug. I said, "Spalla what the hell are you doing back in uniform? I thought you got an admin job after your favorite Chief left."

"I did, but I couldn't stand the office politics, I have been through that once, remember? Besides, I am going to retire soon and I wanted the overtime to increase my pension. But what are you doing down in this neighborhood? I know you are working the Townsend and Jessop case, do you have a lead on it here?"

"Spalla, this is Leo Lapaka. He's my new partner since Big Nate left. Yeah we have a lead. What's the scoop on this dump? It looks like a war zone."

"It is, gang bangers, bikers, hookers, and dopers. That's why we are here, to protect the honest residents, if there's any left in there. Last week there was a biker killing in there. It's owned by a group of investors from China. They don't have to live there so they could care less. The management company is in Texas for Christ sake, so they don't give a shit. The City inspectors don't have the balls to revoke the residency permits so it just sits here and breeds crime."

"Well, we have to talk to one of the residents, a possible lead. We believe her niece was murdered. Want to back us up?"

"Hell yeah." Come on Sheldon."

Sheldon was the other cop Spalla had been talking with.

Agnes Cunard's apartment number was 201, second floor east side. We climbed the wooden stairway to the second floor. The stairway creaked and swayed, I thought the damn thing was going to collapse under our weight. We found apartment 201 and knocked and someone inside responded, "Who is it?"

"The police" I said, "We need to talk to you about your niece, Myrna Dobson."

"Just a minute please."

The lady who answered the door was in a wheel chair. She had stringy gray hair that looked like it had not been washed in six months. She was wearing a blue house coat, with the top two buttons missing. Her breasts, that had seen better days, were half exposed, but she didn't seem to care. She had a nasal canella in her nose with an oxygen tank hanging on the back of the wheel chair. She also had a cigarette dangling from her mouth.

We introduced ourselves and she invited us in. As we entered she put her cigarette out in a glass of water she was holding.

The lady said, "Please excuse my appearance, I wasn't expecting gentleman callers. Are you here to see Myrna?"

I said, "Aren't you afraid to smoke with that oxygen tank so close?"

"No, if the dump blew up, it wouldn't be much of a loss."

"That's true, but aren't you afraid for yourself," I asked.

"No, I'm half dead anyway, all I have is Myrna. She helps keep me going."

Oh, brother, I thought to myself, what is she going to do when I tell her Myrna is dead?

The apartment, which was small, dark and dingy had junk piled everywhere. The sink was full of dirty dishes, must have been a month's worth. Cockroaches were climbing on the dishes and sink. Empty Styrofoam cartons littered the kitchen table. Half empty coffee cups were on the front room end tables. Ash trays over flowing with cigarette butts. And a pack of KILZS cigarettes was on the arm of Mrs. Cunard's wheel chair.

"What is it, is she okay? She didn't come home last night but I thought she was out with her boyfriend."

"Mrs. Cunard," I said, "I'm afraid we have bad news for you. Myrna is not coming home. We believe she was murdered. Her body was found this morning, lying next to the Patagonia River."

"What? My God, I can't believe it. Who could have done such a thing?"

Then she started to scream and cry. I gave her my hanky, and just like every other distraught woman I had ever given a hanky too, she clasped the hanky like she was clinging to the loved one.

Several minutes went by before Mrs. Cunard was able to compose herself and talk to us.

I started by showing Mrs. Cunard Myrna's driver's license photo and asked her if the woman in the photo was in fact her niece.

Mrs. Cunard said, "Yes, that is Myrna Dobson."

Then I gave her the envelope. She looked at it and started to cry again. Then she opened it. But she was too broken up to read it. She asked one of us to read it her

I asked Lapaka, Would you read the letter please?"

The letter started:

January 22, 2000

Dear Aunt Agnes,

First, I want to thank you for all you have done for me and my kids. At least, while I had the kids. I know that I was not the best niece in the world, but Lord I tried, I just couldn't help myself. Drugs are such a dangerous thing to be involved with. I know they ruined me. Maybe it's a good thing my kids were taken away from me. At least now, they have a chance at a better life.

Second, I was not honest with you. I did help Uncle Justin with his criminal activity. I did it to have money to buy drugs. He always seemed to have lots of money from his junk business.

I know you always suspected that Uncle Justin was responsible for Victor's death. Well you were right. Uncle Justin had both of us involved in some of his criminal activity. The night Victor was killed, I was supposes to be with him, but I backed out. I was too scared.

Uncle Justin was to drop Victor and me off at the Three Points Gun Store. Victor was to break in and I was to be the lookout. Uncle Justin was going to wait three miles down the road so he would not be directly involved. I didn't go and Victor got killed because there was no lookout.

After it was over Uncle Justin told me when he saw all the police cars heading toward the store he figured Justin got caught, so he ran. He didn't figure on Victor getting killed.

I know Victor's loss destroyed your inner self. I am very sorry that happened to you. You are such a great person, you deserved better.

Enclosed you will find all the details of the crimes we committed as well as photos and plans written by Uncle Justin. Uncle Justin fenced most of the items in the photos through his junk yard.

Please forgive me,

Love Myrna

The letter was written six months before her death.

Mrs. Cunard blurted out, "That bastard, he destroyed everything he ever touched. I knew he was no good when I married him. Now she is gone too."

Then I asked Mrs. Cunard to give us a history of her relationship with her niece.

Mrs. Cunard said, "My sister Joann was Myrna's mother. Joann and her husband were killed in a traffic accident about twenty-five years ago. Myrna was ten. My ex-husband and I took Myrna in. We didn't want her raised in a foster home. Both of my husbands had been raised in foster homes, and they didn't like them.

My son, Victor was alive then and about the same age as Myrna. Victor was from my first husband. Anyway we thought they would be good for each other. You know, brother and sister. But after a while they each went their own way. Myrna dropped out of school and got hooked up with some druggies and became a drug addict. She had three kids, but because of her drug habit the state took the kids away from her. She had her first kid at eighteen. She had three kids by three different men. A real mess, no support, no one to fall back on but me."

"Do you know any of kid's fathers?"

"No, she wouldn't tell me anything about the fathers. But men were after her all the time. She really was quite beautiful, like her mother, but the drugs ruined her. Sores all over, teeth missing, skinny and paranoid."

"Do you know the whereabouts of Myrna's kids?"

"All I know is that they were raised in foster homes. They are old enough now to be out and on their own. Beth, the oldest should be about twenty, the two boys, Eddie and Ernie are probably teenagers."

"You mentioned that Myrna was out with her boyfriend, who is he?"

"I don't know, she never told me. She always went out to meet him. She never brought him here. But who could blame her, look as this dump. I wouldn't bring a man her either, if I could still get one. He was probably another no good drug dealer, that's all she seemed to hang out with."

"You said both of my husbands, what did you mean?"

"I was married twice both of them were raised in a foster home."

"What happened to them?"

"My first one or Justin?"

"Let's start with Justin."

"I divorced him about twenty years ago for several reasons. Justin was kind of antisocial, did not like rules. He always wanted to do stuff outside of the rules. Not that I knew he was a law breaker, but I had the sense that he was. He would never tell me anything about his business, even when I worked there. All I could do was paper work. Never knew where stuff came from or who it was going to."

"If you were doing the paper work, how come you didn't know what was going on?"

"Because he would come up with phony names for his dealings. It was like he was trying to hide stuff from the authorities. You know, like taxes from IRS and refusing to buy dismantling permits for cars and trucks."

"What about this criminal activity with Myrna and your son?" Lapaka asked.

I kind of suspected he had Victor involved in some underhanded dealings, but not burglary. But I didn't know until just now that he had Myrna involved too. As the letter said, Victor was killed in a burglary by the owner of the gun shop. I thought my ex put him up to it. I could not prove it and he always denied it of course. The letter proves me right on that one too. I Left him because he was a womanizer. He started chasing around on me. That's how I met him. I cheated on my former husband. I guess the term, what goes around, comes around, is true. Justin was such a smoothie. Very charming. Talked me right out of my pants."

"What do you mean?"

"I was happily married to Jason Cunard."

"Your last name is still Cunard, did you take your former married name back?"

"No, I married Justin Cunard."

"What? They both have the same last name."

"Yes, they were brothers."

"What?"

When Mrs. Cunard said her husband's names were Justin and Jason, Lapaka and I instinctively looked at each other and knew immediately they had to be the same guys that the kids had heard the night they found Carsey Jackson's body.

"They were brothers. I know it sounds awful. But I fell for my husband's brother. They had similar looks. But were very different in every other way. On the outside, Jason, was the stuff shirt. Always perfect. Always careful, never took a chance. But in reality he was a brute and he was a bully. He knocked our son Victor and me around all the time. I know he used to bully Justin all the time.

Justin was the opposite. He was daring, devil may care, the real rouge, but at the same time, very gentle. Always treated other people with respect. I don't know why, but I fell for him. Jason caught us in bed and that ended our marriage."

"What happened to Jason?"

"He died several years ago from brain cancer."

That stopped me cold. If Jason was dead, how could he have helped Justin dump Jackson's body?

"Where is Justin?"

"You're kidding right?"

"No, we are not kidding, where can we find Justin?"

"He is in the state prison, doing life for Armed Robbery, kidnapping and Assault. I thought you guys were the police, don't you know anything?"

"Prison?" How would we know that? This is the first time we heard his name."

"Yes, he has been in prison for years."

"What did he do, what happened, how did he get caught?"

"When the police officers came to my house the night Victor was killed they told me he was shot by the owner of a business he was burglarizing. Several days later a detective showed up at my door and wanted to talk to me about Justin. He told me that he had been investigating Justin for some time and was pretty sure he is the one who set up the burglary that got Victor killed. So you see, I already knew Justin was responsible. All the letter does is confirm it."

"I was stunned, I couldn't believe what the detective was telling me. Victor's death just about destroyed me. I knew in the back of my mind Justin knew something about it. But he was so smooth he convinced me he had nothing to do with it. I knew he was lying, I always caught him lying. I finally had enough."

"One night I overheard him planning to rob the Gaylord Bank. He mentioned Victor's name, I knew then that he was involved in Victor's death. I called the detective who came to see me and gave him all the details he needed. They staked the place out and caught him. That detective shot his ass too. It's a shame he didn't kill him. He always was on the police list of small time crooks but they could never catch him until I told them about the bank robbery."

"So you were the informant?"

"Yes I was. I got even, didn't I?"

"I would say you got more than even."

"Do you remember the names of the police officers or detective?"

"The detective gave me his card but I don't know that I still have it. It's been over twenty years ago. One thing I remember about him though, he was really skinny, I felt sorry for him, he looked like he never ate. I thought at the time someone needed to feed this man."

My God, I thought, was it Bones? It can't be, or could it?

"Let's go back to the junk yard. What kind was it?"

"He was a junk man. He dealt in all kinds of junk. Pipes, car parts, housing material. You name it, he would buy and sell it. It did not matter what it was. Today they call it recycling, back then they called it junk."

"How long had he been in the business?"

"All his life I guess. He was in it when I married his brother. That's how Justin and I got so close, he gave me a job in his junk yard. I did the books once in a while. But I never knew he was selling stolen stuff. I understand that when a junk dealer buys something, there is a chance that what he buys could be stolen property. I did not know he was actually involved in stealing and selling stolen property."

"Where was the junk yard?"

"It was out in Mobile, he had ten acres out there. It was really secluded, now I know why. No law enforcement out there. He could buy and sell whatever he wanted and no one checked."

"What happened to the yard?"

"He lost it when he went to prison."

"What prison is he in?"

"I don't know and I don't want to know. I want nothing to do with that bastard. He has done enough damage. I haven't heard of or seen him in years. I wish the ass hole was dead."

"A couple of more things Mrs. Cunard, where do you get your cigarettes?"

"I got them from Myrna, and she gets them from her boyfriend, or at least she did get them from her boyfriend. I guess I will have to buy my own now."

"Have you ever heard your ex-husband use the term "WITCH," in regards to any of his businesses?"

"No, but I know he has a tattoo of a star on the heel of his left foot, with the word "WITCH" around it. I saw it one day when he was sleeping off a drunk."

"Did he ever tell you what it meant?"

"I asked him about it but, he told me it was none of my business, and I was never to mention it again."

Before we left Mrs. Cunard gave us the documents that Myrna left for her with the letter. They were useless in this case but it would give us a reason to go to the State Prison and talk to Justin Cunard.

As we went the door Mrs. Cunard yelled, "Wait a minute, your hanky."

"Keep it." I said, "I have lots of them."

"Thank you young man." She said.

"Young man! I'm sixty three years old, that's the first time I have been called young man in years." I said to Lapaka.

He laughed, as he said. "Maybe she is half blind too."

✑ CHAPTER TWENTY-THREE ✑

As we left Mrs. Cunard's apartment we thanked Spalla and Sheldon for backing us up and then headed for our office.

On the way to the office, Lapaka said, "Now we have three WITCH connections. Townsend, Cunard and the Mayor's WITCH account. But how in the fuck are they connected?"

"I don't know, but one thing for sure, we will have to keep digging. Another thing I don't get? If Justin Cunard is in prison, how could he be involved? Hell he's doing life. And Jason Cunard is dead, he couldn't be involved." I said.

Lapaka said, "Do you suppose the kids had the right names? But how would two other people with the same names be at the same crime scene?" What's wrong with this picture Cod, what are we missing?"

"I don't know, it doesn't make sense. This case gets more bizarre as it goes on. I wonder if the detective Mrs. Cunard described was Bones. That would really be a coincidence. Well maybe Bones can answer that for us. I seem to recall that he did shoot someone once, or at least was involved in some kind of shooting, it's been so long ago I can't remember the details."

It was well after 2000 when we got back to the office. Everyone was gone. We checked our e-mails and phone messages. Nothing of importance on either one, so we left the office. I dropped Lapaka off at Rolanda Jacob's house and went home.

When I got home Louise was waiting up for me. I apologized for being so late, and as usual she was very understanding. She even fixed me a garlic bologna sandwich and a rum and coke. I wolfed them both down and fixed myself another rum and coke.

After the second drink I told Louise that I was beat and headed for the shower and then to bed. Louise stayed up to watch Dave Letterman.

The next morning I was up at 0600 ready to leave when Louise came out. I told her what we had learned from Mrs. Cunard and the possibility that Bones may have shot Mrs. Cunard's former husband.

Louise said, "Well you and Bones have been on the job a long time, maybe he did shoot the guy. I am sure you and Bones have run up against the same crook more than once."

She was right about that, I arrested the same guy three different times for three different crimes. During the third arrest the suspect said to me. "Overture, if this keeps up we are going to be closer than brothers."

I told Louise I had to go, kissed her good bye and left.

I picked Lapaka up at 0700 and we went to our office.

I told Lapaka, "We need to see Bones first thing."

"Amen to that."

We were in the office at 0730 and went straight to Bones' office. He saw us coming and waved us in.

"How are you guys?" He said.

"We need to talk." I told him.

"What's on your mind?" He asked.

"As you know, Myrna Dobson was the dead girl dumped at the Patagonia River. Her car had been impounded by a young state police officer. Lucky for us, that officer saw us at the crime scene and stopped to ask us if we needed any help. That's how we found out about the car. He had it impounded for being illegally parked in the rest area. He actually connected our victim with the car he impounded."

"When he searched the inside of the car he found a purse with her identification in it. But, more importantly, he also found a baggie of meth with guess what in the bag? KILZS cigarettes. KILZS cigarettes are the only evidence we have that connects all four of the homicides."

"When we searched the trunk of the car we found an addressed envelope to the dead woman's aunt. Her name is Agnes Cunard. Does that name ring any bells with you?"

"It certainly does. If it's the same woman, she blew the whistle on her husband years ago because he was responsible for getting her son killed during a burglary attempt. She told us about a bank he was going to rob, we staked it out and caught him. I shot his ass, and then put him away for life. I got him for kidnapping, armed robbery and assault. I had been after him for years on small time stuff but could never prove any of it. But she paid off big time. Man that was over twenty five years ago."

"Yeah she told us about some skinny ass detective that contacted her during the investigation. She also said she called that same skinny ass detective and set her husband up to get even with him for her kids death."

Bones said, "That skinny assed detective was me. Cunard was a class "A" asshole back then, do you know she was married to Cunard's brother and Justin Cunard took her away from him? What a family."

"But what does all this have to do with the Townsend and Jessop killings?" Bones asked.

"Two things, first, Cunard has the tattoo WITCH on his left foot and the KILZS cigarettes. Both Myrna Dobson and Mrs. Cunard smoke KILZS cigarettes. According to Mrs. Cunard, Myrna got them from her boyfriend. It stands to reason that the boyfriend, whoever he is, is a suspect. And Mrs. Cunard told us she saw the tattoo of the word WITCH on Cunard's foot.

"Don't you mean "Person of Interest?" Bones said, as he started laughing.

"Knock off the political correctness bull shit Bones. I meant what I said, he's a fucking suspect."

"I know, I know, I'm just pulling your chain."

"Don't you think that the KILZS cigarette connection and the tattoo are just too much of a coincidence to pass up?"

"Yes I do."

"Also, the kids that found Carsey Jackson's body said that they overheard the names Justin and Jason from whoever dumped Jackson's body." Lapaka added.

"Are they sure? It couldn't be the Cunard's, one is dead and one is in prison. But that is one big coincidence. You better follow up with those kids and make sure they are right."

"I know, it doesn't make any sense." I said.

"Have you found out where the cigarettes came from"? Bones asked.

"No, the lab and Big Nate are doing research on that."

"Mrs. Cunard also told us that her ex, Justin Cunard was a junk dealer when he went to prison."

"You are right, I forgot about that. I believe he had a place out in Mobile. You don't think he's the killer do you? How could he be? He's doing life." Bones said.

"We don't know if he is involved either, but we are going to have to find out what prison he is in and go talk to him. Do you want to go?" I asked Bones.

"Hell no. Why would I want to see that jerk?"

"Okay, just asking, I thought maybe you might want to renew your friendship with him."

"Shut up you old fart." Bones said.

"Well Lapaka and I need to interview him. I'm sure Connors will want to go along."

"Listen Bones, I said. When we had our meeting with the Mayor he never mentioned that he knew Townsend. Have you thought any more about it? Why do you suppose that was?"

"I don't know."

"Has the Chief said anything about when we can interview the Mayor?"

"No he hasn't, and I am getting tired of waiting, hang on, I'll call him right now."

"Hey Chief, Bones here. What about the interview of the Mayor?"

"What, tell him to go fuck himself." Bones then hung up.

Bones looked at us and said, "The Mayor's lawyer said he does not have to be interviewed, and the Mayor has some kind of political immunity. And if he was to be interviewed we would have to submit the questions ahead of time so the Mayor and his lawyer can review them."

"What a bunch of political bull shit." I said

"I agree." Bones said, "But what can we do."

"I know what we can do. Leak it to Rolanda Jacobs, Lapaka's girlfriend from the Register. Then he will be forced to answer."

"No way, get more evidence." Bones said.

"Okay."

❦

Lapaka and I decided to ask Connors to accompany us to the state prison. She was more than anxious to talk to Cunard.

We arrived at the prison at 0900 and parked in one of the "Police Only" parking slots. The three of us exited the car and headed for a large cyclone fence enclosure that had a single pedestrian gate that was separated from a large double gate that was used for vehicle access.

Two County Jail buses were lined up waiting to enter the double gates. The County buses were full of convicted felons being transferred to the State Prison.

Prison inmates in bright orange coveralls with black letters emblazed on them that said, "State Prison Inmate," were busy grooming the grass and flower beds. Two armed Correctional Officers on horseback were supervising the inmates. There was no doubt that these men were convicted criminals.

There was a buzzer on the pedestrian gate post with a sign that said, "Ring for Entrance." Before we could ring the buzzer a loud voice boomed over a speaker. "May I help you?" Christ, I thought it was Darth Vader talking.

I responded, "Yes," I am Detective Cod Overture, I am with Detective Leo Lapaka and Special Agent Isabel Connors, we are here to see the Warden."

"Are you armed?"

"Yes we are."

"Please return to your vehicle and lock you weapons in your car trunk and then come back to the gate."

"10-4," I said.

As we returned to the gate, we heard the gate buzzer come on and the gate unlock. I pushed on the gate and the three of us entered an enclosed passageway that was about six feet wide and twenty feet long. The gate automatically shut and locked behind us. At the end of the passageway was a second gate. The entire area was encased in cyclone fencing and double rows of razor wire, even the overhead. I thought, nobody could get out of here.

As we approached the second gate another buzzer went off and the gate unlocked.

The Darth Vader voice boomed again, "Enter the gate and approach the window. Take the forms from the sliding tray and fill them out at the table to your right. Then put them in the tray along with you identification."

After the Correctional Office in the control room was satisfied as to who we were he returned our ID's and issued us "Prison Visitor Passes." Then he said, "You must wear these passes at all times while you are here. Please proceed to the metal detector on your right."

The Correctional Officer at the metal detector was about 6' 4" and at least 210 pounds. From the look of his arms he must have been a weight lifter. He looked like a US Marine. I probably could have shaved with the crease in his uniform shirt. I wondered to myself, why is this guy here, why isn't he a cop? I should try to recruit him I thought.

The Marine looking Correctional Office instructed us to take everything out of our pockets and place them in one of the plastic bowls on the table next to the metal detector. And he re-iterated everything. I am telling you these guys do not fuck around. They treat everyone like convicts.

We finally got through the screening process and were escorted to a large steel door that looked like a bank vault. The Correctional Office escorting us gave a signal to an armed Officer on the wall who then lowered a water bucket to our escort Officer. Inside the bucket was the key to the door. The Officer took the key unlocked the large steel door, put the key back in the bucket and the Officer on the wall pulled it back up.

What a system. They have electronic surveillance, razor wire and computers. But they still use a rope and a bucket to deliver keys. Whose brains storm was this? But when you think about it, the top of that wall was a safe place for keys. It was at least thirty feet high. Spider man couldn't have scaled that damn wall.

The Correctional Office pushed the door open and told us to go on in. Once inside the prison we faced a long hall with gray cement block walls on both sides. I heard the steel door slam shut and lock. Even though I have been in law enforcement for over forty years, when that steel door slammed shut, I got the eeriest feeling I have ever had. I felt like a trapped rat.

I must have looked pretty nervous because I heard a voice behind me say, "Don't look so nervous Overture, they'll let you out."

I turned around and there stood Paco Peliteer. "What are you doing here Paco?"

"What's wrong with you Overture, are you so old and senile that you forgot that I'm the department's prison gang intelligence officer?"

"Holy shit Paco, I just never thought about it. I have been so wrapped up with the Townsend and Jessop killings that I haven't thought about anything else."

"Yeah, I understand. How is that case coming, any leads?"

"That's why we are here. I think we might be getting close. By the way this is Special Agent Isabel Connors she is with DCIS, and you probably know Lapaka."

I looked at Connors and said, "Paco is our department's gang intelligence officer. His expertise is prison gangs. He travels around the country giving seminars to other police agencies about prison gang activities."

Paco said, "Nice meeting you Agent Connors, and yes I know Lapaka. How have you been Leo?"

"I'm doing okay Paco, thanks for asking."

"Do you guys need my help with anything? I have an office here if you need to use it."

"I have a question," I said. "How do you stand this place?"

"You get used to it, and I get to go home at night."

"How about taking us to the Warden's Office."

"Sure follow me, I will introduce you."

⮑CHAPTER TWENTY-FOUR⮐

Paco led us the rest of the way down the hallway. The hallway floor was impeccable. It shined like new marble. The inmates who clean these floors must spend hours at a time just waxing. Not much they could do with the drab grey walls though. Dull grey cement blocks, with no decoration of any kind.

At the end of the hallway, on the left side, was an Oak door that opened into the warden's office. The door was adorned with the warden's name in gold letters. "J.J. Irish, Warden." I noticed, oddly enough, that this door did not have any locks. How strange I thought, the place full of crooks and no lock on the wardens door.

Paco opened the door and we all entered. But it was not the warden's office. It was a large open area that contained several desks with women sitting at them doing administrative work. Several inmates in the bright orange coveralls were milling around doing maintenance work.

The ante room had several offices off to each side. One was for the Deputy Warden, one was for the Associate Warden, and one was for the Administrative Assistant.

I asked Paco, "How much brass do they need to run this place?"

Paco said, "Hey, it's a bureaucracy, nothing bigger that a state prison system."

At the other end of the ante room was the Warden's real office. It encompassed the whole width of the ante room. The wall between the warden's office and the ante room was glass, which afforded the warden a view of the ante room as well as any approaching visitors.

The warden saw us approaching and got up and invited us into his office. Paco made the introductions, excused himself and left. The warden ordered coffee and soft drinks, which were delivered by an inmate wearing orange coveralls.

Warden Irish was a short portly man who looked about sixty five but was actually fifty two. The stress of running a prison had not been kind to him. He had large puffy bags under his eyes and what little hair he had left was grey. He was probably forty pounds overweight. But he was a natty dresser, he wore a dark blue pin stripe suit, white shirt with cuff links, and a plain powder blue tie. He was articulate, he choose his words very carefully, as if he did not want to divulge too much information. Irish kept referring to me as sir and Isabel as ma'am.

Finally I said, "Warden, I don't know about Isabel, but you are making me feel old with the sir stuff, please call me Cod."

"Me too." Echoed Isabel.

"All right," he said with a smile. "Cod, Isabel, how can I help you two."

"Well, warden. We are looking for an inmate named Justin Cunard. We were told he has been in the state prison for about twenty years or so. We need to talk to him about a case the three of us are working. It involves the theft of federal surplus property. I didn't mention the homicides."

"Cunard, no way. I was a new Correctional Officer when he came in. He has been here about twenty five years. He has grown old in here. I would trust him with my life. But anyway he is not here, and before we go any further I want to call in one of our investigators to sit in, do you have a problem with that?"

"No I don't, do you Isabel, Lapaka."

"No" Isabel said.

"Me either," echoed Leo Lapaka.

The warden then called someone and asked for an investigator.

Then the warden said, "Is Cunard a suspect. If so I need to know about it."

"No not yet, we just need to talk to him. Where is he?"

"He's not here, I don't know where he is, no one does."

"What does that mean?"

"It means he is an outside trustee and out working somewhere, it could be anywhere."

"Isn't he doing life for armed robbery, assault and kidnaping?"

"Yes he is."

"Then how could he be an outside trustee?"

"He has been here twenty five years and has worked his way into a trustee position. It's based on a classification system. Over the years an inmate acquires points for good behavior and trust."

"When an inmate acquires enough points, they are evaluated by a "Board of Wardens" who then decide who should be made outside trustees. Cunard was an inside trustee first, and then he was made an outside trustee. Inmate Cunard actually saves the state and prison system a lot of money with his work."

"What does he do exactly?"

Before the warden could answer his investigator showed up.

Warden Irish made the introductions. The investigator's name was Dan Packard. We learned Packard had started in the prison system as a Correctional Officer and worked his way into the Investigations Division.

Packard told us that prison investigators are not "Certified Peace Officers," and as such cannot file criminal charges or get warrants. He explained that he has to take his cases to the local police department and then they file the charges. Kind of a cumbersome system he explained. He went on to tell us that the department was working toward getting some of the investigators who have a police background certified as "Peace Officers."

Warden Irish explained to Packard why we were there.

Packard agreed with the Warden, "No way," he said. He is an old grandfatherly type. He wouldn't risk his trustee status. He wouldn't hurt a fly."

I said, "Getting back to my question about Cunard, what does he do exactly?"

Irish said, "As I said, he is an outside trusty, his job is to pick up fire trucks from the military bases and take them to the small communities around the state to assist them with fire problems."

173

"As I understand it then, he is inside but he is out. Kind of like inside/out?"

"You could say that. He probably spends more of his time out than he does in. He spends his nights in."

"Who supervise his outside trips?"

"No one, he is a trustee, he is on his own."

"Where does he hang out when he is here?"

"In the motor pool, he has an office out there."

"Are you telling me you have an inmate who is an outside trustee and he has his own office in here?"

"Yes I am."

I felt like asking Warden Irish if Cunard had a fucking secretary, but I thought that might piss him off, and there was no sense in doing that. Instead I continued my normal questioning.

"Why is that?"

"Because he does a lot of stuff for us. He gets us a lot of free equipment from the bases. As I said earlier, he saves the state and the prison system a lot of money. For example, if we need blocks or concrete for a project, Cunard acquires those items for us."

"Where does he get this stuff?"

"I don't know. All I know is that he is good at it."

"So that earns him the run of the state?"

"In my opinion, yes, and I am the final say."

"Does he drive a white semi-truck with a white trailer?"

"He drives a white semi-truck but he has a flatbed trailer."

"Is the truck marked "State Prison?"

"No it is unmarked. Most organizations and individuals that we do business with do not want vehicles in their parking lots that say state prison on them. It is not a good business image. So we thought it best that the truck be unmarked."

"That's convenient for him. Does he wear an orange jump suit?"

"No, he wears the typical prison uniform of denim pants and chambray shirt with no markings."

"So then, no one he deals with would know he is a state prison inmate."

"No they wouldn't."

I couldn't believe what I was hearing. A convict with a semi-truck to run around the state in and has his own office in the prison. What was more insane was that no one checked on him. He could do anything he wanted. Who would know?

I looked at Isabel and said. "Isabel do you have any questions for the warden?"

Isabel said yes. "Warden, do you know who Cunard interacts with at the bases?"

"No, he is on his own for that. I go by what he tells me."

"What does he tell you?"

"Not much, I don't pry into what he does."

"What if he is lying to you?"

I have never caught him in a lie, have you Dan?"

"No I haven't."

"That's all I have for now." Isabel said.

One more question I said. "What kind of cigarettes does Cunard smoke?"

J.J. Irish said, "As far as I know he doesn't smoke. Dan have you ever seen Cunard smoke?"

"No I haven't." Packard said.

I said, "We appreciate your help Warden. And if it is okay with you, I would like to contact Dan if we have any further questions. We really don't need to take your time."

"That would be fine with me."

I got Packard's phone number and we left.

"Oh warden, Just a couple of more questions." I said, "Please do not tell Cunard we were here looking for him."

"We won't tell him anything."

Yeah, I bet I thought.

"And the other question is, do you know if Cunard has any tattoos?"

Just as I asked that question Irish was taking a drink of his coffee. When he heard the question, he gagged and spit coffee all over his desk. I thought he was going to have a stroke. His face turned beet red and he started to tremble.

I said, "Are you okay?"

"Yeah, Yeah, I just burnt my mouth with the coffee, I didn't realize it was so hot. But to answer your question, as far as I know Cunard does not have any tattoos."

We thanked the warden for his time and Investigator Packard escorted us to the main entrance of the prison and we left.

When we got outside I said, "I wonder what made the warden so nervous about the tattoo question?"

"Maybe he lied about it. Maybe he knows Cunard has a tattoo." Connors said.

ᑲᕋᑐ CHAPTER TWENTY-FIVE ᕋᕋ

Outside the main gate Lapaka jumped all over me. He was pissed off because we didn't wait around for Cunard to return.

"You heard what the warden said, Cunard gets supplies for the prison. He is not going to give that up, it makes him look good with his bosses."

"Yes, I heard him, that's why we should have waited and confronted him."

I said, "Look, we were on the Warden's turf. This whole thing stinks to me. An inmate with a truck and his own fucking office. That does not add up. For all we know everyone in there is on the take. The Warden said, I would trust him with my life. How does someone in the criminal justice system trust a convicted felon with his life? That warden is not going to give us anything about Cunard."

"Then what are we going to do?" Isabel asked.

"We are going to have to follow Cunard and find out where the hell he goes. We can put three two person teams together and follow him. He goes around all day committing crimes and returns to prison at night. No wonder we couldn't find him. A thief and probably a killer and the fucking prison is his hideout and the warden is his cover. John Dillinger never had it that good. He has no outside records, no bank accounts, no utility bills, and no phone bills. At least none that we know of, none we can subpoena."

And then Lapaka says, "Who is John Dillinger? Just joking, just joking, don't get in an uproar Overture. But you are right about that, it's a perfect cover. Who would believe this? Who would believe a prison inmate doing life could be an outside trustee.

"No one." I said.

"If it's him, where do you suppose he hides his cash?" Lapaka said.

"I don't know. Probably not in a bank. Maybe he buries it."

"Well if he hides the property on the Mayor's ranch, maybe the money is there too."

"What about the cigarettes, the warden said Cunard doesn't smoke?" Lapaka interjected.

"I don't know about that. This case gets crazier all the time." I said.

"Most guys escape from prison, this guy escapes to prison." Connors said.

"No shit, I can't believe this." I said.

As we were getting in our car Paco yelled at us. "Wait up he said. Did you have any luck?"

"Yeah, we found out that the warden loves our suspect and thinks he walks on water. This guy is a convicted felon, doing life for armed robbery, assault and kidnapping. He is allowed to be an outside trustee with his own truck and a fucking office in the motor pool for Christ's sake. What's up with that?"

"Listen Cod, when I was first assigned to this unit I had heart burn myself over the way some of these inmates are treated. I tried everything to get moved to an outside office. But how do you do that when you are working prison gangs? You have to understand the prison mentality."

"These men and women are with these inmates day in and day out. Sometimes they become friends. Hell every once in a while a female will come up pregnant by an inmate. And a male guard will fall in love with a female inmate. These inmates are doing time. That's all they have is time, time to finagle, time to scheme and time to plot. They live to take down correctional officers."

"Do you know inmate Justin Cunard?"

"I see him around once in a while but he is usually gone in his semi. I know he is well liked by the warden. I know from time to time he brings vehicles in here and the other inmates dismantle them."

"What kind of vehicles?"

"Trucks, cars, and sometimes Jeeps."

"Military Jeeps?"

"Yeah."

"Are you telling me he is running a chop shop in here?"

"I never looked at it that way, but I guess you are right."

"Where does he get the vehicles?"

"I have no idea."

"Where does he do this?"

"In the motor pool, where else."

"Who does it"?

"Other inmates."

"What do they do with all the parts?"

"The prison sells them through state surplus."

"Oh yeah, right." I said.

I said, "The killer has been leaving KILZS cigarettes at each crime scene, we suspect Cunard. But the Warden told us Cunard does not smoke."

"I've seen him smoke." Paco said.

"You have?"

"Not very often, but one day he was leaving in his truck and he had a cigarette in his mouth."

I thought, why did the Warden say he doesn't smoke?

"Can you get in his office and look around for KILZS cigarettes?"

"I'll try."

"Paco." I said, "We are having a meeting tomorrow morning, can you come? We are going to need your input on how to deal with the Prison system. Also I need you to get us a picture of Cunard, without anyone knowing."

"I'll be there with a picture, I have access to prison records, no one will know," Paco said.

"Yes, name it and we will be there." Isabel said.

"0900 at Palm Springs. Do you know where that is Paco"?

"Yes sir. See you tomorrow."

The next morning at 0900 we met in the conference room at Palms Springs.

Bones had brought the Chief and Paco Peliteer showed up with ten copies of Cunard's picture. I gave one of the photos to Connors for her file.

And then Paco said, "You won't believe this, but I could not get into Cunard's office, he is the only one who has a key."

"You can't be serious?" I said. "A convict in prison, and he is the only one with a key to his office. Unbelievable."

"I'm as serious as a heart attack." Paco said.

Victoria and Nate were there before the rest of us. They had set up the podium and had drawn some kind of chart on the blackboard.

We all sat around bull shitting and having coffee before we actually started with the official meeting, if you want to call it official. It was really a lets kick around what we have so far meeting. Kind of a way to determine what we really had and what we needed to accomplish.

Before we started I introduced Paco to the investigative team as the Department's Prison Gang Expert, who works for our department but is actually based at the state prison.

I said, "It looks as if we may have a break through on this case. From the information we have gathered so far it appears that the main suspect may be a prison inmate who is doing life for assault, robbery and kidnapping."

"His name is Justin Cunard. But the kicker is, he is an outside trustee. He has his own semi-truck supplied by the prison. He is allowed to roam the state at free will with a semi-truck to do jobs for the state and local communities."

"He also has his own office inside the prison, figure that one out. His job is to take military surplus equipment to small cities to help them in any crisis situation they may have. For example, if they need firefighting equipment or snow removal equipment, his job is to deliver the equipment to the particular city in need."

"Before he went to prison he was a junk dealer. What does that tell us? He knows the value of the surplus property he was supposed to deliver to the cities. Quite obviously he converted some of that property to his own use, and some to the state prison system."

"In addition to what I just said about the possible suspect we have four killings including two police officers. At all four crime scenes we have found KILZS cigarette butts that ties these crimes together. But we were told Cunard does not smoke. We also found a Jeep tire print at the scene where Carsey Jackson's body was found."

"We know the suspect has access to military property, so the tire print is important. We have information that the Mayor, Lance Wilson, has military property stashed on his ranch. Also that the Mayor received money from the sale of a crane. One of the victims, Myrna Dobson, was the ex-niece of the suspect. We know she provided KILZS cigarettes to her aunt, the suspect's former wife."

"There are a couple of gaps. One is the cigarettes. If Cunard does not smoke, and we were told by Warden Irish that he doesn't, who left the cigarettes? But Paco said he has seen him smoking, not very often but once or twice. The second gap is the names Justin and Jason. The kids who found Carsey Jackson's body heard the names Justin and Jason."

"At first we thought if Justin Cunard is in prison he couldn't be involved. But now we know he is an outside trustee, so he could be involved. But what about Jason, he has been dead for years, he could not have been there."

"It gets worse. To top it all off, she left her first husband, who happened to be the suspect's brother, for the suspect. God what a mess."

"But there are some interesting connections. Officer Townsend has a tattoo of a star with the letters JJ in the center of the star and the word WITCH surrounding the star on his left foot. The Mayor has referred to one of his bank accounts as his WITCH account. We learned from Mrs. Cunard, Justin's ex-wife, that he has the word WITCH on his left foot. Both of these tattoos are on the bottom of the foot so they cannot be seen by just anyone."

They all sat there in silence. You could read the questions before they were asked.

Finally the questions came.

"How does someone doing life for violent crime become an outside trustee?" Sonya Harris asked.

"How does an inmate get assigned a semi-truck?" Jared Bellamy asked.

"How does he have his own office, I have to share mine." Big Nate said.

"I can't answer that, but maybe Paco can. I looked at Paco, and told him, "The floor is yours."

Paco started. "First, the prison system, whether we in law enforcement like it or not, is a member of the Criminal Justice Community. They play a very important role in the System. They take care of the people that you and I do not want in our neighborhoods, namely convicted felons."

"Even though the prison system is in the same system as you and I, they are not treated as equals. They don't get the same pay, they don't get the same benefits and they are not usually as well respected by other members of the Criminal Justice System."

"But believe me there are some very sharp individuals in the correctional system. They work hard, they are honest, they go home at night just like you and I and they have families."

"However, due to the nature of the prison system, which is really a closed society, the staff members are with inmates every hour of every day that they work. They sometimes have a tendency to get lax with inmates, and that's when problems arise. There are cases of male Correctional Officers falling in love with female inmates and vise versa. That causes severe problems in the prison system."

"In the case you are working, you have an inmate who is a lifer. He was made an outside trustee because he met all of the prison requirements of becoming one. However, over time he changed the rules to suit himself and no one in charge of this inmate did anything about it."

"There are also rumors going around the prison that this particular inmate was saving the prison money by acquiring equipment the prison needed, at no cost to the prison. So what you have then, is a prison official who is saving the state money, which makes him look good in the eyes of his bosses."

"So the official, in this case the warden, makes a decision that this inmate can do whatever the hell he wants because it is cost effective for his unit. Then what happens? The inmate is rewarded with his own office. It really looks like it got out of hand, and from what I have been hearing, this inmate has more clout with the warden than some of the staff members."

"I will tell you this, Wardens wield a lot of power in the prison system. I don't know what evidence of a crime you have, but you better have your ducks in a row before you take any of these guys on. If it is J.J. Irish, I am sure he has his back covered somehow."

After Paco finished I asked Big Nate to fill us in on what he and Victoria had uncovered. Big Nate being the nice guy that he is said. "I think Victoria should do the honors, she did most of the work."

With that, Victoria got up to present the findings of the background investigation. It was obvious that she was somewhat nervous, I didn't know if she had ever given an investigation presentation before. She stuttered a little bit and her face flushed, but then she settled down and started.

"At first I was tasked with researching all the case files of Officers Townsend and Jessop in an attempt to find a connection between them and any old suspects that they may have put away. I researched about fifteen years' worth on Townsend, and about six months on Jessop. Jessop was a rookie, like me, so he did not have very many arrests. I was given some information concerning KILZS cigarettes and certain cases to look for, but I came up empty. Oh, and before I forget, Nate found out that KILZS cigarettes come from The Republic of Mordova. The only way to get them is via the internet, there are no outlets in the US. I also created a time line but that was no help either."

"Then Big Nate was brought on board and a decision was made

to conduct brand new backgrounds on anyone connected with this case. We started with Jessop because he was the newest employee. We found nothing on him to tie him to anyone."

"Then we did Townsend, Bingo, we may have hit the jackpot, at least we think we hit the jackpot. During our background investigation of Townsend we learned that he was raised in an orphanage from the age of five."

"Townsend's father killed Townsend's mother and then committed suicide. His father did this in front of Townsend, remember he was only five years old, it must have been traumatic for him. But he survived. The orphanage was originally called "Fontaine House." The name was later changed to "SOK," which means "Save Our Kids.""

This home for kids is still in business. But it is no longer called an orphanage, it is referred to as a safe haven for kids. It sits on 150 acres out in Queen Creek. The woman who now runs the place is Jerilyn Richardson.

"According to the Register of Contracts and Deeds, Jerilyn Richardson is the daughter of the woman who started this home. Her name is Sylvia Fontaine. Mrs. Fontaine is now 86 years old, she turned the home over to her daughter when she retired. We called the home and found out that Mrs. Fontaine still lives on the property, she has her own little cottage in the back."

"We also did a search on the home itself. This is where it gets interesting. About nine years ago Mayor Lance Wilson donated 150 acres of land to Fontaine House. Why would the Mayor do that? For political gain? Could this be a coincidence, or was the Mayor a foster kid at Fontaine House himself? To find that out we would have to ask the Mayor, or go to Fontaine House and search their records."

"We also went to the Library and researched all the old newspapers. We found an article on the Mayor and his donation to "SOK". There were photos of the Mayor with Mrs. Fontaine and Mrs. Richardson accepting the donation."

"There was even a blurb in the paper about changing the name of the home to Lance Wilson Way, but the Mayor nixed the idea. According to the paper, when the Mayor gave his speech, he referred to the place as Fontaine House, not SOK. Which I think is important, how would he know the original name was Fontaine House unless he had lived there?"

"Then we called the home to inquire if they had records from years ago, under the guise of looking for a lost relative."

"We were told that some of the records were retained on site and some have been archived."

Big Nate said, "We did not want to push the lady we were talking to. Besides I figured you and Lapaka would want to interview Mrs. Fontaine, and Victoria agreed with me."

"But we did one more follow up with Personnel," Nate said. "We wanted to look at Townsend's original application. We talked to Donna Douglas, she dug up Townsends original police application from her Computer Archives. You probably won't believe this, but one of Townsend's references on his application is none other than Mayor Lance Wilson. That is one unusual connection, don't you think?"

"What?" I blurted out. "The Mayor was a reference for Townsend? When the Mayor first ordered me back to Homicide he never even mentioned that he knew Townsend. That could have been an over site. But, being a reference for Townsend, that he would not have forgotten."

"And yes that is one very big connection. Now we will have to subpoena Townsend's banking records, just to make sure he was not dirty."

I asked the Chief, "Chief, did you know the Mayor was a reference for Townsend?"

"No I didn't."

"Well if his lawyers will not let us interview him we are never going to find out the truth."

I asked Nate, "Is there any way to find out who ordered the cigarettes? Is there a web site we can check?"

"No, I already tried that, the Lab said the "Cigarette order site" is hidden behind other sites somewhere in Europe to avoid the Federal Cigarette Tax."

"Wonderful." I said.

"We need to go to Queen Creek this afternoon, maybe they will give us the names of anyone else that was there with Townsend. If not we will subpoena their records. As a matter of fact, I think we are going to need a lot of subpoenas."

"But Cod, I have a luncheon date with Rolanda."

"Cancel it, and don't tell Rolanda where you are going."

"Okay boss."

"And quit calling me boss, damn it. We are equals."

"Okay, okay."

"I cornered Paco and asked him to get me Cunard's schedule, if he had one, without tipping anyone off. We need to follow him Paco, to find out what the hell he does."

"No problem he said."

I called Victoria and Big Nate into my office and gave them copies of Cunard's photograph and told them to canvas Southern Avenue and see if anyone will identify Cunard as attempting to sell them surplus property. Run it by the little person at the transmission shop at 4000 Concord.

"Okay, we'll get on it."

ꙮ CHAPTER TWENTY-SIX ꙮ

After we hashed everything over Lapaka and I headed to Queen Creek to see Mrs. Fontaine. I knew I had heard of the home before, but never gave much thought to it. When we got there I was surprised. It was a pretty impressive campus. They had a football field, a baseball field and a gymnasium.

The driveway leading to the main building was long and curvy. It was lined with tall Ponderosa Pine trees and large boulders that were painted white, the boulders were adorned with the names of children, and the names were painted in black. I didn't know the meaning of the rocks but I intended to find out before Leo and I left.

The driveway led to a visitor's parking lot that was outlined with black steel poles with white chain draped between the poles. We parked and started for the entrance.

The main building was red brick with large white columns framing the oaken door. There was a sign on the door that read, "Save Our Kids, Welcomes All New Comers."

We entered and approached a small desk with an information sign. The young man sitting at the desk must have been a resident because he looked like he was ten years old. He asked if he could help us. Lapaka and I identified ourselves and asked to see Mrs. Fontaine. The boy said, "Missy is not here now, I will get Mrs. Richardson."

The boy left and a few moments later a woman appeared. She introduced herself as Jerilyn Richardson, the owner of the home. She looked like she was in her sixty's. She had gray hair, cut short, wore glasses and walked with somewhat of a limp. She had on a blue dress with a white sweater. She asked the nature of our business.

I said, "Mrs. Richardson we are here to see"……at this point she cut me off and said. "Please, call me Jerilyn, last names are too formal." I said, "Okay," And continued with, "Jerilyn, we are here to see Mrs. Fontaine, we need to talk to her about some of your former residents."

"Oh, mother, my goodness, I thought you were after me for

traffic tickets I didn't pay. As she started laughing, just kidding, you know. But mother may still be walking. My mother is 86, and still walks five miles a day, lifts weights and still drives her old De Soto. She should be out back if she is done with her walk. I'll take you out there, she will be happy to have visitors. Her last visitor was here about two months ago."

Lapaka asked, "Who was that?"

"I think he is your boss, the Mayor. He was raised here you know."

I was absolutely stunned. It was true, the Mayor was a resident here at one time. He had to have been here the same time as Townsend. No wonder he gave them all this land. We had our connection at last.

When we got to the little cottage Mrs. Fontaine was out on the porch tending to some potted plants.

"Mother," Mrs. Richardson said, "You have visitors from the police department they want to talk to you about some of our former students."

"Oh, is it about Mike?" She asked.

Mrs. Fontaine was a slightly built woman, 5' and about 110lbs. She had short curly gray hair. Her eyes were deep set and cocoa brown. It was hard to believe she was 86 years old, she looked 60. She wore dark horned rimmed glasses with a silver chain attached to them that draped around her neck. She wore a black silk blouse and silver shorts. She had a pleasant smile and a twinkle in those old brown eyes.

I said, "Partly, we are investigating the murders of Officers Townsend and Jessop as well as three other victims. We want to talk to you about Townsend's time here."

Mrs. Fontaine was very gracious, especially when we told her we were investigating the Townsend and Jessop murders. She invited us in and prepared tea for us. She also took a shine to Leo, she said he reminded her of a kid she used to have, who was killed in the Vietnam War. His name was Allen Provost, his name is painted on one of the rocks that line the driveway. Our kids who didn't make it, their names are painted on the rocks. Our way of remembering them."

I had my answer to the names on the rocks, I didn't have to ask the question.

"Poor Mike, I was at the funeral you know. My daughter did not think it was a good idea for me to go. But he was my kid, I had to go."

Then she started to cry. I thought to myself, here goes another hanky, as I handed it to Mrs. Fontaine.

Between sobs she said, "Mike was the first kid who ever called me Missy. Then all the other kids picked it up. I have been called Missy ever since. Then she started to laugh, it was a sentimental laugh, as if she was thinking about something that Mike Townsend had done when he was a boy.

"My daughter, Jerilyn got really mad at me because I drove to the funeral, I even drove in the procession. I drove my old De Soto. I bought that car new in 1948. Mike loved that car. He used to wash and wax it for me. He made that black paint gleam. I was going to leave it to him when I died, but now it's too late. You know, I never felt that the kids here were my foster kids, I always felt like they were my very own. I loved all of them, even the Cunard brothers."

"So you were the one in the Black De Soto?" Lapaka said.

"Did you see me?"

"Yes in the funeral procession. I wondered who owned that old car."

I had to jump back in or I would have lost my train of thought. I also gave Lapaka a dirty look for interrupting.

"Mrs. Fontaine," I said. "You mentioned the Cunard brothers. Who are they?"

"Oh yes, Jason and Justin, they were brothers. Jason was the bully of the group. He even bullied Justin until Justin beat the hell out of him over that chubby J.J. Irish. Justin was one of those that we failed with. He ended up in prison you know?"

"Did you say J.J. Irish?" I asked.

"Yes, he was one of the group that was here. He was here with Mike, Lance, Porter and the Cunard brothers."

"They all did pretty well. Mike became a police officer and

Lance became the Mayor, but as I said, we failed with Justin. But five out of six isn't too bad."

"Are you talking about Mayor Lance Wilson and Porter Homer?"

"Yes."

"Are you telling us that Lance Wilson, Mike Townsend and Porter Homer were foster brothers here?"

"Yes I am."

"Who else was here with them?"

"Well I mentioned the Cunards, and J.J. Irish, I don't know what happened to J.J. The next time I see Lance I will ask him if he knows."

"You see the Mayor?"

I didn't want Mrs. Fontaine to know that we already had some of the information she was giving us, especially about the Cunards, so I played dumb with the questions. I knew Lapaka was probably wondering why I just didn't tell her we already knew most of this. But this was the first time we had officially heard that all of the players in this case were raised together as foster kids. I wanted her to keep talking.

"Oh yes, he comes by here quite often, him and Porter. So did Mike. Remember, in their eyes I was their mother and they were brothers. Lance was here about a month ago, it could have been two. Time goes by so fast for me now I can't seem to keep track of what's going on. Why do you think we have this big place? Lance donated the land."

"Mayor Wilson gave you this property?"

"Yes he did. He said it was for saving him and setting him on the path to becoming the Mayor."

"Does anyone else come by?"

"Yes, since he got out of prison Justin comes by. He is working for the US Post Office now. He looks so good in his Post Office Uniform. He always comes by with his big white Post Office truck. He gave us a couple of old Army Jeeps that we use on the property. His brother Jason is dead. They say he had a heart attack over losing his wife to Justin."

"Jason lost his wife to Justin?"

"Yes. Jason caught his wife and Justin in bed and that ended his marriage. He died a couple of years later."

"Do you have any other information we should know about?"

"If you have a chance to talk to Justin ask him what happened to J.J. Irish. Justin was J.J's protector."

"Justin's brother, Jason, was always bullying J.J. but J.J. was kind of like a wimp, he was afraid to defend himself. I told you earlier that Justin beat the hell out of Jason over J.J.. Jason was trying to put J.J.'s head in a toilet bowl, Justin caught him and beat the hell out of Jason. After that, the five of them, Mike, Lance, Porter, J.J. and Justin created what they called the "The Fontaine Five." It was their way to protect each other."

"Let me get this straight, Mrs. Fontaine, are you telling us that the Mayor, Lance Wilson, Officer Mike Townsend, Porter Homer, Justin Cunard and J.J. Irish created a group called the Fontaine Five?"

Then it hit me. The FF in the star, it meant the Fontaine Five.

"Yes I am. You know there is always a bully in every group of boys and girls. Ours was Jason. After that beating, Jason changed. Suddenly he became very cautious about everything he did. It was like he shriveled up. We never had any more trouble from him."

"Who came up with the idea for the Fontaine Five?"

"It was Mike Townsend, he was like the informal leader. Mike was the biggest, he was the go to guy when there was trouble. That's probably why he became a police officer. He was the enforcer."

I couldn't believe what I was hearing. This case gets more fucked up all the time.

Shortly after that Jerilyn Richardson came in and announced to us that it was time for her mother's afternoon rest period. "She is 86 you know. She needs her rest. But feel free to come back anytime."

Mrs. Fontaine said. "Oh Jerilyn, quit fussing over me. I am just fine."

"No." I said. "You have been generous with your time. We don't need to keep you from your rest. We appreciate your help. If we need anything else we will call and let you know we are coming."

"I must say Detectives, of that group of boys we are talking about, they did pretty good. One is the Mayor, one is the Mayors Assistant, and Mike was a police officer. The Cunards became business men. J.J., I don't know what happened to him. But now two dead."

"J.J. is a Warden in the State Prison Mrs. Fontaine. He did quite well too." I told her.

"I do have one more question Mrs. Fontaine." I said.

"Do you know what the term WITCH means in relationship to the people we are talking about?"

"No, I don't."

"How about tattoos, were they allowed?"

"No, tattoos were absolutely forbidden. Anyone caught tattooing was expelled and sent to A.L. Holmes State School for boys. We would not allow the kids to ruin themselves with tattoo ink."

That explained why the tattoos were on the bottom of the feet, so they would be hidden. I thought to myself.

Then she started to cry again, only this time uncontrollable.

Jerilyn sat down next to her mother and cradled her in her arms.

And we silently left Mrs. Fontaine to her memories.

"Detective, your hanky." Mrs. Fontaine yelled as we were leaving.

And just as I have always done before, I said. "Keep it Mrs. Fontaine, I have plenty."

I said to Lapaka, "The tattoo, the "FF" in the center, it means the "Fontaine Five." But what do the other letters mean?"

"I don't know. Let's find the Jeeps before we leave and get some photos and numbers."

"Okay." I said.

192

We found them behind the main administrative building being washed by the kid who was at the desk when we arrived. I told the kid he was wanted inside and he left.

While we were searching the Jeeps my phone buzzed. It was a text from Paco. "Cunard is leaving tomorrow at 0500. He does not have a schedule, he tells Irish he's leaving and leaves."

"Thanks" I sent back.

I gave Lapaka the info from Paco.

We checked the Jeeps and discovered that the ID plates had been removed. All we could do was take photos. We did that and left.

As we headed out the drive way Lapaka said, "It looks like we have our connection."

"It certainly does. And the Mayor, Porter Homer and JJ Irish are right in the middle of it."

"If Cunard is leaving the prison tomorrow at 0500 are we going to follow him." Lapaka asked.

"Yes we are, we have no choice."

"How about the balls of Jason Cunard, to show up here dressed like a mail man, conning that old woman." I said.

"Well he's a convict, that's what convicts do, they con people." Lapaka said.

"I hope if I live to be 86, I will look just as good as Mrs. Fontaine." I said.

"I thought you were 86," Lapaka said.

"Respect your elders," I responded.

Then we both started laughing. If you don't laugh once in a while, this job will drive you crazy.

When we got back to the office Bones was gone. I called his home and filled him in on what we had been told by Mrs. Fontaine.

"It's all coming together Bones, it has to be Cunard. There is no other possible solution. He's got the means, the freedom and the protection of the prison. Paco told us Cunard is leaving the prison tomorrow morning at 0500 Lapaka and I are going to follow him. I am going to call Connors and ask her to go with us."

"Okay." Bones said, "But be careful."

"Check"

"Leo," I said, "I still can't figure the cigarettes. If Cunard doesn't smoke, who in the hell left them?"

"Paco said he saw him smoking. Maybe Cunard does smoke, just not at the prison."

"What smoker can control a smoking habit that good?"

"I don't know, it was just a thought." Lapaka said.

"Well I'm going home to sleep on it." I said.

Later that night my phone rang, it was Lapaka.

"I figured it out. I couldn't sleep until I figured it out." He said.

"Figured what out?" I asked.

"The tattoo of the star. 'WITCH,' Wilson, Irish, Townsend, Cunard and Homer. The first initial of their last names spells WITCH."

"I'll be damned. Good job Leo. I bet every one of them has the same tattoo. No wonder JJ Irish gagged on his coffee when I asked him about tattoos. But how do we find out? We would need a search warrant, unless they are in custody, and I don't think that is going to happen. Not now at least. But it is one more connection. See you in the morning. And thanks." I said.

ᴄᴰ CHAPTER TWENTY-SEVEN ᴄᴗ

The next morning at 0430 Lapaka, Connors and I met at Palm Springs and picked up the undercover electrical truck. And of course, Lapaka brought us some of that damn Kona Coffee. But you know what? I was starting to like the stuff. I guess it must take a little getting used to.

At 0500 we were parked a block west of the main gate. We were backed into a driveway of a wrecking yard office with a clear view of the main entrance to the prison.

At 0515 the big white semi exited the main gate of the prison and headed east on County Highway 6. We followed at a safe distance just barely keeping the semi in sight. The semi entered the Interstate Highway and headed north. Excellent for us, more traffic to give us cover. I was worried about our vehicle however, it did stick out like a sore thumb, and maybe we should have used a sedan instead of a truck. Too late now though.

Justin Cunard drove twenty miles north and exited the Interstate at the Congress Street Exit. He drove three blocks west and stopped at Mason's Storage Facility, 300 West Congress. He punched a code into the gate lock from the cab of the truck and drove in. It was too early for anyone to be on duty at Masons.

Cunard was wearing normal prison jeans and prison chambray shirt when he entered storage room 126A. When he exited he was wearing a Postal Uniform and he was carrying a brown shopping bag and two large square items. He placed one square item on the driver's door. He walked around the front of the semi and placed the second square object on the passenger door. There were magnetic signs. U.S. Postal Service Signs.

I said. "This asshole is really brazen."

Lapaka said, "The more brazen you are, the more people you can con."

"I can't fucking believe this." Connors said.

195

That was the first time I heard her cuss.

Cunard entered the semi and drove to the rear of the storage facility. He pulled up next to a white enclosed trailer and stopped. He exited the semi, unhitched the flat bed and hitched the white trailer to the semi. He retrieved the brown bag from the semi cab and deposited it in the rear of the trailer. As far as we could tell the trailer was empty.

He entered the semi-truck and headed back to the Interstate Highway. Cunard drove another fifteen miles north and exited at the Jane Station Exit and stopped at Johnson's Truck Center.

After leaving the storage facility I called Victoria Redondo to have her and Big Nate obtain a search warrant for Cunard's storage facility at 300 West Congress, locker 126A. But first I wanted to know about the photo ID canvas on Southern Avenue.

Victoria said, "We have positive identification from ten people that Cunard was trying to sell them surplus property. They all said he was a postal employee. All except the little person at 4000 Concord, she was positive he was a city worker. But she did identify Cunard as the one."

"Good job," I said. "More probable cause."

As additional probable cause I told her to use the photo identifications as well as the fact that the renter of the storage room was an incarcerated inmate, who as an outside trustee was dealing in stolen military property and a possible suspect in five homicides. That he was hiding his identity as a prison inmate by wearing a US Postal Service uniform and placing US Postal Service Signs on his truck doors. I told her to have Big Nate help her with the warrant procedure.

"Let me know as soon as you have the warrant."

"Okay," she said.

When Cunard arrived at the Johnson Truck Center he parked in the back of the center. He exited the semi and opened the trailer doors, retrieving the brown shopping bag and went inside the truck stop. Lapaka, who was dressed like an electrician, followed Cunard into the truck stop. I parked in the rear of the truck stop within view of Cunard's semi. Connors and I went in to join Lapaka.

Lapaka took a seat at the counter, Connors and I took a booth.

We could both see Cunard arguing with the man who was at the counter. Finally the counter man called a woman out from the back room and they all started discussing something, what, we didn't know. I am here to tell you, Cunard was not very happy, he was really pissed off.

The woman returned to her office and came back holding a ledger. She showed the ledger to Cunard and the counter man. This action seemed to satisfy Cunard. Cunard then gave the brown shopping bag to the woman who took it into her office, she was followed by Cunard. What happened in there we have no clue. About five minutes later Cunard left the woman's office and went to his truck, again driving north.

We followed. I told Lapaka, "We need to pull off, he is going to burn us."

"I agree." Connors said. She also said. "Let's go back to the truck stop and talk to the lady with the ledger."

Why not, I reasoned.

On the way north Justin decided to call Jason.

"Jason, it's me again."

"What is it this time Justin?"

"That fucking weasel at the truck stop has been stealing the money."

"What money?"

"The money I have been getting from the sale of the military stuff. Why do you always act like you don't know what's going on?"

"I have to cover my ass you know."

"You do not, you asshole."

"How much did he take?"

"About $18,000."

"How do you know?"

"Because I count it each time I put money in the bag, and I haven't taken any out."

"What are you going to do about it?"

"I told that little prick he had better return it. But what else can I do? I can't report him to the police. He told me his wife is the one who took it. He said he had it at home in a safe and she took it to pay bills."

"Kill the fucking thief."

"Kill him?"

"Yep, that's what I would do, Kill him."

"Okay." That ended the call.

When we got back to the truck stop Connors approached the man at the counter, identified herself and told him that we needed to talk to him and the lady in the back room.

"What for he asked"?

"Because we believe you have been dealing in stolen federal property. You and the girl in the office back there and the truck driver you were arguing with. You know the trucker in the fucking post office uniform. This guy, as she showed the man Cunard's photo."

That was the second time I heard Connors cuss.

Paynter's face turned ash white, it looked like he saw a ghost. He started sweating profusely, he was scared shitless. He couldn't get the words out, he just stood there and stuttered," but, but, but, but."

"Get the woman out here, Connors yelled in his face."

The man wasted no time in calling for the girl in the back room.

When she came out, Connors badged her too and said. "We need to talk to both of you. Where should we do it?"

We can use my office." The man said, slowly regaining his composure.

We all sat at a large round table. The young woman identified herself as Heather Kolling, the bookkeeper and office manager for the Johnson Truck Stop. He identified himself as Lavelle Paynter the General Manager of the Johnson Truck Stop.

Connors did not miss a beat. "Why was the truck driver arguing with you?

Ms. Kolling said, "The truck driver leaves money here. He has accused us of taking some of it. I started keeping a log to prove he was wrong. But he doesn't believe us. He keeps his own books, but he's wrong. But he says it happened before I started keeping the log. That could be, I don't know what was going on before I got involved."

"Go get the log, we need it."

Ms. Kolling was back in seconds with the log.

"What about it Mr. Paynter"? Connors asked.

Before anything else was said, Paynter blurted out, "I only took 18,000 dollars to pay bills."

"What?" Connors said.

"Yeah I only took $18,000 to pay off credit cards. I didn't think he would miss it. He brings money in here all the time."

"Are you telling us that you took $18,000 of Justin Cunard's money?"

"Yes, I took it, Ms. Kolling had nothing to do with it."

"Why do you keep it here?"

"Just a service we provide. All the truckers leave stuff here."

"Where do you think he gets it"?

"He said he had a side business of selling surplus property. I even bought a Jeep from him."

"How much did you pay for it?"

"For keeping his money he only charged me $500.00."

"Where is it?"

"In my garage at home."

Connors said. "What is your address, I am going to seize the Jeep as evidence."

"2020 Brighton Road, but what about my $500 I paid for it."

"After stealing $18,000 from Cunard I don't think he will give you a refund." Connors told Paynter.

When Connors said that to Paynter, I couldn't help it. I just busted out laughing.

"Did he give you a bill of sale?" I asked.

"Oh no."

"Ms. Kolling have you ever bought anything from him?"

"No I haven't."

"Has he ever given you anything?"

"No."

"Where is the money kept?" I asked.

"In the safe, in the back room."

"Go get it, we will give you a receipt. It is being confiscated as evidence."

Paynter went and got the duffle bag, it was full of money. We counted it in front of Ms. Kolling and Mr. Paynter and had them sign the receipt. $23,000 total.

Paynter asked. "Am I in trouble?"

I said. "You should probably talk to a lawyer."

"What am I going to tell him when he comes back?"

"Tell him the truth, that the police took it."

"What if he doesn't believe me?"

"Show him the receipt."

Then we left.

I told Connors and Lapaka, "In forty-three years in law enforcement that is the first time a suspect ever confessed without me asking him a question."

Connors said, "He stole, stolen money, is that even a crime?"

"Hell I don't know."

Victoria Redondo called us on our way back from the truck stop. She had the warrant.

I told Nate we would meet them at Masons in two hours.

We arrived at Masons at 1700, Nate, Victoria, Sonya Harris, Jared Bellamy and JR Benoit were waiting for us when we arrived.

Victoria Redondo gave me the Search Warrant to review before I presented it to the Masons Storage Facility Manager. I noticed that the warrant had been signed by Superior Court Judge, June Waterman-Briner. Judge Waterman-Briner has been on the bench for over twenty five years. She was a strict Constitutionalist, so I knew if she signed the warrant it had to be valid.

Judge Waterman-Briner's husband Clifton was an engineer, who since his retirement, has been busy producing recordings and musical productions He also volunteers with "Friends of Criminal Justice."

I met them both years ago at a Constitutional Law Seminar at The University of Arizona, where Judge Waterman-Briner was the keynote speaker. Her husband had accompanied her to the seminar. I was lucky enough to be seated at the same table with them during the seminars ending banquet.

I presented the warrant, as well as a picture of Cunard to the manager of Masons, Howard Snell.

Snell looked at the picture and said, "That guy's name is Gregory Pauper, at least that is what we have on our records. He has two adjoining rooms. There is a door in the storage rooms that connects them. He comes in quite often. Is he in trouble?"

"You can't imagine Mr. Snell." I said.

Snell got out his bolt cutters and cut the lock off of Cunard's storage room.

When I entered the room I was amazed at what I saw. Cunard had installed closet organizers for all his clothes and uniforms. He had postal, county and state workers uniforms hanging on the closet rods. Next to them hung Cunard's prison garb. Blue denim shirts and pants.

The shelves held boxes of KILZS cigarettes, state and city magnetized door signs, and several different government license plates. And where are license plates made? In the state prison. This Cunard had more damn reach than Wilt the Stilt. Was this guy ever supervised by the prison system?

Victoria Redondo located a three drawer filing cabinet, marked "USAF," behind a large wooden desk. The drawers contained documents detailing where the military property came from, where it went and how much Cunard made on the sales. He was smart, he put where it went, not to who it went. No names, just towns. And a detailed map of where he had stashed most of his property in Callaway County.

One document listed the Correctional Officers that Cunard had "Loaned Money" to. There were four names, all low level positions. No supervisors were listed. One guy he "Loaned" 2000.00 dollars. Loan my ass, I thought.

There were entries indicating that he had been paying prison inmate trustees to dismantle the stolen vehicles. Another entry listed the payment of one V8 engine for an inmate's father, for holding $5000.00 of Cunard's money.

Lapaka found a damn photo album showing Cunard with people he was selling the military property too. Like new car salesmen do, standing there posing in front of the damned stolen property.

I thought to myself. This Cunard has really got balls. He must feel that he is untouchable. But why? Who is protecting him? It has to be the Warden? The Mayor wouldn't be that dumb. He is so brazen it's unbelievable. How can a prison warden allow this to happen? When this hits the papers the shit is going to hit the fan. This is going to involve a lot of people.

In the middle of the Southern wall was the door Snell told us about. The door was unlocked. I opened the door and found the adjoining room. This room had two 1941 Harley Davidson Military Motorcycles and two Willy's Jeeps.

Against the back wall stood a large black safe. The safe door was ajar. I pulled the safe door open and there they were. Four boxes of 38 Caliber Ammunition and two 38 Smith and Wesson Revolvers. There was also a clear plastic bag containing bloody US Postal Uniforms.

I looked at Lapaka and Redondo and said. "This is enough, we have to get this guy. Put out an APB, we have to nail his ass before he kills someone else."

Lapaka said, "He has to come back here to change his clothes before he goes back to the prison, why don't we just wait until he gets here?"

"Yeah, that's true." I said.

Connors said. "What about the guy at the truck stop? If he has been stealing the money, Cunard may go after him."

"You're right, we need to go back to the truck stop. Victoria, I want you to call for the evidence unit and stay here until they secure these rooms. When they get here tell them to take everything.

"Okay, I sure will." Victoria said. "But what if Cunard shows up?"

Connors said. "Let's leave Harris, Benoit and Bellamy here with Victoria just in case anything goes wrong."

"Okay, good idea."

"Nate, you better go with us."

"Lapaka you go with Connors, I will take Nate with me."

"10-4" Lapaka responded.

We got in our cars and headed for the Johnson Truck Stop.

ᑲᐟᐠ CHAPTER TWENTY-EIGHT ᕼᐧᐧ

After leaving Johnson's Truck Stop Cunard continued on to Callaway County and his storage lot at the Mayor's Ranch. He loaded three Jeeps that he had buyers for, and headed back to the Johnson Truck Stop. He had arranged to have the buyers meet him at the rear of the Johnson Truck Stop. He delivered the Jeeps and was paid $1000.00 per Jeep.

But this day he would have other business at the Johnson Truck Stop. After delivering his contraband to the unsuspecting buyers he waited at the rear of the truck stop for Lavelle Paynter, the little prick who had been stealing his money.

When Paynter clocked out it was starting to get dark. Paynter headed to his vehicle. He was intercepted by Justin Cunard, who stuck a 38 Caliber Revolver in his back and ordered him into his car.

"Where is my money? I know you have been stealing it."

Paynter started squealing, "I only took $18,000."

"Why did you even look in the bag?"

"I wanted to make sure I wasn't holding anything that was illegal."

"What did you do with it?"

"I lost it at the Casino."

"That's original. Too bad."

"Wait, Wait," Paynter screamed. You need to know something else.

"Yeah what's that"? Cunard asked.

"The police were here, they took your money and the ledger Heather Kolling was keeping."

"You're a fucking liar, the police don't know shit about me. You took all my money didn't you?"

"No, No, go ask Heather."

"Fuck you, I don't need to ask Heather, she is the only honest one around here. I know she wouldn't have taken it. Get in your car and drive until I tell you to stop."

"What for"? Where are we going?" Paynter asked.

"Have you ever heard the term going for a ride? Do you know what it means?" Cunard said.

"Don't, I'll pay you back, who will take care of my wife? She is an invalid." Paynter begged.

"I said drive."

They drove three miles north and exited at the Cortaro Road Exit. Cunard ordered Paynter to park under some Tamarack Trees.

"Give me the keys and get out."

Cunard went to the rear of the car and opened the trunk.

Paynter knew what was coming next as he pissed his pants.

Cunard ordered Paynter into the trunk of his car. Then he lit a KILZS cigarette.

Cunard told Paynter. "You told me your wife was an invalid, now she is a widowed invalid." As he shot Paynter twice in the back of the head. And uttered, "Fucking thief, that's what you deserve."

He closed the trunk, got behind the wheel of Paynter's car and drove back to the Johnson Truck Center. He parked next to his semi, and went into Johnson's to talk to Heather Kolling, but she was gone.

Cunard went into the truck center store and bought a can of heating sterno and lighter fluid. Went back to Paynter's car. He opened the trunk and sprayed lighter fluid all over Paynter's lifeless body, lit the sterno wick with a KILZS cigarette and set the sterno in the trunk next to Paynter's body and closed the trunk. He then threw Paynter's car keys as far as he could. Cunard got in his truck and left, heading back to Mason's Storage to change and pick up his flatbed trailer.

On the way back to Masons Justin Cunard called his brother Jason.

"Jason, it's me. I killed the little ass hole just as you said."

"Where?" Jason asked.

"I kidnapped the fucker and made him drive to a secluded spot under some Tamarack Trees at the Cortaro Road exit. I put him in his car trunk and shot his ass."

"Where did you dump him?" Jason asked.

"I drove his car back to the truck stop and parked in the rear of the parking lot. I bought some sterno and lighter fluid. I squirted the lighter fluid all over his dead ass and lit the sterno and put it next to his body. He should be on fire by now."

"What did you do that for? All that will do is create attention." Jason said.

"There you go again, second guessing me." Justin said.

"Look Jason, this guy had the balls to tell me that the police were at the truck stop and took the money. Can you believe anyone would come up with a story like that? The police have no clue who I am or where I live. How would they know about the money?"

"Are you sure about that?" Jason asked.

"Of course I'm sure, they haven't got shit."

"Who else knew about the money?" Jason asked.

"Heather Kolling, Paynter's secretary."

"Did you talk to her?"

"No she was gone when I got back to the truck stop."

"Maybe you better go back there and find her." Jason said.

"I can't, I'm running a little late. I will find her tomorrow."

"Okay." Jason said.

When we arrived at the Johnson Truck Center there were three fire trucks and two Callaway County Deputies controlling the fire scene. And one of the deputies was as big as a barn. It was Bowden. What the hell is she doing here? I wondered.

I said, "Look Nate, there is Deputy Bowden, she is your white twin sister, only she has hair."

"No shit, I didn't know women came in that size." Nate said.

I got out of the car and yelled, "Hey Bowden, what are you doing here?"

"Overture, how are you? Why am I here? This is just inside Callaway County."

I introduced Bowden to Big Nate.

"I thought I was the biggest thing in this county." Bowden said.

"You were until I got here." Big Nate said. As they both started laughing.

Then Bowden asked Nate. "Are you married big fella?"

"Yes I am. I am very married."

"Just my luck. You handsome ones are always married." Bowden said.

Just then the Fire Department Captain came up to us, stopped, looked at Bowden and Big Nate and said. "Whoa, I'd hate to have to feed you two. But, you would be great backups."

And then said to Bowden. "Someone told us that this car belongs to the truck stop manager, but we have been unable to find him."

I said. "Have you checked the car trunk?"

"No, why?"

"I have a hunch he might be in the trunk." As I looked at Bowden and said, "You may have another homicide."

"No way she said."

"Trust me Bowden, I can smell it."

Nate chimed in with. "If Cod said he can smell it, you better believe it."

The Captain yelled at one of the fireman, "Pop the trunk."

He did.

And there he was, in all his burnt glory, dead as a door nail.

I said. "I told you Bowden. You better get Deputy Dog up here to help you."

"Shut up, you old fart." She said, and started laughing again.

Then she said. "The jokes on you Overture, your department hired Cochran. A lateral transfer. He has to attend your academy just to learn your reporting procedures and Chain of Command."

"Good for him. Do you want us to help you with the crime scene?" I said.

"Sure I can use all the help I can get."

The identity of the body we didn't know for sure, but I was willing to bet a month's wages it was Lavelle Paynter. The only way we could positively identify this body was with dental records or DNA.

Isabel Connors came over to look in the trunk, smelled the dead burnt flesh and immediately tossed her cookies. I couldn't help but chuckle, bad ass fed, getting sick.

I got on the horn and called Victoria Redondo. "Victoria." I said. "We missed Cunard. I think he is heading back to the prison which means he will have to stop at Mason's to change. When he gets there take him into custody. I think he committed another homicide. And for God's sake be careful, he's armed and dangerous."

Lapaka was nosing around the parking lot looking at all the semi-trucks. I saw him bending over and picking things up. He would look at whatever he picked up, and then throw it down. He did this three or four times. Finally he came back smiling.

"Look what I found." He said.

A partially smoked KILZS cigarette butt.

"Well it looks like Cunard was here." I said.

"But he doesn't smoke, remember what the warden said."

"Yeah I know, but Paco said he does. Who is leaving the cigarettes if it isn't Cunard?"

"I don't have the slightest idea." Lapaka said.

"Lapaka, you and Connors beat feet back to Mason's and help get Cunard. When you get him, take him to Palm Springs, to isolate him. Nate and I will stay here to help with the crime scene."

"I looked at Bowden and told her we would be up soon to search the Mayor's property."

"I'll be ready, just call and let me know."

"I think things are going to start moving fast now. I'm going to call Bones to fill him in. We're going to have a lot of work to do in a short period of time. We need subpoenas for all the suspects financial records and we need to get them before the "Fontaine Five" have a chance to get their ducks in a row. I guess with the death of Townsend, it's the "Fontaine Four" now."

Big Nate said, "Financials can be tracked down by Rocky Mountain Information Network. All we have to do is give them names and Social Security Numbers and they will do a worldwide search."

✂ CHAPTER TWENTY-NINE ✄

When Justin Cunard got back to Mason's it was well after dark. He stopped at the gate punched in his code numbers and drove the big semi to the rear of the storage facility to swap trailers. He then headed to his storage unit to change clothes and stash his weapon. When he got out of the truck he removed the magnetic signs and walked over to the storage unit door to unlock it.

That's when it hit him. The lock was gone! *What the fuck is going on* he said to himself? Did someone break in?

Then Cunard heard the screeching tires and saw the storage facility light up like the Fourth of July. And then he heard the loud voices yelling.

"Hands up, this is the police. You are surrounded. Down on your knees, now."

Cunard the killer whimpered like a baby and went down on his knees, screaming, "Don't shoot, don't shoot. My brother made me do it."

It was over in minutes. Justin Cunard the killer of five people, including two police officers was in custody. He surrendered like most criminals, without a fight.

I got the call from Victoria Redondo a little after 2300 that Cunard was in custody and they were on their way to Palm Springs. I told her we would be in route shortly.

I looked at Big Nate and Bowden and told them Cunard was in custody. He was armed when he was arrested. I told Bowden I was sorry but we had to leave. We have to interview Cunard before he lawyers up.

We got to Palm Springs about midnight and went in to talk to Redondo and the Feds about the arrest.

Redondo said, "He gave no resistance. He just started whimpering and screamed at us not to shoot him. We took a 38 Caliber Smith and Wesson revolver off of him. I advised him of the Miranda Warnings. All he would do was cry and ask to talk to his brother Jason."

"Jason? He's been dead for about eighteen years."

"Well, that's all he would tell us."

Isabel Connors and I went into the back room where the holding cell was and introduced ourselves to Cunard. I informed him that we suspected him of the killing of five people, including two police officers as well as the theft of government property. I read Cunard the Miranda Warnings.

Cunard was not going to be an easy target to interrogate; after all he was a seasoned, hardened convict who had been in prison for over twenty years. He was not going to tell us squat. So I gave it my best shot.

"Cunard," I said, "We are not going to pull any punches with you. This is what we know about you."

"You are a convict doing life without parole. You were made an outside trustee by Warden J.J. Irish, to deliver surplus military property to local communities. That you were in the junk business before going to prison. You stole your brother's wife."

"We know Myrna Dobson was your ex-wives niece. We know about Victor's death at the Three Points Gun Store. We know about the Fontaine Five and who you were raised with at Fontaine House. And you know who I'm talking about, Mayor Wilson, Porter Homer, J.J. Irish, your brother Jason and of course Officer Townsend."

Cunard said, "Is Bones George still working for the police department? He shot me you know. That's why I'm in prison, he put me away for kidnapping and armed robbery. Look at the scars." Cunard then pulled up his shirt and showed us the bullet wound scars from twenty some years ago.

"Yes he is, he's my boss."

"How is he, is he still skinny?"

"Yes, but this isn't about Bones, this is about you." I said. "Let's cut the bullshit Cunard. We have you cold. We have the weapons, the bloody uniforms, the KILZS cigarettes left at every crime scene, all the documents from your storage rooms, and the locations of the remaining stolen property. We know you stored it at the Mayor's Ranch."

Connors said, "What we don't know is how you pulled it off,

that's what you need to tell us."

"Take your shoes and socks off Cunard."

"Why."

"Because you are in custody and I want to search you, now take your shoes and socks off."

When Cunard has his shoes and socks off I told him to stand facing the wall. I had him lift up his right foot. No tattoo. I told him to lift his left foot. There it was. The "Star Tattoo with the letters FF in the middle and the initials WITCH.

"What does the tattoo stand for?" I asked.

"It was part of a ritual. I can't tell you anything else."

"Justin, we know Townsend had the same tattoo. We figured out what FF and WITCH stand for, you may as well tell us."

"I know you can't do anything to me. I am already doing life, and there is no death penalty in this state. As long as I accept the fact up here, as he pointed to his head, that I am in prison for the rest of my life, there is nothing you can do to me. So I may as well tell you."

And then Cunard opened up.

"This all started a long time ago at Fontaine House. There were six of us that became very close. Lance Wilson, Porter Homer, JJ Irish, Mike Townsend and my brother Jason and me. But Jason started bullying the rest of us. He picked on JJ Irish the most because he was the smallest. He was even smaller than Porter Homer."

"One day I caught him trying to force JJ's head in one of the toilets, well that pissed me off and I beat the fuck out of Jason. That ended his bullying days, at least on us."

"Years later when he married Agnes he bullied her and his kid Victor. I know he used to beat the hell out of her. She would come to work with black eyes, she always had an excuse, but I knew it was him."

"When we were at Fontaine House we decided that we should ban together for protection. Townsend was the biggest, no one fucked with him anyway, and we wanted him to be the enforcer. So we created the "Fontaine Five." We excluded Jason because he was an asshole. We were kids then, this was meant to be a lifelong commitment to protect each other no matter what or where we were. Like the Musketeers, "One for all and all for one." We even cut our fingers and became blood brothers, like the Indians did in western movies. We did the tattoos at the same time."

"After we left Fontaine House we kept in touch with each other for a long time, but finally we drifted into our own little worlds. Wilson went into politics, and took Homer with him. I went into the junk business and Wilson got Townsend into law enforcement. I completely lost track of JJ. I didn't know what happened to him."

"Not until I got sent to prison. I ran across him one day in the yard. He was a fucking Correctional Officer. I couldn't believe my eyes. He filled me in on what the others were doing. I saved his ass from my brother while we were in Fontaine House. Well he never forgot that and started taking care of me in prison. The higher he went in the system, the better off I was. Finally, he became the warden, and he made me an outside trustee. Hell, he even gave me a semi-truck to drive and my own office."

"My job was to take surplus military property to the cities that needed extra equipment. Surplus property, are you kidding? To me it was like a candy shop. I used to be in the junk business. My eyes were suddenly filled with money signs. JJ let me do whatever I wanted so long as I gave stuff to the prison. JJ started a prison slush fund with some of the cash. It made him look good. He wanted to be named the Director. That's why he let me do it. I had it made. I was outside more than I was inside. I was making money for me and the Prison."

"After I started making money for the prison I decided to keep some for myself. I could buy anything. No one ever challenged me. I could do anything. The internet, the bank accounts, the storage facility, and the junk dealers. They all thought I was a government worker. I was never ever searched when I returned to prison. I had Carte Blanche. It is hard to believe, but I had it made."

"It got too big, the operation I mean, I had nowhere to put all the stuff I was getting. I had it at the prison for a while but I had to move it. JJ called Porter Homer, and Homer arranged for the land up North."

Connors asked, "Why the Postal Signs and Uniforms?"

"Because the cops don't stop postal vehicles."

"What's the Mayors role in this?" I asked.

"Really nothing, he took some of the money for letting me use his property, but that's it."

"What about the crane that was sold to a South African?" Connors asked.

"That was arranged by Porter Homer, who cut the Mayor in."

I asked, "Why the killings?"

"I had no choice. I was afraid Townsend would recognize me and blow the whole operation. Besides, he tried to get out of the Fontaine Five. He was a turncoat. He didn't keep his blood brother vow. His partner and the bartender were collateral damage."

"Why did you dump the bartender in Callaway County?"

"Because it was close to where I killed him."

"Where was that?"

"On the Mayor's property, where I stored the military stuff."

"Why did you kill the homeless veteran?"

"I killed the homeless guy because he was a witness to the Townsend killing."

"What about Myrna Dobson?"

"My niece wanted to blackmail me, the crooked bitch. She wanted $100,000. No way was I going to pay blackmail. So I capped her ass."

"Why did you dump her in the Cienega River?"

"Because it was handy. I killed her in the back of the trailer at the rest area, which is close to the river."

"And the prick at the truck stop. He was a fucking thief, he was stealing my money. I couldn't very well go to the police and tell them Paynter was stealing my stolen money, now could I? I took care of it myself."

"But why did you burn him?"

"To give him a taste of hell."

"You call those people thieves, you stole millions and committed six murders. What do you call yourself?" Connors asked.

"I'm a business man, I've always been a business man. I was protecting my interests. Kind of like the Federal Government when they bomb someone to protect their interests. It's not my fault they let me do this."

"I don't think that's going to fly in court Cunard." I said.

"Any one at the bases involved in all of this?"

All of a sudden Cunard got this eerie look on his face and demanded. "What is this? Who are you? What the fuck do you people want? What am I doing here? "I need a cigarette; do you have any KILZS cigarettes?"

"Sorry we don't smoke. And we were told you don't smoke."

"I don't know who told you that. I've always been a smoker. My brother Justin is the one who never smoked."

"What the hell are you talking about? You are Justin." I said.

"No I'm not, I'm Jason."

I said, "Jason died over eighteen……." But before I could finish my sentence he changed back to Justin.

"Jason was here wasn't he? He is always interfering in my business. Just like the junk business. He insisted that I give his wife Agnes a job. But he just wanted her to spy on me. I fixed his ass, I stole the bitch away from him."

I said. "What the hell are you talking about Justin?"

"I'm talking about my brother Jason. He is the one who told me what to do. He told me to kill anyone interfering with the operation. I need to talk to my brother."

"What brother." I asked.

"My brother Jason."

"Jason has been dead for 18 years." I said.

And then Jason reappeared.

"Justin is blaming me for this isn't he? That prick never did take responsibility for anything he did. He was always blaming others for his problems. Where are my fucking cigarettes? He never wanted to go by the law, I was the one who was law abiding. I need a cigarette."

And then Justin reappeared.

"No he isn't dead. That's who I bought the cigarettes for. I don't smoke. Jason does. I talk to him almost every day, he tells me what to do."

"What are you talking about? Are you crazy? Jason is dead." I said.

"Give me a phone and I will call him and prove it to you."

Connors gave Cunard her cell phone. He took the phone, and started talking to Jason. He didn't even dial the damn thing, he just started talking.

"Hi Jason, Justin here."

"Yeah what's up Justin?"

"The police have me, I have been arrested."

"Arrested, for what?"

"For killing Mike and the others. Stealing military property. What should I do?"

"You dumb fuck, I told you, you were going to get caught."

"Stop calling me dumb Jason, you told me to do it."

"Well, you are the one who got caught, you will have to take the heat."

"You ass hole, you helped, it was your idea?"

"Yeah prove it."

"I can't, you'll have to tell them."

"Fat chance, goodbye Justin."

Justin Cunard looked at us and said. "Jason hung up on me, he is making me take all the heat. He made me do it. He bullied me. Can we make a deal? I will testify against Jason." And then he cried like a baby.

He thought he had been talking to Jason, asking Jason questions, but he was not getting answers from Jason. He was answering himself. This fucking wacko was talking to himself. This son-of-a-bitch is crazy. He has a split personality. His other self is his brother Jason. Holly shit, he took his brother's persona.

Connors and I looked at each other as if we were crazy. What the hell have we stumbled on to.

Now what the hell do we do? How do we prosecute? Who do we prosecute? Justin or Jason?

ᑯᑭ CHAPTER THIRTY ᑫᑲ

The day after the arrest of Justin Cunard a meeting was held with Judge June Waterman-Briner, the County Attorney, Alexis Woods, Chief Larry Flynt, Bones George, Leo Lapaka and myself.

We presented the Judge and County Attorney with all the evidence we gathered from the Mason Storage Facility. The tattoo evidence tying the Fontaine Five together. The residential documents from the Fontaine House detailing the names of our suspects and when they were residents at Fontaine House. Photographs of the Military Property on Mayor Wilson's ranch land and the documentation of the sale of the crane to someone in South Africa, and of course the Mayor's WITCH account.

After viewing all the evidence Judge Waterman-Briner issued search warrants for the offices, homes and all vehicles belonging to Mayor Lance Wilson, Porter Homer and JJ Irish. Which included all electronic devices in such offices, homes and or vehicles.

What we didn't expect was the arrest warrants that she issued for Mayor Lance Wilson, Porter Homer and JJ Irish.

The Judge said, "I want them arrested and booked. I well determine bail at a later date. What I detest are Public Officials who are corrupt. They are not only corrupt, they could be involved in five homicides. Are we clear on what I want gentlemen and lady?"

"Yes ma'am." We all said in unison.

While we were waiting for the Judge to sign the warrants I suggested to Lapaka that he make an anonymous call to Rolanda Jacobs. That should give her time to get to City Hall before we do.

When Lapaka and I got to City Hall to serve the warrants the place looked like a fucking zoo. There were at least four TV trucks with their antennas raised to about fifty feet in the air. Reporters and camera men were everywhere.

The Mayor was standing on the top step of the building trying to find out what the hell was going on.

When the Mayor saw me he asked, "What the hell is this Detective?"

"This is for you Mr. Mayor. You are under arrest for complicity in the killing of five people and the theft of $300,000,000 worth of Military Property."

Then I read his honor the Miranda Warnings.

He remained silent.

"Lapaka went in and arrested Porter Homer and at the same time Isabel Connors and her agents were at the State Prison taking JJ Irish into custody.

✑EPILOGUE ✑

Of the $300,000,000 in stolen military property, $110,000,000 worth of the property was recovered on the Mayor's Ranch. The recovered property was ordered returned to the military at state expense.

Only $28,000 in cash was recovered. $23,000 from the Johnson Truck Stop and $5,000.00 from an inmate's father who was holding some of the money for Justin Cunard.

One year after his arrest Justin Cunard was declared incompetent to assist in his own defense. He was sent to a state institution for the criminally insane, where he will be treated for his mental illness.

Even if he recovers from his mental illness he may not be tried by the State for his five brutal killings. This state has no death penalty. I was told by an anonymous source, in the prosecutor's office, that State prosecutors are reluctant to waste money prosecuting someone already doing life without parole.

There will be no Federal prosecution of Cunard because of his mental illness and the fact that the feds believe he was acting under orders of the State Prison System, who benefited from his theft of the military property.

The Defense Criminal Investigative Service does not incarcerate anyone, they opt to fine their criminal suspects. As of yet, DCIS has not levied any fines. They are still searching for the remaining money and property.

JJ Irish, who never benefited personally from Cunard's criminal activity, was forced into retirement because of his lapse of judgment and never realized his dream of becoming the Director of the State Prison System. He had the same tattoo as the others. He was not tied to the killings.

The State Department of Corrections Director was forced to resign due to the political fallout over his failure to properly supervise the prison system.

The four Correctional Officers on Cunard's payroll were terminated for cause and not allowed to retire. They were not prosecuted because they were taking orders from Warden JJ Irish.

Porter Homer, who was the Mayor's Aide and the individual who arranged for Cunard to stash his stolen property on the Mayor's ranch, was sentenced to five years in prison for aiding and abetting a felon. He was not tied to the killings. He also had the tattoo.

Three years after Mayor Lance Wilson was indicted on a felony charge of Wire Fraud, involving the transfer of $50,000, he pled guilty to Attempted Wire Fraud, and was sentenced to three years in prison and agreed never to seek public office again. He was abandoned by all his political allies. He had the Fontaine Five tattoo.

The Mayor's WITCH checking account in the Caymans along with his tattoo were the last two nails in his coffin.

Prior to his plea agreement he survived two hung jury trials and refused to resign as Mayor. But the cost of two trials left him bankrupt, he had no choice but to accept the plea agreement.

Baylor "Bones" George has been offered the position of Director of State Prisons, he is currently considering the offer.

Victoria Redondo was returned to the patrol division where she is currently patrolling the south side of the city.

Carole Bowden was elected Sheriff of Callaway County, the first woman ever elected as a County Sheriff in this state.

Former Callaway County Deputy Sheriff Shelby Cochran is now a full-fledged member of this department assigned to the North Side Patrol Division.

Leo Lapaka and Rolanda Jacobs are married and have a son. They named him Leo "Cod" Lapaka.

Leo Lapaka is still my partner in Homicide.

Mike Townsend's widow and Henry Jessop's parents received generous financial settlements from the State for their loss.

Agnes Cunard and Myrna Dobson's children also received financial settlements from the State.

There is still public outrage because Justin Cunard has not been brought to trial.

Big Nate and Leona Randal are currently on Safari in South Africa. Louise and I are with them, we are riding on the second elephant. Nate and Leona are on the lead elephant. This trip has two purposes. One, to keep our promise to Nate and Leona, and second, for me to contemplate retirement. I just might do that. I just might retire and write a book.

Then my phone rang, it was a message from Bones. "Call me ASAP."

Now what?

 **THE END**

ABOUT THE AUTHOR

Gerald "Doc" Holloway has had two illustrious careers in public service. As 43 year police veteran, he rose through the ranks from Patrol Officer, Criminal Investigator, Sergeant, Supervisor of State Police Air Rescue, Chief Criminal Investigator and

223

finally Chief of Police. Gerald's second career was the United States Navy. He qualified on Submarines and went on to attain the rank of Chief Petty Officer as a Master at Arms in the Navy Police Service. He retired from the Naval Reserve with eighteen years of Honorable service.

Gerald graduated from the University of Arizona in 1974 with a BS in Criminal Justice.

He has been married to his High School sweetheart, Patricia, for 52 years. He spends his leisure time visiting friends, family, and former police colleagues. He also plays the guitar, but his favorite activity is interacting with his eight grandkids.

Gerald and his wife Patricia divide their time between their home in Arizona and a summer home in Eastern Michigan.